MY GITFIDDLE SUMMER

My Gitfiddle Summer

DAVE DONELSON

MY GITFIDDLE SUMMER
Copyright © 2025 by Dave Donelson.

All Rights Reserved. Published and printed in the United States of America by Donelson SDA, Inc. No part of this book may be reproduced, copied or used in any form or manner whatsoever without written permission, except in the case of brief quotations in reviews and critical articles.

For information, contact Donelson SDA, Inc.
44 Park Lane, West Harrison, NY 10604

FIRST EDITION

ISBN 978-1-963813-18-0

Disclaimer : This is a work of fiction. All events described herein are imaginary, including settings and characters. Any similarity to real persons, entities, or companies is purely coincidental and not intended to represent real places or living persons. Real brand names, company names, names of public personalities or real people may be employed for credibility because they are part of our culture and everyday lives. Regardless of context, their use is meant neither as endorsement nor criticism: such names are used fictitiously without intent to describe their actual conduct or value. All other names, products or brands are inventions of the author's imagination. Donelson SDA, Inc. and its directors, employees, distributors, retailers, wholesalers and assigns disclaims any liability or responsibility for the author's statements, words, ideas, criticisms or observations. Donelson SDA, Inc., assumes no responsibility for errors, inaccuracies, or omissions.

Dedicated to Nora Raleigh Baskin,
who gave me the idea
and years of encouragement

PROLOGUE

I bet you want to know why this guitar has a bullet hole in it. Yep, that's what it is all right, an honest-to-gosh hole made by a 32-caliber slug. In case you didn't guess, I didn't put it there myself, although I sure was there when it happened. It was in the heat of battle, so to speak, one summer a long time ago. Bear with me and I'll tell you all about it.

You don't know me, but that's okay—not many folks do. I'm just a small-town guitar picker you probably never heard of unless you hung out in some of those beer joints out on Highway 36 more than a few years ago. I'm Daniel Freemont. I wrote a few songs back in the day, mostly on whatever scrap of paper was handy. Tried it a few times on a typewriter, but that didn't work so good. Clacking those keys around threw me out of my rhythm. You can fake a rhyme in the lyrics, but you gotta put proper tempo in a tune if you want it to swing. I sold a few of those songs and kept the rights to some of the others and it's the few dollars I get in royalties that butters my bread today. That and my Social Security check.

I'm an old wreck now, but I had my time in the sun. You may not believe it looking at me, but for a while I was a headliner on the biggest television show in country music. You probably think it's the *Grand Ol' Opry*, but, no, I played on the *Ozark Jubilee* out of Springfield, Missouri. Yep, it was the biggest—and the best. I made my debut in 1956, the year after the program went from local radio to national television. On the ABC TV network, no less.

I can see you're not impressed. That's okay. You're entitled to your opinion—you wouldn't be the first one that thought I was full of bull hockey. This here Martin D-18 guitar with the bullet hole is the same one I played back then. My dad gave it to me, God rest his troubled soul wherever he is. Me and this guitar have been on the road together ever since I went hunting for Dad that same summer. You see, not long after he gave it to me, he ran away and left my brother and me living in a cellar with my Mom. I found out later why he had to sneak out of town, but I gotta tell you it was a rough summer for all of us when he skipped. Of course, if I hadn't gone looking for him, I never would have been on television with the *Ozark Jubilee*, so I guess it all worked out in the end. Except for Dad, I suppose.

Oh, yeah, sorry. I distracted myself. Us old guys do that a lot. This bullet hole in my guitar? Well, I'm not getting any younger, so I guess I ought to tell that tale while I've still got all my strings.

~ 1 ~

It happened the summer when Elvis topped the charts with "Hound Dog" and Mickey Mantle won the triple crown of major league batting. Mom and Dad got divorced in the spring, which is why her and me and my little brother, Willy, lived in the cellar beneath my Aunt Mae's tavern. It was a lightless cave, a place Willy believed was home to monsters, so Mom left the bathroom light burning all night. There weren't any monsters, of course, except for the one Mom brought home one night not long after school let out for the summer.

The evening began quietly enough. Mom had a date, so we ate supper early. She warmed up some navy beans with a ham hock on the two-burner hot plate in the tiny kitchen. We ate a lot of beans. Sometimes she cooked noodles with ox tails or goulash or made some hoppin' john—anything that could be cooked in one pot and stretched over several days. She served whatever came out of the pot with store-bought bread or corn fritters because we didn't have an oven to bake anything.

"Thanks for watching Willy, tonight," Mom said as she put our bowls on the table. "I'm going out with a guy who drives a real snazzy Chevy—it's a '53, almost new! Pretty cool, huh?"

"Yeah, I guess," I answered. Inwardly, I groaned. I filled my mouth with beans so I wouldn't say what I really thought. Since the divorce, Mom met a lot of men in the tavern upstairs where she waited tables for Aunt Mae. She worked there because she didn't have cash to rent the cellar apartment. She went out with a few of the men she met, but they never amounted to much. I may

~ 1 ~

have just finished the eighth grade and been only twelve years old at the time, but I knew that the kind of guy who hits on a waitress in a neighborhood tavern isn't looking for anything more than a good time in the back seat of his car. In Mom's case, they usually disappeared as soon as she mentioned her two kids.

"Don't be such a sourpuss, Daniel," Mom said, reading my scowl. "Give the guy a chance."

"Sure," I said. "Sorry."

"Willy needs a bath tonight. Will you help him? My friend will be here in a minute and I have to get dressed."

She filled our biggest pot with water and put it on the hot plate. The cellar didn't have a hot water heater, so we boiled water in the kitchen and carried it in a bucket to a galvanized laundry tub next to a floor drain at the end of the hallway where Willy and I slept. The tub was barely large enough for me to sit in with my knees drawn up to my chin. Willy always went first so Mom or I could wash him. When it was my turn, the water was usually tepid and cloudy and the bottom of the tub was full of grit that stuck to my bare butt.

A car honked outside and Mom gave each of us a quick peck on the forehead on her way out the door. I cleared the table and washed the dishes while the water for Willy's bath came to a boil. When it was hot, I poured it into the tub and added some cool water to keep it from scalding him.

"I don't feel good," he said as I pulled his t-shirt over his head. "I want Mom."

"You'll see Mom when you get up in the morning," I said. Willy was only six, about half my age. He was not old enough to hang around with but plenty old enough to be a pain in the ass. I gave him a quick scrub, rinsed and toweled him off, and told him to put on his pajamas. "We can listen to the radio when you get in bed, okay?"

He nodded and crawled into the bottom bunk where he slept. Our bedroom wasn't a real room, but rather a passageway to the stairs that went up to the tavern. Mom and Aunt Mae had cleaned it out when we moved in. It was connected to the other two rooms in the cellar apartment through a bathroom equipped with a toilet and doors at either end. Mom found the bunk beds at a second hand shop and covered the dirt floor under them with a sheet of loose linoleum so we wouldn't track dirt onto our bed sheets. Our beds were opposite a run of open-backed wooden stairs that climbed to a trapdoor in the tavern floor, our ceiling. The wooden trapdoor was thick and heavy and I could barely push it open over my head. Every time I did, I expected it to fall back to crush my skull and knock me toes over teacups down the wooden stairs. I would probably break an arm or a leg in the process, I knew, and lie twisted on the dirt floor at the bottom of the stairs until I died in a pool of blood. I had a lot of dark thoughts that summer.

Danger lurked in a locked room at the end of the passageway, too. It held the compressors that chilled the beer coolers upstairs, chugging and rumbling all the time with whirling wheels and swishing belts that would slice off a careless finger in less than a blink. The room was dark even when you pulled the string for the light bulb in the ceiling. The dirt floor was damp and critters scurried around, always just out of sight, and if you touched anything, your hand came back grimy and greasy. We were supposed to stay out of the room. Willy wouldn't even go near the door. "There's bugs in there!" he would exclaim with wide, popping eyes. I knew how to jiggle the lock until it opened and went in sometimes just to show him I was not afraid.

Once he was in bed, I pulled Willy's covers up to his chin. "Feel better?" I asked.

"A little. Are you going to play the radio?"

"How about if I play my guitar, too?"

"Like Dad does?"

"Well, I'll try."

"I miss him."

"Me, too. You be quiet now and I'll play some music in the front room where the radio is. You can listen from here."

It was Saturday night and time for the *Ozark Jubilee*, my favorite program. While the radio tubes warmed up, I sat on the threadbare sofa and tuned my guitar so I could play along. Next to getting my dad back home, my not-so-secret greatest desire was to play on that program someday. When I tuned in, two sisters from Jonesboro, Arkansas, were singing a ballad in close harmony about lost love. I found the key they were singing in by listening for the last note in the chorus and finding it on my guitar, a trick Dad taught me. That's usually the root note in the key, he said, and it will be the name of the major chord for the song. "Once you know the key, you listen for the chord changes and you can accompany almost anybody." It doesn't always work, but this time it did.

As I played along with the sisters and then with another song sung by the star of the show, Red Foley, I visualized myself on stage with them as the music carried me to a life without the ugly problems that drive families apart. I imagined playing a duet with Dad at the *Ozark Jubilee*, me chording rhythm guitar and singing the melody while he picked fancy licks and harmonized the vocals.

By the time the program was over, Willy was snoring lightly and my mind was in a place where I could sleep, too. I checked to make sure the front door was locked—Mom had a key, of course—and tiptoed into our room so as not to wake Willy. I put my guitar into its case and stowed it at the end of the bunks, climbed up to my bed, and pulled the string on the bulb in the ceiling. I rolled over in bed to shade my eyes from the bathroom light and slipped into sleep.

I sat up in bed, suddenly awakened by the sound of someone rattling the front door. Most nights, I heard creaking floorboards and customer chatter from the tavern above me, but now it was late and long past closing time. I told myself the sound had been in a dream. I had no idea how long I had been asleep but I knew it wasn't long enough. I laid back down and closed my eyes. Before I could drift off to sleep, the lock in the front door clicked and, a second later, Mom giggled and a man snickered. The door closed with a slam followed by a thud as if something had fallen against the wall in the living room. Someone smothered a laugh. "Shhh, The boys!" Mom said. She had gone on several dates since the divorce, but this was the first time she'd brought anybody home.

All was quiet as they shuffled down the hall past the bathroom's other door to Mom's room. Her bedroom door closed, but it did nothing to hide their murmurs and whispers. Then came the creak of springs as first one of them, then the other, found a place on her bed. I was wide awake by then, but I laid very still, queasy as I imagined what was happening in the next room. I knew what men and women did—I had seen plenty of magazine centerfolds and I wasn't ignorant—but somehow I never put my mother's face on one of those glistening naked bodies.

Sheets rustled and the bedstead groaned as they settled into whatever they were doing. After several minutes of heavy breathing without words, the man whispered something to Mom. He must have had his mouth right next to her ear, because I couldn't understand him. Mom whispered back, "Keep it quiet. The boys are in the next room." The man snorted, but she shushed him and somebody turned over in the bed. I hoped it was Mom turning her back to him, but I knew it wasn't. The headboard bumped hard against the wall and the guy's breathing got louder. Mom said something urgent, but her voice was muffled as if her mouth was covered. The headboard slammed against the wall again.

"Ouch!" Mom whispered. "That hurts!"

Willy woke up and cried out, "Mom! What's wrong?"

"Hush. It's all right," I said as I climbed down from my bunk to settle him.

The wall reverberated again and Mom hissed, "Stop it!"

Bedsprings squealed and heavy feet hit the floor in Mom's room. "Goddammit!" the man muttered. "Where are my shoes? I've had enough of this!"

Willy sobbed, "Mom! I'm scared!"

"Everything's okay, Willy," Mom called back. "I'm fine. You boys get back to sleep."

Willy whimpered. I burned to run into Mom's bedroom and pound the guy to a bloody pulp, but I couldn't leave my brother. Before I could move, Mom's door flew open. The guy stomped through the apartment and the front door slammed behind him.

Mom came to our door pulling on her bathrobe. She took Willy into her arms and reached over to stroke my hair. "Everything is all right," she said. "Let's all go back to bed." In the light from the bathroom, I saw angry red finger marks on her cheeks and neck.

I climbed up the ladder into my bunk and pulled the covers over my head. I felt like my life was a train that was hurtling off the rails. Then I remembered that tomorrow was Sunday. Dad was coming to see us—I hoped.

$$\sim 2 \sim$$

Late the next morning, Dad showed up at the door for his weekly visit. Willy squealed and ran across the front room to jump into his arms, eyes sparkling as Dad crushed him in a bear hug. Mom's eyes sparkled, too, but that may have been something I imagined because I wanted it to be true. Dad was tall but slim—I'm built like him—and Willy was pretty big to be carried around in his arms, but Dad didn't care. He was still giving Willy a big squeeze in the doorway when a very shiny Chevy pulled up to the curb and the driver honked the horn. Dad gave Mom a quizzical look, but before he could ask, she said she had to go. "You boys have fun and be good," she said as she gave Willy a kiss on the forehead.

"That must be her new boyfriend," I said after she left. I felt an urge to tell Dad about the events of last night, but thought better of it. There was no point in making him feel any worse.

"Nice car," Dad said. He stared out the door with a confused look as the driver peeled his tires on the asphalt and drove away with Mom. "Oh, well, what are you going to do, huh?" Dad didn't have a car. He got around by cadging rides from friends or on the city bus, which only cost a dime but sometimes took hours to get you from one part of town to another. The bus stopped right in front of the tavern, though, so that's how Dad came to see us.

As you may have gathered by now, I pretty much grew up with a part-time dad. Oh, he was there when I was real little. I remember him carrying me piggyback and sitting me on his lap to read a book or listen to the radio, but by the time I got older and Willy came along, Dad was hustling pretty hard trying to put food on the table by playing in various bands in bars and dance halls. That meant he was gone evenings and didn't get home until the early hours, so he slept in late during the day—the times when I wanted him to fun around with me. Even before all this happened, his music career had taken a hard left without a turn signal and Mom divorced him. He was even more part-time after that.

Turning away from the door, Dad shook his head as if to clear it and stood Willy back on the floor. "Okay, boys, what are we going to do today?"

"Pickin' and grinnin'!" Willy shouted. Dad brought his guitar every Sunday and had turned his lessons for me into a game that included Willy. I jumped up to get my guitar out of its case.

"Okay, Daniel's the picker!" Dad exclaimed, feeding into Willy's excitement, "And Willy, you're not only the grinner, you're going to be the strummer this week! I brought something for you."

He opened a paper grocery bag he'd carried in with his guitar case and took out the strangest instrument I'd ever seen. It looked like something a blindfolded monkey would glue together in the dark.

"What's that?" Willy asked.

"This is a gitfiddle," Dad answered with a big grin. "I made it out of an old violin and a ukulele with a cracked body I found in the second hand store. It should be just the right size for you." The body of the conglomeration had the fancy curlicue shape of a violin and the neck had frets and tuning keys like a uke.

Dad handed it to Willy and showed him how to hold it. He'd tuned it to an open chord so Willy didn't have to do any fingering, but he could still make music by strumming.

"Let's play, 'Billy Boy,' Dad said. "Daniel, we'll play in G"

"Got it," I answered, and started picking.

Willy jumped right in, playing along with me more or less in time to the song. He strummed energetically with Dad sitting behind him and reaching over his shoulder to move his hands. I wondered if my face had borne the same look of bliss when I was Willy's age and Dad cradled me on his lap with my first guitar.

Dad and I took turns singing the verses. My voice had changed over the winter, but it still cracked every once in a while if I reached hard for a high note. Dad always said not to worry, I'd be through puberty soon enough. I finished my last verse okay and we all joined together for the end of the chorus, "She's a young thing and cannot leave her mother." Willy ended with an extra hard strum and WHANG! one of the gitfiddle strings broke.

"Oh no!" he cried.

"Don't worry," Dad said. "I'll put a new string on it and bring it back next week. Now you can be a drummer. Go get yourself a spoon."

Dad took out his own guitar and put its empty case on the floor for Willy to beat on. Willy always wanted to use one of Mom's pots, but the guitar case made a less irritating thump.

Dad had taught me to play by learning chords and playing songs by ear, not scales and musical notation exercises, because that's how Grandpa taught him. He showed me how to finger basic chords with visual names I could remember like pump handle C, chicken G, and D the V, then how the 7th chords led from one chord into another like D to D7 into G or G to G7 into C. Once I learned to form them on the fretboard, he'd name a song and tell me to try some chords while I sang the melody in my head. "You know the song, so you can tell if you're playing the right chords by the way it sounds," he said. The songs were simple tunes—two or three chords and a melody you could hum or whistle like "Billy Boy." It didn't matter if I got it right the first time, Dad would just keep playing and nodding to me as I floundered along until I eventually sensed the chord changes and found the progressions. He didn't so much teach me to play as he helped me teach myself.

Willy started pounding on the guitar case and Dad strummed his guitar a few times. "Here's a good song, Daniel. You should work on this lick." He played a few lines of "Lovesick Blues," a big hit song for Hank Williams. "When you get to the end of each line in the chorus," he explained, "you walk your fingers to the first chord of the next line by playing the steps on two strings, not just one. Like this." He played three beats, plucking two strings at the same time on each, until he played the full chord on the fourth beat. It sounds easy, but it's not. Every guitar player can step up or down to the next chord one note at a time, but adding that second note for harmony breaks the usual fingering. It also dressed up the song quite a bit. Dad used it on a lot of songs—it was his signature lick. Anyone hearing that lick knew right away who was playing it.

Dad's sound was also different from most guitar players' because he didn't use a flat pick or his fingers to strum and play. He wore a thumb pick on his right hand and—something very different—brass picks on his fingers like a banjo player. When I got past the basic strumming stage, he gave me a set of finger picks, too, and showed me how to use them. Most guys in bands play electric guitars, but Dad and I didn't need amplification. Our guitars rang out with those brass finger picks.

In case you haven't noticed, music fills my head all the time. I play music, I sing it, I hear it even when nobody's there to make it. It's as if my brain is a juke box that never stops playing. Mom said music runs in Dad's family, that the men all have it. My grandpa played fiddle for square dances and such and his music runs in my dad's veins. Dad performed every morning in a string band on KFEQ, a local radio station. When he could get gigs, he played at dances and bars and other places around town at night. Dad sensed the music in me and taught me how to play on an old Silvertone from the Monkey Wards catalog when I was hardly bigger than the guitar. When I got good enough to not embarrass myself on that beater, he gave me this beauty, his old guitar, when he got a new one. "Treat it with respect," he said. "It's a Martin D-18 just like the big stars play." He showed me how to finger-pick it and I followed him down the path to earning a living in the music business. He taught me how to play when I was about the same age as Willy.

I tried to play Dad's signature two-note harmony transition lick, but stumbled on it pretty badly. "Just keep at it. You'll get it," Dad said. He opened his guitar case and took out a thick notebook. "Here, you can see where I use it on this song in my fake book." He flipped to the page with "Lovesick Blues" on it and pointed to a double line he'd drawn over some of the chord changes.

Willy jumped in to say, "Hey! That's not a fake book. It's a real book!"

"You're right, Willy," Dad chuckled. "It's a real book for fakers like me. That's why we call it a fake book. It's for us poor uneducated pickers who play by the seat of our pants." He closed the book and started to put it back in his guitar case, then handed it to me instead. "Tell you what, Daniel, why don't you hold on to this for a few days? Copy some of the songs you like and make your own book. Just keep it safe and don't lose it."

"I'll take real good care of it!" I promised. "But don't you need it?"

He busied himself putting his guitar into its case and latching the lid. "Well, uh, I'm not going to play for a few days," he said. "The guitar will be in the shop for some repair. You can use the book in the meantime."

"Repair? What's wrong with it?" I thought Dad's guitar sounded great, but he was the expert, not me.

Curtly, he said, "There's some buzz from the second fret. Didn't you hear it? The fret wire needs to be replaced and the others leveled and polished so they all match."

Surprised by his tone, I just said, "Oh." But his answer raised another question and I plunged on to ask it. "But what will you play for the radio program?" From the quick frown he gave me, I knew I had touched a real nerve. To make amends, I quickly added, "I know! You can play mine."

Now Dad looked like a trapped animal. "What? Oh, yeah, well, uh, that's okay. I'm just going to take a few days off."

His tone was as tense as a fiddle string but I took a chance on making him mad with yet another question. "Dad, when I get good enough on these songs, can I play gigs with you? We could go on the road together."

His eyes softened. "You're good enough now, son," he said. "but it's not as easy as that. You're not old enough for a lot of places where I play because they serve hard liquor. There are other complications, too. Besides, your mom needs you around here."

"But that won't be forever! Maybe you could work things out with Mom. Then we could all be a family again and you and I could play together all the time."

"I wish we could," he said, looking down at the floor. "But it won't work that way for us now. I love your Mom and you and Willy, but, well, there are things in the way."

"Like what?" I demanded.

He sighed. "For one thing, I'm embarrassed to admit it, but money is really hard to come by for me right now. I can't pay my own bills, much less support you guys."

"If it's just all about money, I can work!" I said. "Aunt Mae pays me to sweep out the tavern. I could sweep Joe's barbershop next door, too." My plan sounded lame even to me.

He smiled. "Don't give up on me." He lowered his voice to just above a whisper. "It's a secret, but I'm working on a deal that could solve all our money problems. I've had a little setback, but it's all going to be straightened out soon."

My life brightened. "What is it?"

"I can't tell you now, but I will as soon as it's all set." He put a finger to his lips. "Don't say anything to your Mom, okay?"

"Okay," I answered and turned to Willy. "That means you, too."

"Huh? What?" he said. He'd been busy trying to play the broken gitfiddle with his spoon.

Dad packed away his guitar and put the gitfiddle into its bag, muttering something to himself about the guy with the Chevy.

Before I could tell him what I thought about the guy, Willy spoke up. "I don't like to sleep here, Dad. It's scary. I want to live at your house."

"Willy, I sure wish you could," Dad said. "But I only have a room in a boarding house and I share it with another guy." He smiled as he thought of something. "Speaking of my roommate, he has a car. What would you guys think about going fishing this week? Daniel, you could invite your buddy, Rusty, too. Wednesday maybe?" He caught me by surprise, but I jumped to answer yes right away.

~ 3 ~

My criminal career began the next day. It was a chicken-and-egg kind of thing. I don't think I would have become jailbait if Dad had stayed married to Mom, although I guess you never know. Don't get me wrong. I'm not making excuses for what I did or anything else that happened in my screwed up life. Mom said it's not my fault they got a divorce and I pretty much believed her. And Dad went missing later all on his own, so that wasn't my fault either. And as for my first big crime, I confess to it, but I refuse to flush myself down some giant toilet of guilt.

The thing is, I got caught stealing. It was a simple deed of need, not greed, a need that Dad confirmed when he said money and the lack of it had caused him and Mom to split up. And even with one fewer mouth to feed, it was clear Mom was having trouble putting food on the table with the tips she earned waiting tables and by taking in ironing for some kindly neighbor ladies who knew she could use a few extra nickels and dimes. It was also a crime of opportunity. That morning, I came across a dozen empty pop bottles behind a grocery store just waiting to be stolen, so I pinched them. And that's how my criminal career began. The felonies came later.

Aside from the divorce and what followed, the summer had started okay. School let out as always at the end of May and my buddy Rusty and I had three full months to get ready for high school in the fall. We'd survived junior high together, and he'd kept me from losing it when Mom and Dad split up, so I figured we could handle whatever else happened as long as we stuck together.

I spotted the pop bottles while I was waiting for Rusty in the vacant lot behind the grocery store. The store's owner, a fresh-off-the-boat Italian guy everyone in the neighborhood knew as Bruno, stashed them in a fenced space next to the dumpsters until the delivery truck arrived, when they would be traded for full ones. The chicken wire fence wasn't much of a deterrent. All I had to do was climb over, throw the empties one-by-one back out into the weeds behind the store, then climb out and gather them up. The deposit on the bottles was two cents each, which doesn't sound like much, but a full case of them would bring almost a half dollar. That was real money in those days. Heck, you could buy a hamburger in a restaurant for fifteen cents!

Rusty skidded his bike to a stop next to me and I told him my plan.

"Toss them over, and I'll put them in your bag," he said. "The trusty Rusty brain figures that will be twice as fast, right?"

"Right," I said, then added with a grin, "But how do I know you won't run off and sell them yourself while I'm stuck on the wrong side of the fence?"

"Would I ever do something like that?" He smiled as innocently as he could and, of course, I believed him. Maybe his red hair and freckles and the gap between his two front teeth made him look harmless. Or maybe I just knew what kind of a loyal friend he'd been throughout grade school and into junior high. Rusty and I bonded over many things like chess and Superman comics from the day we first met in the fifth grade.

I climbed over the fence and threw a bottle back over. He caught it and we were in business.

"So, are you going to sell them back to Bruno?" he asked.

"Nope," I answered. "I tried that last week. He just took them anyway and told me to pound sand. Said he wasn't born yesterday."

Rusty chuckled. "I guess he's not as dumb as he looks." He caught another bottle. "Speaking of which, don't you think he looks like President Ike with a Yosemite Sam mustache?" Dwight Eisenhower had been elected almost four years earlier, when Rusty and I were still in grade school.

I tossed the rest of the bottles over the fence and climbed out. Rusty was handing the bag to me when the store's backdoor creaked open and Bruno came out with a bucket full of vegetable trimmings destined for the dumpster. I tried to stash the bag of bottles behind some tall weeds but I wasn't fast enough.

"You brats! You stealing from me?" Bruno shouted.

"Oh, no sir!" Rusty said, trying to look like an innocent angel. "We would never steal anything. That's against the law!"

"Hah! You steal my bottles! What you got in that bag? Give it here." Bruno dropped his bucket of garbage and snatched the bag out of my hands. The bottles clanked inside. "See! You a thief!"

"No, sir, Mr. Bruno, we're not thieves!" Rusty protested. "We found these up the street a few minutes ago. We were bringing them to you for the deposit." He grinned and added, "There are ten of them, so you owe us twenty cents." I ducked my head and bit my lip.

The grocer glared at him, speechless.

"Bah!" Bruno exploded. "I give you twenty smacks on your butts! Get out of here! I catch you again, I call police. I know where you live, you little snots."

"Yessir," I said. I shoved Rusty into motion before he could say anything else. Bruno could have the bottles in the bag. They were his, after all. Rusty picked up his bike and we headed across the vacant lot. I felt Bruno's eyes on my back until we were well up the hill into the weeds.

The lot was overgrown with knee-high grass and thistles that hid busted pallets, rusty cans, and a remarkable number of old tires. We followed a foot path beaten down by folks like us who didn't have cars to take them to the big new supermarket on the other side of town. The path cut through the lot from their homes on the next block to Bruno's grocery store and Aunt Mae's tavern across the street.

Rusty grunted as he pushed his bike up the hill. I walked behind him, turning every few steps to see if Bruno was searching for the rest of the bottles in the weeds. He wasn't looking, so they were still there. I'd have to be careful going back to get them, though. I thought about waiting until dark when the store would be closed, but that might be even more dangerous since Bruno lived in an apartment over the store and could easily spot me from there. I'd have to bring a flashlight, too, which would be like shining a beacon for him. With the way my life was going, he'd be sitting in his bedroom window with a sniper rifle waiting for me.

"That was close," Rusty panted as we got to an old, forgotten peach tree that stood in the back yard of an abandoned house. The ground beneath the tree was littered with peaches that had already fallen. The fruit was sweet and easy to reach for me since I was pretty tall for my age. Ants crawled everywhere while bees gorged on the fallen fruit. I spotted two peaches about ready to drop and gave one to Rusty. I looked mine over closely for worm holes, then took a big bite. The peach skin popped in my teeth and the sweet, syrupy juice flooded my tongue. I leaned forward to keep the sticky mess from running down my chin.

Rusty just chomped down and let the juices flow until a glop landed on his t-shirt. He swallowed, grinned, and broke into an off-key rendition of "When It's Peach-Pickin' Time in Georgia," a Jimmy Rodgers song. Rusty tried to finish the tune with a pathetic yodel. I laughed until I choked.

"What?!" he protested. "You don't like the entertainment?"

"Two things wrong with it," I said. "One, we live in Missouri, not Georgia. And two, you sound like a coyote getting castrated."

"Sheesh, everybody's a critic!" He tossed his peach pit in my direction.

"You know it," I said with a grin. "Someday I'll show you how that song is supposed to sound—the way Dad taught me—as long as you promise not to sing along."

"My old man taught me to play music, too" Rusty said. "Go ahead and pull my finger. I'll play you a tune in the key of fart."

I laughed again but, when Rusty started looking for another peach, I couldn't help but think about Dad and Mom and money. It wasn't fair. Dad was the center of my universe, until one day he wasn't. And it was all because he couldn't make a living doing the thing he loved. As Mom had explained many times, "He's a musician. He only makes money when he has gigs and sometimes there aren't any."

Rusty burped, bringing me back to the real world. "I got to go," he said, mounting his bike. "See you later."

"Hey, wait," I said. "Do you want to go fishing Wednesday with my dad and me?"

"Sure," Rusty called out as he pedaled toward home.

I walked back down the path through the weeds toward the grocery store, bending low and hoping Bruno wasn't watching for me. I needed to gather the rest of the bottles while there was enough daylight to find them. Just when I thought it was safe to start searching, Bruno called out, "Hey you! Boy! Come here!"

Damn, caught again, I thought. I started to duck lower into the undergrowth but I didn't see a gun or anything, so I decided to take my chances. I stood up from where I'd crouched behind the weeds and tried to act casual, like I crawled around on my hands and knees all the time.

"You that boy lives across the street in Mae's tavern?" His accent was heavy, but I understood him just fine.

"Yes, sir." Uh-oh, I thought, he's going to rat me out.

"I watch when you move in. You need earn some money?"

That took me by surprise. Wary, I nodded.

"Me, too. When I the same age as you, my folks and me, we come to this country with nothing. Then my papa die and we have even less. I no see your papa." He paused to see if I was going to tell him he was wrong, but when I didn't answer, he said, "You want job?"

"Uh, yes, sir," I said, still on guard. "What kind of job?"

"You get empty pop bottles from inside store, bring out here. Then you sort into cases. Pepsi into Pepsi. 7Up into 7Up. Dr. Pepper into Dr. Pepper. Like that. Capeesh?"

I didn't know what that word meant, but I caught his drift. "I can do that."

"I give you dime every day you work. Deal?"

"Deal!" I stuck out my hand and he shook it.

"Good. Come when I open Monday. In the morning."

"Yes, sir. Thanks, Mr. Bruno."

As I turned to leave, he added, "First job for you Monday, you pick up bottles you throw in weeds today."

He truly is smarter than he looks, I thought.

~ 4 ~

Wednesday as promised, Dad pulled up in front of the apartment in a banged up pre-war Ford he borrowed from his roommate. When Willy saw Dad, he dashed out the front door, almost colliding with Rusty, who rolled up on his bike at the same time.

"Whoa, guys!" Dad said. "Save some of that energy for reeling in the fish!"

The car's dented trunk squealed when Dad opened the lid to put in our stuff. Rusty handed him a fiberglass spin-casting rod and reel and a hefty metal tacklebox. "Nice gear," Dad said.

"Thanks. It's my dad's." Before my dad could ask if Rusty's dad knew the gear was gone, Rusty handed him a coffee can full of shredded leaves and nightcrawlers. "The worms are mine, though. I caught them last night after the rain."

I put my old metal rod and bait-casting reel in the trunk along with a bamboo pole for Willy. Willy's pole didn't have a reel. He couldn't operate one anyway, so Dad tied a piece of line with a hook to the end of the pole. I set a ball of dough bait wrapped in wax paper next to Rusty's can of worms. I made the bait myself because I could never find any nightcrawlers in the hard-packed earth of the vacant lot next to the tavern. As a substitute, I mixed up a fist-sized wad of smashed corn flakes, flour, water, garlic powder, and vanilla extract, a recipe Dad had given me the summer before. He said to let it set for a few minutes until it gets gummy, put a glob on a treble hook and sink it to the bottom, and you can catch a catfish or a carp. Get hungry enough and you can eat it yourself, he said. I nibbled on a bite of it one time and he was right.

As you can probably tell, I loved my Dad more than I could say, but that summer I came to learn he wasn't perfect. Nobody is, I guess, but we can love them anyway. I love him still, in spite of everything that happened.

We piled into the car and Dad drove to a farm pond on the outskirts of town. The pond was at the bottom of a grassy pasture that was bordered by the road where we parked. A lone maple tree provided some shade near the pond and a rough foot path led around to the opposite side of it. Trees and undergrowth on the other side lent an air of mystery and adventure to the open pasture where we stood.

"Let's fish over there," Rusty said, pointing to the other side of the pond.

"That's not a good idea," Dad said. "There are too many tree limbs hanging over the water. You can't cast."

While Rusty and I rigged our rods, Dad cut a piece of line from his own reel and tied it to Willy's bamboo pole. He put a lead sinker and a hook on the line, stuck some of my dough bait on it, and attached a red and white bobber.

"Here you go, Willy," Dad said, helping him lift the pole so the rig reached the water. "If you sit still and be quiet, I bet you catch a whale!"

My own rod and reel were hand-me-downs from Dad, far from something you'd find in *Field & Stream* magazine. The rod was tapered steel and the reel had a spool, crank, drag, and level rewind mechanism. Dad watched me get ready to cast and nodded his approval.

"Bait casting is the ultimate test of a fisherman's skill," he said. "You need an educated thumb and a confident arm. Let's see what you've got." I wound up a slow backswing with my thumb on the reel to keep it from unspooling. I flung the rod tip toward the water and lifted my thumb at the perfect time to let the line spool off. As it raced out, I feathered the spool—again with my educated thumb—to match the speed of the free-wheeling reel to the decelerating flight of the hook and sinker. My baited hook dropped into the water just where I had aimed. "Good job," Dad said as he went back to check on Willy.

The outfit Rusty borrowed from his dad was a beauty, a spin casting reel with a fiberglass rod. I'd seen them in the hardware store and they cost nearly twenty dollars. The reels almost never snarl.

We sat in the sun for an hour, throwing our bait into the water, waiting for some action, reeling it back in and trying a different spot, then another, but didn't catch much of anything. My dough bait got me a small catfish, but it was not big enough to eat and I didn't really want to ride back home with a single dead fish in the car, so I tossed it back. I borrowed a worm from Rusty, but it was much lighter than my dough ball, so when I tried to cast it, the reel snarled as the bait hit the water. I managed to get the bird's nest untangled and started reeling in the line, but the empty hook snagged on something beneath the surface, probably a dead tree branch. Dad took a turn of the line around his hand and yanked. The line sliced his finger and he started bleeding. "Damn!" he said as he used his pocket knife to cut the line. He put his bleeding finger into his mouth and Willy sniffled.

"Hey, buddy," Dad said. "No need for tears. It's only a little cut." Dad started to give my rod back to me, but paused as he thought of something. "Here, Daniel," he said. "I want you to have this. It's time." He handed me his pocketknife. "It's a real Barlow. My grandpa brought it with him when he came over from Flanders and then he gave it to my dad. He passed it on to me and now I'm giving it to you."

I thought about him using it to cut the fishing line when it got tangled. "But don't you need it?"

"I've had it all my life. Now it's your turn."

"Wow, thanks, Dad," I said as I weighed the knife in my hand before slipping it into my pocket.

"Very cool, Mr. Freemont," Rusty said. His attention snapped back to his rod as its tip dipped sharply. "Come on, you monster," he crooned, tensing his grip on the rod for the next nibble. Dad grinned and I shushed Willy so he wouldn't scare the fish away. The rod tip jerked again and, as Rusty yanked it up to set the hook, a motorcycle roared by and backfired when the rider shifted gears as it flew us. At the sound, Dad fell to the ground like he'd been shot. Rusty and Willy were preoccupied with the fish that had taken Rusty's bait, but I was gripped by the scared look in Dad's eyes as he got up off the ground and watched the motorcycle disappear in the distance.

"What happened?" I asked

"Nothing. The noise startled me and I, uh, slipped," he said.

"How do you like this big monster?" Rusty cracked as he held up a sunfish about the size of Willy's tiny hand.

Dad got himself together and said, "Pretty terrifying."

"That's cool. Just the right size. You could take it home in your pocket," I said, trying to lighten the moment for Dad. "It will fit."

"It'll fit in your left ear, too," Rusty said as he cocked his arm to throw it.

"Look out, Daniel!" Willy giggled. Rusty tossed the fish back in the water.

"Let's try the other side of the pond," Dad said. I thought it was strange that he wanted us to fish where he'd said earlier it wasn't a good idea. Then I realized that we would be farther from the road and next to a screen of trees and undergrowth.

I had never seen my dad duck and dodge before, never seen him so afraid he had to hide his head from danger, real or imagined. In my mind, dads were always heroes, never cowards. They always stood up to life's bullies, dealing with the enemies of misfortune, mistrust, and bad luck, able to leap tall buildings or pull the damsel off the railroad tracks just before the oncoming train ran over her. That's what dads were for, why they existed. I thought that included my dad, too, until he left us to fend for ourselves while he dived for cover from a backfiring motorcycle.

The fishing wasn't any better on the other side of the pond. Dad was right about how difficult it was to cast where trees crowded the bank with limbs hanging over the water. He saw me frown the second time I had to use my new knife to cut my line loose and said we might as well call it a day. He led us back around the pond to the car, walking so fast Willy could barely keep up. As Dad drove back home, he constantly checked the rear view mirror on the country roads and swiveled his head at every intersection to look down the cross streets when we got to town.

"Is everything okay, Dad?" I whispered, not wanting to alert Willy or Rusty.

"Sure. Just being careful," he answered. "It's not my car, you know."

"Oh, okay," I said even though I thought Dad could have driven that piece of junk headfirst into a freight train without anyone noticing the damage. I waited a few minutes, then whispered again, "Any news about the big deal you're working on?" He shook his head and put his finger to his lips, then pointed over his shoulder to the back seat where Willy and Rusty were thumb wrestling.

When we got home, we discovered Dad's parking spot had been taken by the shiny Chevy. Dad scowled as he pulled to the curb behind it, but he didn't say anything. We jumped out of the car and Rusty tied his fishing gear to his bike and headed home. Willy and I gave Dad goodbye hugs. "Drive careful!" I called as he pulled away. He didn't wave, so I don't know if he heard me. Knowing he was in some kind of serious trouble made me want to find a place to be alone to figure out what to do about it, or maybe cry a little.

Mom's new flame was sitting on the couch with his arm around her when we came in.

"Here are my boys, home at last!" Mom said as if she'd been counting the minutes. I don't know, maybe she had been. "Daniel and Willy, I want you to meet Larry Kingston, that new friend I told you about."

The guy was dressed like a Hollywood hoodlum. He wore tight black chinos cuffed above his ankles. White crew socks extended into surprisingly small black penny loafers. His white rayon shirt had two big red vertical stripes, one on each side leading to its flared open collar. The short sleeves were rolled up to reveal enough of his biceps to let you know he had big ones. He had a low ducktail with sideburns, too, and a hint of a spit curl on his forehead. When he stood up, I saw he wasn't tall, but his body looked solid, as if he could handle himself in a fight. He stuck out his hand and said with a smile, "Good to meet you, Bub."

'Bub?' Did he just call me 'Bub?' I thought. I ignored the nickname and shook his hand with as firm a grip as I could muster. His hand was stronger than mine by far, though, so I pulled back to keep my fingers from being crushed. "Nice to meet you, Mr. Kingston," I said. I glanced at Mom to see if I could escape yet.

"Hey, Bub, just call me 'Larry'," he said. "Mr. Kingston was my old man." He chuckled and sat back down on the couch next to Mom. "And what moniker do you go by? Danny? Danny-boy? Dan?" At least he didn't intend to call me 'Bub' anymore—I hoped.

"Uh, 'Daniel,' please," I said.

"Then 'Daniel' it is."

I wondered if he pretended to be cheerful like this all the time. Something about his expression bothered me. When I looked closer, I saw that his smile didn't quite match the look in his eyes, which was kind of calculating as if he were checking you out, measuring your likelihood of fighting back if he decided to smack you for some reason.

"Larry is a fire fighter, Daniel. Isn't that exciting?" Mom said. "He works for the city. He's got another job, too, in a garage." That's how he could afford an almost-new Chevy, I thought as she added, "He brought you boys some presents."

I hadn't noticed the brown paper bag on the couch next to him. Almost dismissively, he handed it to me and said, "I figure all boys like cars, right? So I got one for each of you. Didn't want to start any fights, so they're both the same."

"Thank you," I mumbled. I opened the bag and showed it to Willy. Inside were two identical diecast toy Chevrolets. I didn't know what else to say. I outgrew toy cars years ago. Willy grabbed one and immediately sat down on the floor to push it around, making vroom-vroom sounds with his lips.

"Those are models of my car," Larry said. "I couldn't resist."

"Isn't that nice?" Mom prompted.

I mustered as much enthusiasm as I could and said, "Yeah, sure. Thanks, Larry. They're great."

"See, I told you they would like them," he said. He gave Mom's shoulder a rough squeeze.

"Stop it!" she hissed, squirming out of his grip but not pushing him away. "That hurts!"

Her words echoed in my head. That's exactly what she said Saturday night. Was Larry the guy who stomped out of the apartment? I looked closer at his eyes. They twinkled at her protest until he caught me staring. Then they narrowed as if to warn me to mind my own business. Then he smiled.

"Your mom says you went fishing today," he said. "Did you bring home a big mess for dinner?"

I mumbled, "No. We didn't have much luck."

"Well, next time, bring me along and we'll get all the fish you want." If he'd been standing up, I think his chest would have puffed out. When I didn't respond, he raised his eyebrows and asked, "Want to know how?"

"Uh, sure," I said, playing along until I could escape.

"Dynamite, Daniel. Dynamite," he smirked. "You toss a lighted stick in the water and BOOM! The fish float to the top and you just scoop them up." He paused expectantly, then brayed "Har! Har! Har!" Mom joined in. I tried to laugh, too, but all I could manage was a single "ha."

"That's pretty good, Larry. I'll remember that." I edged toward the door to the bathroom. "I need to wash up. Okay, Mom?"

"That's a good idea," she said. "I bet you've got some of that smelly fish bait on your fingers." As I turned to go, she added, "Larry is going to take me out for a ride in his Chevy, Daniel. You'll watch Willy, won't you? There's some of last night's dinner in the fridge you can heat up."

"Sure, Mom. We'll be fine."

After they left, I gave Willy both new toy cars and showed him how to crash them into each other, which kept him happy while I warmed up the leftover beans and corn fritters and turned on the radio so we could listen to *The Lone Ranger*. At the final "Hi Yo, Silver! Away!" I switched it off and packed Willy off to bed. He always slept better after spending the day with Dad.

Once Willy settled down, I went to the front room to wait for Mom to come home. I didn't know exactly what I expected to happen, but I wanted to let Larry know I had my eye on him. Mom, too.

While I waited, I sat down with my guitar to practice with Dad's fake book. There must have been three hundred songs in it. I found a dozen I liked and copied them by hand onto notebook paper I had left over from school. I wrote the lyrics out line by line, then added the chord names over the places they came in the melody just like Dad had done in his book. I copied his playing marks, too, especially the double-note transition licks. There were some other marks I wasn't sure about, but I figured I'd ask him about them Sunday when he came to visit again.

I forced myself to stay awake long past my bedtime until a car door slammed outside, then another one. Our front door opened. Mom walked in giggling, but stopped short when she saw me. Larry bumped into her from behind.

"What the hell!" he said.

"Hi Mom," I said. "Did you have a nice time?"

~ 5 ~

I still get a chuckle every time I remember the look on old Larry's face that night. He huffed and turned on his heel and left in disgust. It was the highlight of my day. On the other hand, the motorcycle thing from the afternoon was just downright disheartening. It's bad enough when you figure out your dad isn't the stalwart breadwinner you always thought, and it's discouraging when your mom tells you he's never going to change, but when you see your dad cowering in fear, well, that just takes the salt out of life.

Dad didn't show up the next Sunday. We didn't have a telephone, although he could have called the pay phone in the tavern and left a message with Aunt Mae. But he didn't. I was worried. Really worried that something bad had happened. I couldn't erase the image of him ducking when the motorcycle raced by and I kept circling back to when he told me he had some "problems" that I wouldn't understand. It's true. I didn't understand, but that was because I didn't know what those problems were. The only thing I knew for sure was that they had shattered our family.

"I want to play my gitfiddle," Willy whined as the time for Dad to arrive came and went.

"Maybe next week," I said, not sure whether or not I believed it myself.

With sad resignation in her voice, Mom said, "Looks like your Dad can't make it today boys. I'm sure he wanted to see you but something must have come up."

"Yeah, I guess," I answered. I desperately needed something or someone to cheer me up. "Mom, could Rusty come over today?"

"That would be fine. But you guys watch Willy, okay? I made plans to go downtown and do a little window shopping while your dad was here." She didn't need to add that window shopping was the only kind she could afford.

"You go ahead and go, Mom. I'll take care of him."

After she left, I went upstairs to the tavern and called Rusty, then Willy and I sat down on the sofa in the front room with *Charlotte's Web*, one of the books Mom had checked out for him at the library. They had been reading it together all week and were deep into the story. I read with him the way I remember Mom reading with me when I was little. She would read a sentence aloud, then I would read one while she ran her finger under the line, taking turns. That's what Willy and I did. He was only going to be in second grade in the fall, so he stumbled a bit over some of the big words, but I helped him along. When we got to the part where Wilbur the pig wins the prize at the fair and Charlotte tells him she is dying, Willy whimpered and put his little hand flat on the page.

"What's wrong, Willy? Are you sad about Charlotte?" He didn't answer, so I put my arm around him. "It's okay. This is just a story."

"I know, " he sniffled. "Everybody lives happy ever after like always." He sniffled again and said, "That's baloney."

"What's the matter?"

"Nothin'. I'm okay." I didn't know how else to make him feel better, so I moved his hand out of the way and read a line on the page. When I pointed to the next sentence, the one he was supposed to read, he said instead, "Daniel, where did Mom go?"

"What do you mean?"

"She got dressed up like she was going on a trip. Did she go far away?

"You heard her, Willy," I said, trying to sound calm and matter-of-fact. "She just went downtown to look in the stores."

"Are you sure?" He screwed up his face and a tear trickled down his cheek. "Will she come back?"

"Of course she's coming back. Mom won't leave us."

"Dad did!" he sobbed, stabbing me in the heart. "If Mom goes away too, who will take care of me?"

I stifled my own sob as I pulled him to me. "I will."

"Promise?"

"Yes, I promise."

We sat in silence and held each other close.

"Hey, boys! How they hangin'? cracked Rusty when he came in. He took one look at Willy and me and raised an eyebrow to ask what was going on. I closed the book and gave Willy a squeeze before I stood up.

"So what have you cooked up for today?" I said as cheerfully as I could.

"The trusty Rusty brain has been hard at work," he answered. "And it came up with a cool game I bet Willy can play. What do you say, sport?" Willy gave a whoop like he always did when we included him in whatever we were doing.

Rusty led the way through the kitchen and out the back door to a patch of bare dirt where Willy sometimes played with his cars. He found a stick about as long as my index finger and told me to sharpen one end of it with my new pocket knife. That's what tipped me off to what he had in mind. He took the sharpened stick from me and pushed it into the dirt so only the top of it showed.

"Kneel down here with me, Willy," he said. "This game is called mumblety-peg."

"That's a funny name!" Willy giggled.

"Yes it is. It's a funny game, too."

"Can I play?"

"Sure, but you have to be careful and do exactly what I say. Okay?"

"Okay!"

"We take turns throwing this knife so it sticks in the ground. Think you can do that?"

"Yes," he said, reaching for the knife in Rusty's hand.

"Wait! Let me show you." Rusty held the knife by the handle and speared it straight down so the point of the blade stuck in the dirt. He nodded to me, so I drew it out and handed it to Willy handle first.

"Your turn," I said. "Hold it like this and throw it down like Rusty did." He tried to imitate Rusty but the knife landed on its side. The tip of the blade was under a little pile of loose dirt, though, so I said, "It's in the ground! Good job, Willy!"

He clapped his hands and said, "I won!"

Rusty laughed. "Not yet. We take turns until somebody misses. If Daniel and I miss, then you win."

"My turn, now," I said. I picked up the knife and threw it into the ground. Rusty went next, then Willy took a turn and did a little better. We went around two more times until Willy showed signs of boredom. Before he lost focus, I threw the knife deliberately to land it on its side. "I missed, Willy!"

Rusty picked up on my cue and did the same. "Oh no!" he cried. "Willy wins!"

"Yay!" Willy yelled. He jumped up and danced a jig in the dirt, waving his little arms in the air.

I laughed until he settled down. "Now for the best part," I said. "Do you know why the game is called mumblety-peg?"

"No, why?"

"Because Rusty lost, so now he has to pull that peg out of the ground with his teeth." I pointed to the sharpened stick I had made when we started. "You'll hear him mumble when he does it."

"Wait a minute," Rusty protested, putting on a show for Willy. "I wasn't the only one who lost!"

I grinned at him and said, "But it was your idea, so chow down on that peg, Mr. Genius."

"Yeah," Willy giggled, "Bite that stick, mister genie bus!"

"Okay, you two. Here I go!" Rusty put his hands behind his back and leaned over until his nose touched the dirt. He made a big show of grunting and rooting around like a pig trying to find the pointed stick while Willy whooped and laughed at the sight. Finally, Rusty sat up and grinned so we could see the stick between his teeth. With a big "Blaah!" he spat it out.

Delighted, Willy exclaimed, "You got dirt in your mouth! Let's play again!"

"That was fun, but I've got to take my dirty mouth home," Rusty said. "Maybe I'll come back for a rematch next week."

"Come on, Willy. Let's go inside," I said as Rusty left. "I'll fix us some supper."

"Yay!" Willy yelled. "Supper!"

That night after we'd been in bed for a while, Willy started whimpering and muttering in his sleep. From the few words I could make out, he was dreaming about Dad. I tossed and turned sleeplessly. I couldn't decide if I was mad at Dad for not showing up or worried about him for the same reason. I have to tell you, I felt like I'd been living a real, live nightmare. First, I had to listen to my Mom in bed with her drunk boyfriend and hear the jerk hurt her or something. I still cringe whenever I think about how she cried out. Or how she brought him home again. I mean, what was wrong with her? Then Dad disappeared on us without so much as a "see ya later." And it wasn't only me that was having nightmares. It was all piling up on my little brother's shoulders, maybe messing him up for life. It might have been summertime, but the livin' sure wasn't easy. I dropped into fitful sleep trying to imagine how I could find my dad. He may not have been the most reliable guy in the world, but he was the only hope we had.

~ 6 ~

On Mondays, Aunt Mae didn't open the tavern until dinner time. That was the only time she could stay off her feet for a few hours and recuperate from the busy weekend. Mom took the whole day and evening off from waiting tables, too, although she spent the afternoons ironing clothes for the neighbor ladies, who did their laundry in the morning, then brought the damp shirts and whatnot to Mom to be ironed. She charged a nickel for each item. That doesn't sound like much, but she was fast and could make a few dollars in an afternoon.

Monday was also the day when Aunt Mae did her books, took inventory, ordered beer, pop, and bar snacks for the week, and generally got the tavern business affairs organized. I worked for her on Mondays, too, after I sorted Bruno's bottles. She paid me to sweep the floor and empty the garbage cans in the morning while she sat at a table in the corner of the room in her robe and slippers, her hair in curlers, drinking coffee and smoking Winstons and making notes in her ledger. She had a heavy mechanical adding machine with a paper tape that would run clear across the floor by the time she was finished punching its keys and cranking its iron handle.

Sweeping the floor was a smelly job. I had to get on my hands and knees under the bar with a whisk broom and dust pan to gather up the trash that had missed the garbage cans. The wooden floor boards had been soaked by spilled beer for many years, so I had to hold my breath against the sour odor. Next, I sprinkled saw-dust dampened with red oil on the tavern floor and swept it from the back of the room to the front with a push broom. By the time I reached the front of the tavern, the sawdust was black with the dust and cigarette ashes it had picked up. I wasn't sweeping rose petals, but the work took my mind off everything else for an hour or so. Finally, I dragged the stinky garbage cans to the curb.

"Another job well done, Daniel," Aunt Mae said as I came back from stowing the broom and can of oiled sawdust in the back room. "You did your fifty-cents-worth for sure. You know how the register works, so get your pay out of the till. Help yourself to a candy bar and a cold pop, too. Then come here and visit for a few minutes."

When I came back and sat down at her table, she said, "How are you guys getting along down in that cellar?"

"Pretty good, I guess. Willy gets scared of the dark sometimes, but he's just a little kid."

"I heard some banging around a few nights ago. Are you sure everything is all right?"

"Yeah. That was Larry. He got mad and left in a huff." I was too embarrassed to tell her what he was doing there and not sure I should say anything about Mom.

"How's your mom? He didn't hurt her, did he?"

"I don't think so. She said she was okay."

She gave me a long, knowing look. "You're pretty grown up for a boy your age." As if to herself, she added, "I guess you have to be, don't you?" She paused as if deciding whether or not to tell me something, then she added, "This is a small burg we live in, you know. I heard that Larry's ex-wife was fooling around with other guys on the days and nights he was on duty at the firehouse. It got pretty ugly before he divorced her. Of course, that doesn't let him off the hook for treating other people wrong." She reached across the table to lay her hand on my arm. "If he hurts your mom, you come and tell me, okay? She won't say anything, so it's up to you to let me know."

"Why won't she tell you herself?" I asked.

"Lots of reasons, but sometimes because it's hard for a woman to admit she picked a loser," she said. I took a sip of my Dr. Pepper while I tried to figure out what she meant, but before I could frame another question, she said, "I've been thinking about getting one of those new television sets for the tavern one of these days. What do you think about that?"

"Wow, that would be incredible!"

"They tell me it would only get one station, but that would be better than nothing, right?"

"You bet!" I said. "How soon will it be here?"

"Now, don't get your shorts in an uproar. I haven't even decided for sure, much less ordered it. Maybe we'll have one before you go back to school this fall." She paused and squinted at me with a little smile. "In the meantime, your birthday is next on the calendar. Anything you been wanting?"

"Gee, I don't know," I said, stalling for time while I pondered the possibilities. The only thing I could think of that I really wanted was for Dad to come home, but how could I ask for that? Finally, I said, "Rusty has one of those new spin-cast fishing reels. I think they're only a few dollars."

"I'll look into that," she said. She took a sip of coffee. "You know, I hear you playing your guitar and singing downstairs sometimes. You sound pretty darn professional. How would you like to play a few tunes here Friday night?

"Really!?"

"Yes, really!" she chuckled. "I don't have a stage, but we can just stand you up here next to this table while you play. Liven up the joint a little bit."

"That would be great!" Then I visualized myself playing in front of a crowd while everybody watched and my stomach seized up a bit. "You really think I'm good enough?"

"Sure you are! I hear you banging that guitar and singing and sometimes I can't tell if it's you or the radio." I remembered Dad saying I wasn't old enough to play with him in taverns like Aunt Mae's. When I asked her about that, she waved it away. "We only serve beer, so we'll pretend that stuff doesn't matter."

"What should I sing? Dance songs?"

"Well, the Friday night crowd is mostly working men and their dates. They come after dinner and have a few beers. They can't dance in here, though. There's not enough room. But, yes, they like lively tunes. Don't forget they like love songs, too. You know, ballads and such that put them in a romantic mood."

"Okay. I'll take a look at my fake book. It's got some of each." Then I thought of something else. "Would it be okay if I put out a tip jar? You know, just in case?"

Aunt Mae laughed and shook her head. "Good God! Don't tell me you're another deluded soul who thinks he's going to make a living playing the guitar! Oh, you poor thing."

I grinned. "Thanks! Dad said I was getting good enough before. . . ," my voice broke a little as I realized what I was about to say. I swallowed and finished by adding, "Good enough to play with him on the radio."

Aunt Mae patted my hand. "Well, he would know. Your dad is a crackerjack guitar picker. He could have made it big, you know."

"Aunt Mae, can I ask you something?"

"Anytime, sweetheart."

"Where is Dad?"

She wasn't expecting that question, but she didn't hem and haw about an answer.

"Somebody told me they heard him playing at some bar in the south end of town Saturday night. The guy who told me about it was drunk, though, and he couldn't remember the name of the place. It's down by the stockyards, I imagine. I don't know if your dad is still around or not. He hasn't been on the radio station lately. There's no live music. They're playing records every morning now."

"Is he in some kind of trouble?"

She took a deep breath and said, "Daniel, I just don't know. I hear he borrowed some money or something from the wrong people. Then something happened and he can't pay it back. And these people don't take kindly to 'I'll pay you tomorrow' for an answer. I don't think he blows his money on booze and drugs like some guys, but he's a musician and there are lots of temptations."

"Can't we help? I'd give him everything I earn."

"I know you would, honey, but there's nothing you or your mother can do for him. She knows that and that's why they got a divorce and that's why you guys are living here."

I couldn't say anything more without crying and I didn't want to cry. What I wanted more than anything was to find out why my dad hadn't shown up Sunday. Bad news overrules good news, don't you think? I get my first gig, a real one with an audience and everything, and the next minute I find out my dad is a bum with bill collectors chasing him. I tried not to pass judgment on Dad as a provider for his family, even though that was supposed to be a man's job—his first and only duty—back in those times. Oh, some women worked, but mostly out of desperation when their men didn't hold up their end of the bargain. Plenty of people condemned folks who couldn't or wouldn't follow the "rules" about who was supposed to be the breadwinner and who was a housekeeper, but I was too young to see why. All I knew was that both Mom and Dad struggled with life pretty much every day. I wanted to help them out somehow.

Anyway, it wasn't long until I found out there was a lot more to the story about Dad and his problems. Before I could ask Aunt Mae anything else, Rusty came in.

Rusty came to play pinball on Mondays after I'd finished working. We played on a used "Gottlieb Knock Out" pinball machine in the back room of the tavern where Aunt Mae kept it out of sight since it was technically an illegal gambling device. When Rusty arrived, I got some painted nickels from the jar next to the cash register. The red nickels were for Aunt Mae's personal use. She got them back from the guy who owned the machine when he came to empty it and collect every week. She split the rest of the take from the machine with him. She did the same thing with the phone company with painted dimes for the pay phone on the wall in the tavern.

Rusty played first. He pulled back the spring-loaded plunger, chanted "Yowzah!" and released it, sending the chrome pinball shooting up the lane, through the gate, and around the top of the board. As soon as the ball bounced off the first bumper, he started maniacally pushing the flipper buttons. The bumpers flashed, bells rang, numbers flipped on the scoreboard. Rusty's strategy was to punch the flipper buttons as fast as he could no matter where the ball happened to be rolling. By accident, that often kept the ball in play. He didn't register a high score, though, since pure chance ruled where the ball went when it rolled into his aimlessly flailing flippers.

I couldn't focus on the game because I couldn't get all the tangled up emotions out of my head. The more I thought about Aunt Mae's customer saying he saw Dad playing Saturday night, the angrier I got.

"Yowzah!" Rusty yelped again and launched another pinball, bringing me back to today as it disappeared off the board. "Your turn," he said, stepping away from the machine.

I pulled the plunger and launched my ball, but forgot what I was doing before it even hit the first bumper. My anger at Dad just wouldn't let me go. It was all mixed up with worry about him, too, which just made me angrier. Aunt Mae said maybe he owed money to the wrong people in town. Could that be part of his big secret deal? I had to find out.

"Hey, knucklehead," Rusty said. "What are you doing?" I had let the ball meander down the table undisturbed until it disappeared into the "no score" hole.

"I can't concentrate on this," I said. "I'm going to Dad's apartment and see if he's there. Do you want to come?"

I got my bike out of the storeroom. Rusty took the lead. We rode north on Twenty-second Street, down the hill through the first few blocks of tiny, old, frame houses, then on a level stretch to the railroad tracks. The street made a slow climb from the tracks through the town's dying center, a neighborhood of mostly African-American homes where we had lived before Dad got his steady radio gig. We stopped when we reached the boarding house where Dad lived, which was next door to a pawn shop appropriately called "I Buy Anything." One look in the front window confirmed its name. The shop was full of old lamps and busted chairs, questionable radios and assorted hubcaps, bike wheels, and ugly statuettes that nobody would ever, ever want in their living room. Everything in the shop was the same color—a peculiar mix of brown and dusty gray. The old guy who owned the place didn't have much time for kids and their nonsense, but he would give you a nickel if you brought in a piece of junk metal he could re-sell to the scrap yard. "I Buy Anything" was the pawn shop where Mom and Dad bought my beat-up old bike years ago.

It was also the store where Dad found the broken violin and ukulele that became Willy's gitfiddle. I stopped in shock when I passed the store window and saw the gitfiddle itself sitting on top of a pile of old records and yellowed sheet music. The world crashed around me.

"What's wrong?" Rusty said.

"That's Willy's!" I pointed at the instrument behind the glass. "Dad made it for him."

"What's it doing in that place?"

"That's what I'm going to find out." A cow bell clanged as I pulled open the door. The proprietor was bent over the counter, tinkering on a rotating fan with a screwdriver.

"The guy who made it traded it to me," he said when I asked where he got the gitfiddle. "Very peculiar, he was. Lives next door, I think. I remember selling him a busted fiddle and a ukulele last month, then he showed up a few days ago with a real nice guitar he needed to pawn. Asked me if I'd hold it 'til Saturday, so I gave him a hundred bucks for it but told him I wanted a full week's vig for every day I held it without putting it up for sale."

The pieces fell into place. Dad's guitar wasn't in the repair shop; incredibly, it was in the pawn shop. I was shocked he would part with it. It wasn't just how he made his living, his guitar was his very soul. "Where is the guitar? Do you still have it?" I asked.

"Oh, he came back and got it Saturday, just like he promised. Didn't have all the vig, though. That's how I got this." He pointed to the gitfiddle. "Said he'd buy it back one day soon." He cackled, "Sometimes it seems like I just buy and sell the same crap over and over."

"Did he say when he'd be back?" I asked.

"Nope. I haven't seen him since."

Now I was really mad at Dad. How could he solve his money problem by selling Willy's gitfiddle? How could he do that! If Willy found out, it would break his little heart.

Rusty could see the storm building in my face. "How much do you want for it?" he asked the proprietor.

"Well, with what he owed me, I'd have to get twenty dollars out of it to make it worth my while. You in the market for a gitfiddle?"

"Not at that price," Rusty said.

"Maybe I could do a little better. What'll you give me?"

Rusty looked at me, silently asking if I had any money. I gave him the two quarters I had earned that morning from Aunt Mae, then scrounged around in my pocket until I found the dime I made at Bruno's. Rusty took two dollars out of his own pocket, what was left of his allowance for the month, and held it out to the man.

"Sorry, boys, but you'll have to do a lot better than that."

"Forget it," I mumbled. "It doesn't matter anymore." Sadness and disappointment tempered my anger. I needed more than ever to talk to Dad and find out what had gone so wrong. "Let's go check the rooming house."

We went next door and Rusty rang the doorbell. He stood aside to let me do the talking when a big, burly woman in threadbare blue overalls opened the door.

"I ain't got time to be buyin' no magazine subscriptions," she said. "I got rooms to clean."

"No ma'am," I said. "We're looking for John Freemont. Is he here?"

"Johnny Freemont? Him and his no-good roommate skipped out this morning. You just missed him. Packed all their junk in that old Ford and skedaddled without paying the rent." She paused and squinted at me. "A couple of other guys came looking for him, too. Rough characters. You with them?"

I shook my head, suddenly scared speechless by what Aunt Mae had said about Dad owing money to the wrong people.

Rusty said, "No ma'am. Mr. Freemont is Daniel's dad. Do you know where they went?"

She bent down and stabbed a stubby finger into his chest. "Nope, but if you see him, you tell him he owes me five dollars. Hear?"

"Yes, ma'am," Rusty said as he scrambled backwards, bumping into me.

I pedaled home in a fog but by the time we got to the tavern, I knew where I had to go.

~ 8 ~

You don't see many gitfiddles now. Everything's got to be digital or electronic or molded out of space-age polymers or some such. I don't care. I'm still an acoustic picker through and through. There ain't nothing like the mellow sustain of a note struck on a string laid across a rosewood bridge on top of a seasoned spruce face. Bits and bytes just can't capture it. Sorry, I got off the story again. I was thinking that my life that summer was kind of like that gitfiddle. It was cobbled together from broken parts and got shoved around from one dark and dusty pawn shop to another. And just like Willy's gitfiddle, I broke a string, too.

Aunt Mae was setting up the tavern for the dinner hour when we came in that afternoon. "Back for more pinball?" she said. Her hands were deep in a crockery bowl of hamburger that she was mixing with cracker crumbs to make it stretch farther.

"Nope, just checking a phone number," I answered. She shrugged and went back to her work. The pay phone hung on the wall in the doorway to the back room. The phone book hung on a chain next to it. Aunt Mae had said her drunken customer heard Dad playing in the south end of town Saturday night, so there was a chance he would be playing in the same place tonight. Or at least somebody might know his whereabouts. I checked the Yellow Pages under restaurants and bars, looking for ones with addresses on King Hill Avenue, the main drag in that part of town. That's where the stockyards and packing plants were, as well as the small businesses catering to the cattlemen, farmers, meat cutters, and packers who worked there. I found a few joints with addresses that looked to be practically next door to each other.

"You're not going now, are you?" Rusty said. "That's a long way to ride and it's getting pretty late."

"Yeah, but I need to follow what little trail I have while it's hot."

"You going to sneak out?"

"Not exactly. I'm going to your house for dinner, remember?"

"You are?" Rusty asked, giving me a puzzled stare. Then he realized what I was trying to pull off and broke into his big gap-toothed grin. "Oh yeah! I forgot!"

I tore the page with the restaurant listings out of the phonebook, folded it up, and stuck it inside my shirt. We went downstairs to ask Mom if I could eat at Rusty's. She said that would be fine as long as Rusty's mother didn't mind.

"It was her idea, Mrs. Freemont," Rusty said, getting into the scheme in a big way. "My dad got one of those new kettle grills that burns charcoal from a bag. He's going to cook hot dogs tonight!"

"Well, aren't you just about the most up-to-date family in Missouri!" Mom teased. "Go on, you two, and stay out of trouble."

We got our bikes and headed in the direction of Rusty's house. As soon as we were out of sight, I pulled over to the sidewalk.

"Pretty smooth," I said. "Thanks!"

"Yeah, the trusty Rusty brain has its moments," Rusty grinned. "Listen, I'd go with you but it's my mom's birthday, so I better get home for dinner for real." He paused a minute, then turned dead serious. "Look, I know you miss your dad and everything, but what's the hurry? Why do you need to find him right away?"

"It's not so much him as my Mom." I hadn't told Rusty about Larry and Mom and how he treated her. It was embarrassing, but I had to get it off my chest. "Her boyfriend is a real asswipe. I think he hurts her sometimes."

Rusty winced. "Man, that sucks."

"Yeah."

"Why doesn't she dump him? Your mom's cool. She could find another guy."

"I think maybe she's afraid of him. That's why I've got to find Dad. If he knows how bad things are, he'll get his act together and come back." Telling Rusty didn't make me feel better, but saying it out loud solidified my resolve.

"Gotcha. Well, you be careful down there. That end of town is pretty rough."

"I will," I answered. "See you tomorrow."

I circled the block and pedaled west and south, skirting downtown and heading for the far reaches of the south end of town. St. Joe wasn't a pretty place, except down by the river, and the homes I passed fell into the modest to shabby category, mostly wood frame with some aluminum siding. The neighborhoods I rode through became more rundown the farther south I went. The storefronts had more hand-painted signs, the yards less grass and more hard-packed dirt. The deepening twilight didn't make them any less hard-edged. By the time I got to King Hill Avenue, the streetlights were on and I was wishing my bike had a headlamp like Rusty's. A mile later, I could hear the cows lowing in the stockyards on the other side of the railroad tracks that ran parallel to the street.

The stench from the packing plants made my eyes water but I kept going. I couldn't imagine living in this neighborhood with the smell of blood and defecation and slaughtered animals, but the side streets were all lined with little houses where the men who worked in the stockyards and the women who raised their children led lives not much different from mine. When I passed the sign for Kansas Avenue, I remembered Dad saying he was born on that street. I stopped under a street light on the corner and unfolded the page I had torn from the phonebook.

My first stop was the Pony Express Bar & Grill. It was squeezed between a storage lot for an auto body shop and a small warehouse. The railyard was right behind it and cattle pens were just beyond the tracks. The bar itself was not much more than a hole in a wall that needed a coat of paint. A small faded sign over the door had a cowboy riding a galloping horse to match its name. I tried to open the front door, but it was locked. I shielded my eyes to see through the single window, but the glass was too dirty to make out anything but shapes. Then one of the shapes moved.

I rattled the door and knocked on the glass as hard as I dared. "Anybody here?" I shouted.

"Beat it! I'm closed," a heavy voice answered.

"I need some help!" I yelled and knocked again.

The door swung open and I jumped back. A husky unshaven man in a greasy T-shirt blocked the doorway.

"I'm closed Mondays. Get lost." He tried to shut the door but I blocked it with my foot.

"I'm looking for my dad, John Freemont. He's a musician. Does he play here?"

The man stopped trying to close the door in my face but didn't move aside to let me in. He scowled. A train rumbled along the tracks behind the building.

"You're Johnny's kid, huh?" the man scratched the belly stretched against his T-shirt. "If that booger-eater sent you here to collect his pay, he's out of luck. He don't play, I don't pay. Tell him Harvey said so." He pushed the door against my foot again.

"He didn't send me, Mr. Harvey, sir. I'm looking for him. I've got to tell him something important. Do you know where he is?"

"He played here Saturday, but he only did one set. He took his break, then he never came back. I ain't seen him since. Some of the guys from Angel's Place came in while he was in the john. They went back there to find him, but he was gone. What's that all about? I don't know where he is and I don't care." Harvey shoved my foot out of the way and slammed the door. The lock clicked.

I was let down and encouraged at the same time. Harvey's story didn't make any sense, but if Dad played here two days ago, he had to be around someplace.

Angel's Place was a few steps further down the street, so I walked my bike there. A dozen motorcycles were parked on the sidewalk and a skull with wings growing out of it had been crudely painted on the front window. A few heads turned as I walked through the door, but most of the crowd ignored me, probably because they couldn't see me through the cigarette smoke hanging in the room. A jukebox somewhere in the back blared Bill Haley and the Comets, but I didn't see a stage of any kind. I squeezed between two big guys in leather jackets at the bar and asked the bartender if he knew John Freemont. "He's my dad and I need to find him," I said. The bartender shook his head and turned away to take care of somebody at the other end of the bar.

"Looking for your daddy, huh? Is your mama sure he's really your daddy?" smirked one of the guys next to me. The other one chuckled.

"Yes sir," I answered. At first I didn't catch what he meant. When it sank in, I bristled and started to tell him to keep his filthy mouth off my mom. But I swallowed the urge and stuck to my plan. "My dad plays guitar. Is there live music in here?"

"Nah, just that jukebox full of crap," the first guy answered. "Say, little man, if your mama needs a daddy, send her down here. I'll take care of her."

I clenched my fists, but before I could take a swing at his leering face, the other guy stepped in.

"Wait a minute. Did you say your old man is Johnny Freemont?"

I relaxed my fist. "That's him. Have you seen him?"

"Come with me," he said. "There's a guy back here who knows him." He took me by the shoulder and pushed me through the crowd toward the far end of the small room. The bikers made way for us until we came to a table where a lean, tall man sat backwards in a chair with his legs splayed around it and his muscular arms folded on the back. His forearms were thick with tattoos. The right arm had a snake that wound around it and ended as a skull on the back of his hand. My man stopped pushing me and said, "Hey, Mike, this kid is looking for Johnny Freemont."

"Is that so?" Mike said. "I'm looking for that bum, too." He didn't raise his voice, but I heard it clearly through the rough clatter of the bar crowd. "Do you know where he's living these days? We went to see him this morning, but he moved."

I shook my head. "No, sir," I said as bravely as I could. "I was hoping someone here might help me find him."

"Hmmmm. Tell you what. I'll help you if you help me. How's that?"

I didn't know what else to do, so I nodded.

"If I find him, I'll let you know, okay?" He paused and I nodded again. "And if you find him, you come see me right away. It's a matter of life or death. You know what that means?" When I nodded, he added, "Good. We got a deal?" He held out his hand for a shake from me.

I'd gotten into something way over my head and I didn't know what to do. Was I making it worse for my dad? Was I in danger? I badly wanted to turn and run, but the hulking guy behind me still had his thick hand on my shoulder. Before I took Mike's hand, I squirmed a bit, and screwed up enough courage to say, "Sure, but why do you want to find him?"

A touch of anger darkened his face as he dropped his hand, but then he laughed. "Gutsy, aren't you? Let's put it this way, your dad was a business associate of mine from time to time. Then he got some valuable merchandise from me. Sort of on consignment. Said he would sell it to some other guys he knew and split the profit with me. I don't like doing business that way but I felt sorry for him, kind of. Anyway, I gave him the stuff and that's the last I saw of him. You see my problem?"

"Yes, sir," I said. It still didn't make much sense to me. Why didn't Dad just give him the stuff back? I was really scared.

"Now you know why I need to find him, just like you. So let's help each other out." He spat in the palm of his hand and held it out to me again. "We got a deal or what?"

My mouth was so dry, I could barely raise any spit, but I did the same and shook his hand.

"Yes, sir," I answered, knowing that I would never keep any part of the bargain.

"Good. Anything else I can do for you?" he said. "Do you need a little pick-me-up for the road?" I shook my head. "Then you better go home to your mama."

I didn't hesitate. I ran back outside, trailed by rock 'n roll and raucous cat calls from the guy who talked smart about Mom. I didn't know what time it was, but it was full dark, so I headed for home. I gave the parked motorcycles a wide berth and pedaled from street light to street light on King Hill past the storefronts and industrial buildings. Just as I reached Sixth Street, a cop car rolled up beside me.

"Hey, kid! Pull over."

~ 9 ~

Yep, I ran out of the devil's den and straight into the clutches of the Spanish Inquisition that night. But that wasn't the worst of it.

At the police station, the cop took me to a hard wooden bench next to the booking desk and told me to stay put or he'd stick my butt in the holding cell with the drunks and other degenerates. I sat down right away. I couldn't see the cell, but I could imagine what would happen to me in there. I couldn't go anyplace anyway since I didn't know what happened to my bike after he put it in the trunk of his patrol car.

"We had our eye on you tonight, kid," the cop said. "What did you deliver to Mike?"

Confused by the question, I shook my head. "I don't know what you mean."

"I mean we didn't find anything on you, so you must have dropped it off before we picked you up. Am I right?

"No, sir, I didn't give anybody anything." I was thoroughly confused. What did he think I'd done?

"We saw you go in Angel's Place, so what were you doing there? Trying to score some weed?"

"No, sir," I answered. So that was it: he thought I was buying or selling drugs! A brief scene of crazed teenagers in *Reefer Madness*, the film they made us watch in school, flashed through my head. I shook it off. "I was looking for my dad."

"Well, if that's where your dad hangs out, you're better off not finding him," he said as he sat down at the booking desk and started filling out some forms. I gave him my name and address. When he asked for a phone number, I told him to call the tavern and talk to Aunt Mae. He wrote it all down without comment.

Was I under arrest? I didn't know and I was afraid to ask. Actually, I was afraid to do anything but sit there in dread of what would happen when Mom came for me, assuming she did. The looming disaster was mixed up in my brain with repeated questions about Dad, drugs, motorcycle gangs, all jumbled around with images of the grim jail cell where I might be spending the rest of my life. The only thing that kept me sane was that, when I told him my name and where I lived, the cop nodded like he knew Aunt Mae, so maybe everything was all going to work out somehow.

I stared at the posters and signs on the faded green wall for a while, then shifted my gaze to the floor where the scuffed linoleum was worn through to the wood underneath. Policemen came and went, none paying any attention to me. I glanced repeatedly at the cop behind the desk, but he never looked up.

It was after midnight before Mom came to get me. She didn't have a car and, by the time she got to the police station, my butt was numb from sitting on the hard bench for hours and my brain was exhausted from chasing itself in circles.

"Where have you been?" she cried as she snatched me off the bench and crushed me to her chest. "Are you all right?" she sobbed, barely able to get out any words. She pushed me away so she could inspect me, then pulled me back. I buried my face in her neck. "What did you think you were doing? You could have been killed! Wait till I get you home, you're going to be sorry, mister!" She gripped my shoulders and pushed me out at arm's length again so she could search for damage. "Are you sure you're all right? Let me see."

"I'm okay, Mom." I looked into her face. It was twisted with distress. "I'm really, really sorry." Her eyes and nose were damp and red. I felt tears welling up in my own eyes. "I'm sorry," I said again.

Mom shook me hard to keep me focused.

"What were you doing?" she demanded.

"I . . . I was looking for Dad," I mumbled.

"Looking for your father? What on earth . . . ."

"I need to find him." Tears ran down my cheeks as I sobbed, "I know he's in trouble and I want to help so he can come back and we can all be together again."

Mom pulled me to her chest once more and rocked back and forth. "Oh, Daniel. You can't do anything for him." I sniffled one last time and she wiped my face with a wadded tissue from her purse. The cop brought her a form to sign.

"We could charge him for riding his bike after dark without a light," he said, "but we'll let it slide this time."

"Thank you," Mom said.

"In the future, ma'am, he needs to stay away from the stock-yards, the whole south end, as far as that goes. Day or night. There's a drug gang from Kansas City that's expanding across the state and that's where they dug in first. They are all over that neighborhood and decent folks have no business there."

"Yes, sir," Mom said, then looked at me. "Did you hear what the officer said, Daniel?"

"Yes, ma'am."

"Your boy said he was looking for your husband," the cop said. "What's his name?"

"He's my ex-husband," Mom said. "His name is John Freemont."

The cop made a note. "Why would he be in Angel's Place?"

"I have no idea where he goes or why. I haven't seen him for over a week."

"If he contacts you, please ask him to come to the station. We're trying to get a handle on what that gang is doing and if he's been hanging around there, we want to ask him a few questions."

"Okay," she said. "Daniel, let's go home." She stood up and looked around. "Where's your bike?" I shrugged and looked at the cop, who said he gave it to some guy waiting for us outside.

When we came out, Larry was standing with my bike by his car. I grabbed Mom's arm and pulled her to a stop at the top of the stairs. I whispered, "What's he doing here?"

"I had to call someone to give me a ride, Daniel. Who else would I call?"

"But . . . but . . . he hurt you!"

She looked surprised and confused for a minute, then said, "No, he didn't hurt me. That was all kind of a mistake. When you get a little older, you'll understand. Now, come on, let's get home." She tugged my hand and I followed her down the stairs. "Put your bike in the trunk," she said.

"I'll do it," Larry snapped. "He'll scratch the paint on the car." He lifted the bike by the frame with one hand and carefully turned the front wheel with the other hand so it would fit into the trunk. Anger poured off him in waves. Every muscle was like a spring wound tight. I was afraid he would bend the wheel when he shut the lid, but I wasn't about to warn him. "Be careful when you get in the back seat," he said as he sat down behind the steering wheel. "That's custom upholstery." His car was a two-door, so I had to fold the front seat forward and crawl over it to get into the back. I took extra care to be sure I didn't scrape my feet across his sacred seat covers—much as I wanted to.

"Daniel, don't you want to say something to Larry?" Mom said as she folded the seat upright and sat down in front.

'Uh, yeah, I guess. I mean, uh, thanks for coming to get me," I muttered.

"Sure," he grumbled. He turned his head toward Mom and switched on a smile that made me want to puke. "I'd do anything for this little gal." Mom reached across the seat and put her hand on his arm. We rode the rest of the way in silence.

When we got home, Aunt Mae was downstairs where she had been babysitting Willy. She met us at the front door and, as I passed her, she gave me a quick wink and a little nod to let me know everything would be all right.

Larry left and Mom sent me to bed. She came in as I climbed the ladder to the top bunk. Willy snored softly in the bottom one. Mom whispered, "Daniel, you know I love you. I need you, too. I need you to be grown-up. I'm sorry we have to live like this, but that's the best I can do for now." She kissed me good night. "I know you don't believe me, but your dad is not the solution to our problems."

I crawled under the covers but couldn't go to sleep. What kind of jerk makes his mother get him out of jail? Makes her cry like that? I ached with worry about her—and Dad, too. I rolled over in bed and tried to erase the echo of her sobs, but I couldn't do it. My thoughts whirled to the nasty things that guy Harvey said about Dad. Then the insults from the bikers in Angel's Place came back to me. I wish I had stood up to them when they bad-mouthed Mom. But I didn't. I was a coward and didn't do anything. I just hurt her. And I was no closer than before to knowing where to find Dad or what kind of trouble he was really in.

~ 10 ~

You know what comes next. I was grounded. It was only for the rest of the week and it wasn't the first or the last time in my life I was confined to quarters, but it sticks in my mind to this day because what happened that week was a major turning point in my summer of woe, if not my life.

Being grounded was fine with me, though, since I had no interest in anything after all the trouble I'd stirred up to earn my punishment. All I wanted to do was stay in the cellar apartment and play my guitar and try to forget everything else. For the first couple of days, Mom watched me eat my Wheaties in silence and sink deeper into the black hole I had dug for myself. Finally, she told me she was tired of watching me mope around, so I could invite Rusty over. We could play outside if we wanted, she said, then changed her mind and said we, in fact, must go outside and get out of her sight.

By the time Rusty got there, Willy and I had finished our breakfast of champions and were poking around in the vacant lot that served as our yard. It wasn't much of a playground, but it was all we had. Mom and I had cleared the broken bottles and rusty cans and other stuff off the hard-packed dirt so Willy could play outside when we first moved in, but there were still patches of concrete and rocks buried just below the surface. There were plenty of scrubby weeds, too, but no grass.

Rusty leaned his bike on its kickstand and said, "So, Daniel my boy, how is your incarceration going?"

"Bite me," I said.

"Ah, still a bit down in the dumps, I see. No word from your dad?"

"Nope. Vanished from the face of the earth." I was ashamed to tell Rusty the cops were looking for Dad, too. I still couldn't believe he might be tangled up with drug pushers.

"Hey you guys!" Willy shouted from the other side of the lot where he was poking around in some weeds. "I found a buried treasure! Come here and dig it up."

Rusty grinned and I rolled my eyes, but we went to see Willy's treasure.

"See!" he said, pointing to a rotting board sticking out of the ground. I grabbed it and tried to pull it up, but it was stuck fast.

"We need a shovel, Willy," I said. "But we don't have one." I hoped that would be the end of it.

"Aw come on," Willy whined. "You do it, Rusty."

"I don't know, Willy," Rusty said. He winked at me and turned to look somberly at Willy. "If it is a buried treasure, there's probably a curse on it. You know what that means?" Willy shook his head. Rusty put on his best Bela Lugosi accent. "Anyone who disturbs ze treasure vill haf to eat Brussel sprouts for breakfast efery day for ze rest of his life."

Willy's eyes got wide as he contemplated that prospect. Then he caught on. "You're full of crap!"

"Ha! Gotcha!" Rusty laughed.

I laughed, too, although I added, "You better not let Mom hear you use that kind of language."

The laughter trailed off to silence when Larry's Chevy pulled up at the curb. He honked and got out of the car with an armful of something and a big grin on his face. "Glad to see you're up and at 'em," he called from the sidewalk. "Your mom said you were feeling pretty low so I thought I would come over and do something about it." I was rocked by a wave of unreality.

Keeping his voice low as Larry crossed the lot, Rusty asked, "Is that who I think it is?"

"Yep, that's Larry."

"From what you said, I wouldn't have recognized him. He doesn't look at all like a Neandertal. Although he does kind of walk like one."

"Hi, Willy," Larry said as he came closer. "And you must be Rusty."

"Yes, sir."

"My name's Larry. Nice to meet you," he said, shaking Rusty's hand. "Say, would you take Willy someplace? I need to talk to Daniel for a minute." Rusty looked at me. I didn't know what was going on, so I shrugged and he and Willy walked to the other side of the lot.

"Look, Bub," Larry said when they were out of earshot, "I think we got off on the wrong foot for some reason. Your mom and me got a good thing going and I don't want any hard feelings on your part since I think we're going to be seeing a lot of each other in the future. Can we be friends?" He held out a hand for me to shake.

I wanted to hock up a loogie but I held back. Maybe Mom put him up to this. Maybe he really does make her happy—she sure deserves a little happiness these days. I owe it to her after all the trouble I caused, I thought. Or maybe he means it. The guy's a jerk, but maybe there's a spark of humanity hidden under the spit curl on his forehead. I decided to give him a chance, for Mom's sake.

I shook his hand. "Sure, friends," I said, trying to sound sincere.

"Great! Come on back, you guys," he called to Rusty and Willy. "I thought we'd play a little ball. You know, just throw it around some. I only brought three gloves, so you can use mine, Rusty. I don't need one." He passed us each a glove. "Here, Willy, let me help you with that." Willy had never worn a baseball glove before and his entire six-year-old fist would fit inside the thumb of this one. I was sure he didn't have a clue about how to use it.

I never was much of an athlete. Baseball always looked like fun, but Dad told me he jammed a finger catching a hard throw one time and couldn't touch his guitar for a month. Said he was lucky he didn't break the knuckle. It could have knitted back stiff and the only thing he'd be picking was his nose. I tried to avoid playing games with balls after that.

Rusty pounded his fist into his glove and gave me a rueful smile. The whole thing was redolent of gym class. It was not our favorite place. "Daniel, my boy," Rusty would say as we changed into our gym clothes in the locker room, "it's time for us to gird our loins and do battle with the knuckleheads."

"You can gird your loins if you want," I would always answer, "but I'm going to wear a jock strap. Got to protect the jewels, you know."

Gym class was all about faking our way through jumping jacks and sit-ups and then staying alive during testosterone-fueled ball games where the jocks were out to get guys like us. We knew it. They knew we knew it. The gym teacher knew it, too, but he didn't care. We were logical targets for the cretins. Rusty not only had hair the color of a fire hydrant, he was short and skinny to boot. His legs were almost hidden by baggy blue gym shorts that hung below his knees and were frequently yanked down by the jocks. I was tall for my age, but that just made me gangly and awkward and my legs stuck out of my shorts like a bony-kneed stork. The knuckleheads snuck behind me and yanked my shorts down a lot, too.

Larry probably would have been one of those obnoxious jocks, I thought, but today he was Mr. Nice Guy. He rolled a ball to Willy, who squealed and chased it down, then tried to throw it back. His throw only made it half way. Larry chuckled and picked it up. He tossed it back-handed in my direction, catching me off guard. I snagged it with my bare hand at the last minute. It stung, but not too bad.

"Nice catch, Bub, but that's what the glove is for," Larry grinned.

I bit off what I wanted to say and fired the ball at Rusty.

We played very sloppy four-way catch until a bad throw from Larry slipped out of Rusty's fingers, hit a rock, and caromed up to hit Willy in the stomach. He was more surprised than hurt, but he cried "Owww!" anyway. Larry knelt down and tried to comfort him, but Willy backed away from him and ran to me. Larry sat back on his heels. I dropped my glove and wrapped my arms around Willy. "You're not hurt," I scoffed. "Knock it off and tell Larry thanks for coming over." Willy leaned back to see if I was serious. Me telling him to treat Larry nice confused both of us.

I spent the next two days practicing nonstop for my performance Friday night. I worked through almost every song in Dad's fake book, making myself stop and start over if I made a mistake. I copied several more songs into my own fake book and played them over and over until my throat got hoarse from endlessly singing and my elephant toes—that's what Dad called the calluses on the ends of my fingers—got even thicker from sliding up and down the steel strings.

When worries about Mom and Dad started to intrude, I turned them off with daydreams of playing a duet with him on the radio someday, maybe even on the *Ozark Jubilee*. That would be like Christmas morning and the last day of school all rolled into one. But disgust about Mom and Larry and confusion about the rest of the real world kept intruding. Even when I could put all that aside and work on my music, I worried that my voice might crack at the wrong time. It had been fine since before Dad left, but who knows what it would do in front of a room full of people?

By Friday afternoon, I was a mental mess and didn't know what I wanted. When it came time to set up to play in the tavern, I gave up struggling with my demons. I told Aunt Mae I didn't feel like playing, as long as she didn't care.

Aunt Mae cared—a lot. She also knew it wasn't stage fright that was making me sick.

"Your life may not be fun right now," she said, "but if you want to be a musician, you have to realize it's your job. And real adults do their jobs, even when they don't feel like it." I started to protest, but she read my mind and cut me off. "Your dad's problems are his own, Daniel. And so are you mom's. You have your own life to live. Your mother and your brother depend on you, but you have responsibilities to yourself, too. One of those responsibilities is doing what you promise."

Her words struck home, so I sucked it up and got ready. I helped her move the rear table to one side so I would have a place to stand where everyone could see me but I wouldn't be in the way if they wanted to get to the bathroom in the back. I was afraid my mind would go completely blank in the middle of a song, so I sat up a rickety folding music stand Dad had given me and put my fake book on it just in case. Aunt Mae didn't have a microphone, but she thought I could play loud enough to be heard in such a small room.

The tavern wasn't packed that night but it was busy. Mom was waiting tables. Willy sat with Rusty and his folks in the first booth so he wouldn't miss anything. Bruno and Mrs. Bruno came in and took a booth, too. Larry stood at the far end of the bar. Finally, all the booths to my left were full and the bar to my right had some guys standing waiting for a stool. A few of them glanced my way as I strapped on my guitar and took my place behind the music stand. Just before Aunt Mae came out from behind the bar to introduce me, Mom passed by with an empty tray and threw me a kiss for good luck. I needed it. I'd never played in front of anyone other than my family before and my palms were sweaty and my stomach was turning queasy with stage fright. Before I could run away, Aunt Mae clanged a spoon on an empty beer bottle.

"Can I have your attention, please?" she yelled over the crowd noise. "We got something new tonight, folks! Music by this good-looking young man who happens to be my nephew. You all know his mother, too, my sister, Betty!" She waved in Mom's direction and several people clapped. "So you folks be kind and welcome Daniel Freemont to the Ko-Z-Inn stage, such as it is." A few more people clapped.

I tried to look confidently at the crowd as I hit a hard E-minor chord and let it ring for four beats, then picked up a steady 4/4 rhythm on the low E string by itself. On the third bar, I sang, "Some people say man is made outta mud." Aunt Mae had said most of the audience were working folks, so I figured "Sixteen Tons" by Merle Travis would get a good reception. It was also pretty simple to play so I probably couldn't screw it up. I was right about not messing up, but wrong about the song's appeal. By the second verse, most of the audience had gone back to their drinks and dinners. The clink of beer bottles on glasses and cutlery on plates stepped up. The laughter and conversation grew louder until I was sure no one beyond the next booth and the nearest end of the bar could hear me at all. I finished the song with a last ringing E-minor chord that disappeared in the clatter. Nobody applauded. I hadn't exactly wowed them and I wasn't sure what to do next. Should I bow? Should I thank the audience? Should I run out the door? Finally, seeing that I'd stopped playing, Willy clapped, then Rusty and his parents joined in, followed by Bruno and a handful of others. Mom detoured past me carrying an order for one of the booths. She leaned over and whispered, "You're doing great! Give 'em something hot!"

I gritted my teeth and nodded. I could do this! I looked back toward the crowd just as someone yelled out, "Do you know any Hank Williams?"

"Sure!" I called back. I turned to my fake book again, trying to choose the perfect song. Out of the corner of my eye, I saw Mom step from behind the bar with a tray of drinks. "Here's a Hank Williams tune!" I announced. "This one is for my mom! It's called 'Hey, Good Lookin'!" The crowd got a big laugh out of Mom as she mimed a protest in my direction and came to stand next to the booth with Willy and Rusty. The tune had a real rocking rhythm to it and simple, memorable lyrics that the crowd liked. A few of them clapped along and some even joined in on the chorus. Their attention energized me and I knew at that very moment I wanted to sing and play in front of people for the rest of my life. The applause was genuine this time. The ragged claps punctuated by a "whoop" here and "that's the way" there charged up all my senses. The tavern lights radiated a glow that was reflected in the customer's cheering faces. The scent of beer, the sizzle of burgers on the grill, the tinkle of ice cubes wrapped around me like Superman's cape.

I was getting ready to start another song as Larry made his way to the end of the bar near me and raised his beer bottle in a silent toast. I was still high from the applause so I took it as a compliment and grinned back at him. He drained the beer, took a last drag from his cigarette, and pushed the butt into the empty bottle. "You've got a great future in hillbilly music, Bub," he said. "But you ought to get a real guitar—you know, an electric one—and learn some rock 'n roll." He gave a thick, drunken chuckle and went back to the far end of the bar. I shook it off.

My confident fingers knew exactly where to go on the strings as I picked a simple but lively four-bar intro to another Hank Williams song, "I Saw the Light." As I took a big breath to sing the opening line, I remembered how strong and clear I had sung the first two numbers—not a hint of a crack in my voice. The crowd settled down to hear my song and I was flooded by happiness I hadn't felt for months. I poured my euphoria into the tune and the audience lapped it up. Their applause was even louder than before. I looked around the room and found Mom beaming near the booth where Willy and Rusty sat. She balanced her serving tray on one arm so she could give me a big thumbs up with the other hand.

"More Hank!" somebody shouted from the bar. Before I could answer, the tavern door crashed open.

The room went deathly silent as Mike and two of his biker goons pushed their way through the crowd to stand like three escapees from a nightmare staring at me. Mom darted to my side.

"I don't know who you are, but you better leave him alone!" she warned.

"I don't give a shit about your kid," Mike said. "I came to ask him if he found his no-good father yet." He glared at me. "Where is he?"

"He doesn't know," Mom said.

"Then maybe you know," Mike sneered as he came so close to Mom his tattooed forearm brushed against the empty tray she was holding in front of us like a shield. Larry half-turned on his bar stool but looked away when one of Mike's goons glanced at him. I tried to step between Mike and Mom but she pushed me out of the way.

Bruno jumped up, ignoring his wife's hand on his arm, and stepped out of their booth. "Who you think you are?" he shouted. "You no bully that boy!"

A goon shoved Bruno back into the booth. He struggled to get back up but his wife grasped his shirt and held him down.

Mike kicked my music stand over and the pages of my fake book flew everywhere. "I think you know where Freemont is," he snarled at Mom, "and you better tell me."

"Or what, dirt-bag?" It was Aunt Mae. She barreled through the crowd brandishing the sawed-off baseball bat she kept beneath the bar. "You get out!" she bellowed, "and crawl back under your rock." She raised her bat. "Daniel, call the cops. Tell them there are dead drug dealers littering up my floor."

I dashed to the phone. I had today's dime from Bruno in my pocket. As I put it in the slot, I looked back at the room. One of Mike's goons laughed and made a grab for Aunt Mae's bat. She took a mighty swipe and he jumped back just in time. I dialed the police number stenciled on the wall next to the phone but I must have missed a number because the call didn't go through. "There's a fight in Mae's tavern," I shouted into the phone anyway, hoping no one but me knew the line was dead. "Come quick!"

Aunt Mae cocked her bat again and the biker took another step back. "We made our point," Mike said. "Let's go." The crowd parted as the three men turned and strode toward the door. As they passed the far end of the bar where Larry was cringing, Mike swiveled back to face Mom. He pointed at her. "When that asshole husband of yours comes around, I'll know about it. I'm going to keep an eye on you—and your kids."

As soon as the door closed behind him, the crowd released the collective breath it had been holding. Aunt Mae yelled to the crowd, "Show's over, folks. Sorry about the trouble." Mom stood quivering with Willy in her arms. Mae put her arms around them both, a fierce scowl on her face. I shook with fear, too, barely able to take the guitar strap from around my neck.

Rusty brought me my guitar case. "You okay?" he said. When I nodded, he said, "Your Aunt Mae should bat clean-up for the Yankees." His crack helped.

"That's for sure," I said. Rusty gathered up the scattered pages of my fake book. I tried to fold up the music stand, but it was bent beyond repair. As I was putting my guitar away, I noticed Larry talking earnestly to Mom in the back room. She shook her head once, but he took her chin in his hand and lifted her face to his. She froze. He gripped her upper arms and shook her slightly. I couldn't hear what he was saying, but she finally dropped her head in sad resignation.

~ 12 ~

I lived in lots of places in my long life. The first home I remember was a room over a grocery store where we lived when Willy was born. About all I can recall about the place was a long, narrow wooden staircase on the side of the building that we had to climb to get to the room. I was old enough to navigate it on my own, but after Mom had to haul Willy up those stairs a few times, she got pretty tired of it and so we moved. Most every other place is kind of a blur now, except, of course, for the cellar under Aunt Mae's tavern and then Larry's house. That's where we went after the motorcycle gang crashed my musical stage debut. It was safer there, according to Mom. And besides, she thought Larry would be a good provider. Willy and I didn't get to vote on the matter, and Dad was nowhere to be seen, so we packed up our stuff and became refugees under Larry's tender care.

At first, living in Larry's house was a world better than living in the cellar of the tavern. The house may have been a cheap tract home thrown up to sell to veterans with low-cost mortgages from the G.I. Bill, but it was luxurious in comparison to the hole in the ground where we had been living. The house had windows, so the sun could reach every room. It had a yard with grass, not broken bottles. It had a bathroom with a shower, a real bathtub for humans, not a watering tub for horses, and plumbing that ran both cold and hot water. The house was small but livable for the four of us, with two bedrooms, a living room, and an eat-in kitchen large enough for full-size appliances. Every room in the house except the kitchen and bathroom was carpeted, too. Larry even had a television set in the living room. The bedroom Willy and I shared was large enough to allow both our beds to be on the floor instead of stacked as bunks, which would be helpful a few weeks later when I had to sneak out of the house to start the journey that led to the bullet hole in my guitar.

The only thing wrong with the house was the owner.

"If you want to live in my house," Larry said over dinner the day after we moved in, "You're going to follow my rules." Mom cast her eyes down at her plate. Apparently she knew what was coming. "Dinner is at six o'clock every night. You'll both wash your hands and face and set the table before then. You'll eat everything on your plate and thank your mother for cooking it. You won't leave the table until everyone is finished. Then you'll clear the dishes and help your mother wash them. You got all that?"

I nodded, but Willy just stared at him with his mouth open. Sternly, Larry repeated, "You got that, Willy?" My brother blinked, looked at Mom, then at me, then, very softly, said, "Yes Larry."

"Good," Larry said as he stood up from the table. "There are some other rules, too, and you'll both have chores. We'll go over those later." He went out the back door and sat down in an aluminum lawn chair where he smoked a cigarette while he surveyed the backyard of his kingdom. We learned that's what he did every night after dinner.

"Okay, boys," Mom said. "Let's clean up so we can watch TV before bedtime. I think 'Rin Tin Tin' is on tonight."

Larry's other rules seemed to come into existence only after we'd broken them. Over the next few days, we learned he got to use the bathroom first in the morning so he would have plenty of hot water. And I couldn't leave my bike in the front yard even for a minute—Larry decreed it had to be parked under the eave in the back of the house so our yard didn't look like a bunch of hillbillies lived there. The same rule applied to Willy's toy cars. The first time Larry found one of them on the front sidewalk, he stomped on it to make his point.

At first, I had a lot of trouble figuring Larry out. Later, I found exactly what he was, but in the beginning I didn't know if he was a good guy or a bad guy. Or a good bad guy or a bad good guy. Was he like a barber I could trust, or one I had to keep my eye on in case he decided it would be hilarious to shave his initials in the back of my head. As you may have noticed, with my hairline, I don't have to worry much about that these days. But back to Larry. My gut told me one thing while my brain told me something else. Go with my heart, you say? Well, that's a recipe for calamity. In a situation like mine with Larry, your heart is no good. It just knows what it desires—not why it wants it or if what it wants is good or bad. The heart just wants. It's a useless organ when you have to make tough judgment calls. Sentiment corrupts tough decisions, at least in my experience. And I've had to make plenty of tough decisions.

Which is what I had to do with Larry. Was he a bad guy because he was sleeping with my Mom? Or a good guy because he let us live in his house? One day he was Simon Legree making me work all day for next to nothing, and the next day, well . . . you'll see.

One blistering summer day not long after we moved into the house, Larry found me lying on my bed reading in the room I shared with Willy. He ordered me to close my book.

"You need to cut those weeds behind the garage."

I looked up from my book. "Okay, as soon as I finish this chapter."

"Finish it later. I want them weeds cut right now."

"But the sun's around there. Can't I wait until it's shady?"

"Now, you little turd. I said NOW!"

He clamped his hand around my skinny arm and yanked me up out of my chair. He pushed me through the house and shoved me out the back door. His rock-hard grip left purple welts on my arm that faded by the time I got to the garage.

I swung the cutter whip into the weed stems standing tall and tangled in the hot sun. I don't know why I had to cut them down; they don't obstruct anything in the narrow strip of dirt between the garage and the gravel alley running behind it. But Larry wanted it done, so I did it. Tall, white-juiced milkweed, sticky thistles, tough-stemmed Johnson grass. Who was Johnson, I wonder, and why did he have grass named after him? He must have been a mean man.

I swung the whip again and again. It had a sharp flat blade set at an angle on a flexible steel shaft with a wooden handle that got heavier with every swing. It was slow, hard, hot work. The saw-toothed leaves scratched my arms. The stiff weed stems snapped around my fingers when the blade slashed through them. Dust from the gravel in the alley coated the leaves and puffed into the air along with the grasshoppers who fled the whip, whirring before the flashing blade to new hiding places in the brush. The sun glared off the white side of the garage.

"Watch the blade. Watch your leg. Don't hit your toes," I said to myself as I swung the whip. "If you chop off your foot, he'll just laugh at you." Swish, thunk. Swish, thunk. I was not quite strong enough to drive the blade all the way through the stiff weeds in one stroke, but every time I swung, a few more fell.

"Watch what you're doing," I repeated to myself.

Swish, thunk. Swish, thunk. Swish, CLINK, BANG. The blade drove a piece of gravel into the garage. I had swung too low.

"Watch it, stupid," I muttered

The whip grew heavy in my sweaty hand. Sticky weed sap spotted my scratched arms and dust coated my sun-reddened skin. I finished the job and gasped for breath in the thick air as I dragged the whip back up the hill to the house.

"Did you rake it all up? When I go down there, I better find them weeds in a pile," Larry demanded.

"I will. I just need a drink of water."

"You're a lazy son of a . . ." Larry said, but was interrupted by Mom bringing me a glass of cool water.

"He's going to have a sunstroke," she said while keeping an eye on his expression. I gulped the water down and she added, "And look at his skin. Sweet Jesus, he's all sun-burnt."

"He ain't hurt none," he answered. He pointed at me and said, "Those weeds need to be piled up so I can burn them."

Mom brushed her hand across my brow, wiping away the sweat and gravel dust and flakes of weed. I shivered under her cool touch. She took the glass from my hand and went back in the house. As soon as the screen door closed behind her, Larry grabbed my wrist.

"Let me see your arm," he said loudly so Mom could hear him. "How bad are you burnt?" He yanked my arm out straight for inspection, twisted it back and forth, then slapped my sunburn with his fingers. I gasped between my clenched teeth. "Doesn't look too bad," he grinned, examining his white finger marks on my red skin. He smacked my forearm again, harder, and a weak mewling escaped from me as I shuddered from the pain. "You little pussy," he snarled. He slapped my arm three times, hard and fast, then dropped my wrist and walked away.

I slumped and silently cringed as I cradled my screaming arm. I didn't cry out to Mom; she couldn't help. I sucked it up, left the grass whip where it lay, and fetched a rake to finish the job.

Willy started moping around not long after we started living under Larry's rules. He wasn't sick, but I heard him whimpering in bed sometimes. I asked him if something was wrong one morning, but he just shrugged his little shoulders and trotted off to be by himself. I knew it was tough on him. I could escape on my bike with Rusty, but Willy was stuck at home with no one to play with most of the time. After a few days of this, I found something he could enjoy about our new house—or that would at least make living there tolerable. I showed him how to make himself dizzy by tucking his arms into his small chest and rolling like a log down the embankment in the back yard that slanted from the house to the alley. The first time he did it, he screamed in mock terror all the way down and jumped up at the bottom with his head swimming. He staggered around until his eyes could focus, then demanded to do it again.

"Roll me, Daniel. I want to go faster," he said, so I did.

About the time I got bored watching Willy roll down the embankment, Rusty turned the corner into the alley on his bike. Larry's house was on the east side of town, a long walk but a short bike ride from Rusty's house and Aunt Mae's tavern.

"Hey, boys!" Rusty said as he jumped off his bike. He pointed at Willy weaving unsteadily across the grass. "I think he's getting ready to barf his breakfast." As a matter of fact, Willy did look a little green around the gills.

"That's enough for now, Willy," I said. "Why don't you go inside and see what Mom's fixing for lunch." He climbed the hill and went in the back door without any argument.

Rusty propped his bike up on its kickstand and flopped onto the grass. "So, how's it going in the new house?" he said.

"Not so good when Larry's around. At least he's on duty at the firehouse today, so it's kind of like a vacation for me." Larry didn't have a regular nine-to-five job. He worked 24 hours on duty at the firehouse, then had two days off. When he was on duty he slept at the firehouse and we didn't see him at all. "I have to mow the grass and clean my room and stuff, but that's not the worst thing."

"Let me guess. Larry is the worst."

"You got it. He's a first-class prick."

"What happened?"

"It's not any one thing. It's a bunch of them. He's a little dictator with rules and crap. He treats Willy like dirt. He roughed me up the other day, then laughed about it. Worst of all, I'm not sure, but I think I heard him smack Mom the other day. She denied it."

"Holy crap!" Rusty said. "What are you going to do?"

"Mom says we have to wait it out. He'll get used to us and we'll get used to him."

"You know, you can get used to crotch itch, too, but that doesn't make it go away."

"Yeah, that's pretty much what it's like. But what am I going to do? Get this--Mom says I need to earn his respect."

"How are you supposed to do that?"

"I don't know. Get a job or build a house or something, I guess."

"Hmmm, a job's not a bad idea, you know. You can always use the money. How much is your allowance?"

"Ha! Ha! What a comedian! I get to sleep and eat here—that's my allowance."

"Ouch! What do you do for walking around money?"

"I still sweep the tavern on Monday mornings," I answered. "And I sort bottles at Bruno's sometimes, but that's a long way to ride for a dime."

"The trusty Rusty brain says you need another hustle, my man." He looked around as if the answer were somewhere in the yard, which is where he found it. "You say you mow the grass, right? How long does it take?"

"It's a small yard, so not long, maybe an hour. This embankment is the worst part of it."

"Would you mow it for a dollar?"

"Sure, I guess so, but Larry isn't going to pay me anything."

Rusty ignored me. "And every yard in this block is the same, right?" I nodded when I saw where he was going. "The grass grows on them, too, so get your butt in gear," he said. "I'd help, but I think I'm allergic to grass."

"Allergic to work, more likely!"

"That too. See you later."

I got the lawn mower out of the garage, filled the gas tank, and went door-to-door looking for work. I soon found that most of the neighbors were either too cheap or simply couldn't afford to have someone mow their lawns, although few of them would admit it. I worked my way down one side of the street to the end of the block with no takers and was half way back up the other side before I finally found an old lady who needed some help. Her little tract house was identical to Larry's but it felt like something out of Hansel and Gretel when I rang the bell and the door was answered by an old witch.

Her chin shot up and out, almost meeting the tip of her crooked nose as she loudly demanded through toothless gums, "What do you want, boy?"

"I, uh, I was wondering if, uh, I could mow your grass?" I stuttered. "It looks a little shaggy."

"Shaggy is it?" she screeched. Her eyes bugged out as she looked past me at her yard. "Guess it is! Place has gone to hell since my husband died." She fixed me with a squinty glare. "How much you want? Speak up, boy," she cackled, "I'm deaf in one ear and can't hear out of the other one."

She was an old widow who lived alone. She sure could pass for a witch, though. I looked around her yard as if appraising the property, then said I would do it for a dollar.

"A dollar!" she exclaimed. "I live on Franklin Roosevelt's Social Security. I can't afford a whole dollar." She started to close the door.

"Okay, fifty cents?" I asked.

"All right. Fifty cents. When you're finished, not before."

I went right to work. The yard was just like ours, a small square in front, narrow strips of grass on each side of the house, and another square of lawn in back. Her plot was perfectly flat, so pushing the mower was easy and I finished in less than an hour. The old lady gave me two quarters, then handed me a snickerdoodle.

"Here's a cookie, boy. To keep your strength up." As she closed the door, I made a mental note to bring Willy to her house on Halloween. I went back to soliciting jobs from her neighbors but I got no other takers, so I pushed the mower home, cleaned it up, and put it back into the garage.

When I told Mom I'd earned some money that day, she said she was proud of me and Larry would be, too. Maybe that would lighten him up a little, I thought, but I didn't say so out loud. Somehow, I didn't think he was likely to give me a medal.

Larry's shift at the firehouse ended at six AM. He was waiting for me the next morning when I came into the kitchen for breakfast.

"Did you run the lawnmower yesterday?" he asked.

"Yes," I answered. I wanted to add, "and good morning to you, too," but I didn't.

"What for? You just mowed the grass three days ago. What did you use it for?"

"I mowed some lady's grass. She lives across the street down the block a ways. She paid me." I couldn't figure out why he seemed to grow more angry the more I explained. "I cleaned the mower up afterwards just like you showed me. Did I break a rule?"

"Yeah. A big one," he snarled. "Who said you could use my mower? And my gas? And my oil? Did you ask my permission? You didn't, did you?"

Mom was pouring corn flakes into a bowl for Willy. She stopped and said, "He was just trying to earn a little spending money."

"You keep out of this," Larry snapped. He turned back to me. "You don't touch my tools or anything else in my garage without my permission! Understand?"

"Yes, sir."

"You want a job, I'll give you a job. It is about time you earned your keep around here. Eat your breakfast and get your ass down to the garage." He turned to Mom. "I'll deal with you later." The back door slammed after him.

Mom's hand quaked as she put a bowl of cereal on the table for me. "I'm sorry, Daniel."

"I'm trying, Mom, really, I am!"

"I know. We need him, though, so give him a chance," she said as if she were trying to convince herself as well as me. She brightened and added, "Maybe he's going to teach you how to paint cars. Won't that be something?" I had my doubts, but I kept them to myself as I took my time eating my breakfast.

I pretty much hate cars to this day for no other reason than the misery I endured working on them. I guess nearly everybody—especially guys—takes great pride in their wheels, but all that work I had to do, sanding and cleaning, washing, waxing, jacking them up and crawling underneath to drain the oil—all that dirty stuff—just ruined cars for me. Sure, I own one today, but I don't worship it. My car is lucky if I take it to the car wash a couple of times a year. My dislike for automobiles began that morning.

"All right, Bub. Time to get to work," Larry said when I came into the garage. On his days off, he did auto body repair and painting in the garage behind the house by the alley. Some of the cars belonged to friends of his, others were repossessed cars sent by a bank loan officer he knew. Larry worked sometimes in a big body shop near the firehouse, too, but his own garage was the center of his life. It was big enough to hold a car with room to spare for a mind-boggling collection of tools and supplies in cabinets lining the walls. An air compressor the size of a refrigerator occupied one corner.

He patted the hood of a dark blue Oldsmobile. "I have to paint this beauty tomorrow and you're going to get it ready. Here are your tools." He pointed to a bucket of water with a sponge floating in it, then held up a piece of sandpaper wrapped around a block of wood. He squeezed most of the water out of the sponge, swiped it across a section of the hood, and rubbed the sandpaper back and forth across the surface. "It's simple," he said, handing me the sponge and sanding block. "You keep the surface lubricated with the water and sand it until the paint doesn't shine. Keep moving around until you've sanded the entire car. When it dries, there can't be any shiny spots. Every bit of the surface has to be dull for the new paint to stick. Got that?"

"I guess so," I said. It didn't look like brain surgery. It also didn't look like much fun.

"Okay, Bub," he said. "Show me."

I took the sponge and the block wrapped with sandpaper and tried to do exactly what Larry had done. I squeezed a little water on the hood and rubbed it with the sandpaper. I was surprised at how fine the grain was on the paper. It felt like there was no friction with the paint, almost like I was polishing it instead of rubbing it off. I stepped back to let Larry see what I had done. He dried the spot I had sanded and laughed.

"Do you see that shine?" he asked. I looked at the area I thought I had sanded. It looked like the sandpaper had never touched it. "You got to put some elbow grease into it. And rub and rub and rub. That's 400-grit paper, so it doesn't have much bite. Try it again."

I went at it again, harder and faster, for several minutes. The water turned blue as my sanding finally started lifting the old paint. I stepped back to let Larry wipe it dry and check. When he nodded, I felt a tinge of accomplishment. Then I saw that my frantic work had prepped an area smaller than my hand. My spirits sank as I realized this job was going to take at least all day.

"Every square inch has to look just like that," Larry repeated. "You better not dawdle. I'll check on you later." He disappeared and left me to my work. I could tell he was testing me, expecting me to fail, but I fell to the job determined to prove him wrong.

My estimate of the time, it turned out, was very wrong. It didn't take all day—it took longer. By lunch time, I'd only finished the hood and one front fender. By the time I broke for dinner, the other front fender, the doors, and the top were done, but that still left both back fenders and the trunk. When Mom called out that it was time for dinner, I dragged myself up to the house and cleaned up as best I could so I could sit at the table to eat.

"You still got some work to do, don't you?" Larry smirked.

"Can't he finish in the morning?" Mom asked. "He looks awfully tired."

"Nope. I have to paint the car tomorrow."

Mom started to say something else, then shut her mouth so hard her teeth clicked together. She was distressed and undecided whether to stand up to Larry or just shut up and avoid an ugly scene.

"I can get it done," I said, although I didn't know if I could or not. My arms felt like soggy spaghetti and my back ached from bending over to reach the lower parts of the car's body. I wasn't going to quit, though. I knew that's what Larry expected and I wasn't about to give him the satisfaction of being right.

It was well past midnight when I turned off the lights in the garage and stumbled up to the house. My t-shirt and jeans were soaked with blue water and the skin on my hands was wrinkled beyond prunes. The wet sandpaper had taken its toll on the calluses on the tips of my fingers, too. As I stripped for a shower, I wondered how long it would be before my fingers healed so I would be able to play the guitar again.

$$\sim 14 \sim$$

It was almost lunchtime when I got out of bed the next day. I not only needed the rest, but I wanted to stay under the covers hoping to steer clear of Larry. When I finally got up and went into the kitchen, it was close to noon. Mom handed me two dollars. "He said this is for yesterday." She wouldn't look me in the eye. I didn't bother to calculate what it broke down to by the hour. I just hoped he wouldn't have another sanding job for me any time soon. Mom saw my frown and reached out to lay her hand on my cheek. Her sleeve slid up, revealing a black and blue bruise encircling her forearm like a bracelet. It looked like someone had tried to wring her arm like a wet towel between their two hands.

"You're hurt, Mom!" I said. "What happened?"

"Oh, that's nothing. I reached under the sink and got it caught in the drain pipe." Before I could ask another question, she said, "I know two dollars isn't much, but I think he's got a birthday present for you, too." That didn't brighten my outlook any, but it took my attention away from her bruise.

Through the kitchen window, I saw Larry drinking beer in his lawn chair waiting for the paint on the Oldsmobile to dry. I should have gone out to thank him for the big two-dollar paycheck, but I went back to my room instead. I picked up my guitar with my aching hands and tried to practice a little. The calluses on my fingertips had disappeared. They had built up from hours and hours of playing until the strings couldn't dent them, much less cut the skin. Now, after a day soaking in water and pushing sandpaper, just touching the steel strings was agonizing, but I played through the pain anyway, trying to lose myself in the music where the Larry couldn't find me. I flipped open my fake book and found "Lovesick Blues" with Dad's double lines between some of the chords to signify his signature double-note transition licks. I tried to play the song the way he would, but the special licks were too hard for me. After a dozen tries, I put my guitar back in its case and sat on my bed wishing I knew where Dad had gone. I was still mad at him, but I ached for him, too.

Larry opened my bedroom door. He didn't bother to knock, didn't say "excuse me," didn't do anything to show any concern for me, just opened my door and said, "If you can quit fooling with that guitar for a minute, I've got a surprise for you." He was a little drunk, but not slurring his words or anything. I didn't jump right up, so he snapped, "Come on. Let's go." My present must be coming, I thought. Happy birthday to me.

I followed him out the front door to his spotless Chevy parked at the curb. He opened the driver's door, stood aside like a sarcastic chauffeur, and told me to get behind the wheel. "Your mom said your birthday is tomorrow. I'll be on duty at the firehouse, so I want to give you your present today." He was obviously reciting a speech Mom told him to give. "Get in. It's about time you learned stuff a real man needs to know." I'm sure that snide remark didn't come from Mom; it was an adlib fresh from his own pea-size brain.

"But I'm not old enough to drive," I said.

"Nope, but you're tall for your age so you can see over the steering wheel and your feet will reach the pedals. Get in and let's see if you can grow a pair."

Larry went around to the passenger side while I reluctantly sat down in the driver's seat, tense and unsure what I was supposed to do. The beer on his breath filled the car. "Here's the key," he said. "Put it in, turn it, and start the car." I hunted for a place to stick the key until he finally snorted in disgust. "There," he said, pointing to a spot on the dashboard under all the dials. "That's the ignition switch." I turned the key and the engine came to life. Its roar startled me and I jumped. He laughed.

"Relax," he commanded. "Now put your right foot on the brake pedal and release the emergency brake." There were two pedals on the floor, so I pushed the one on the right. The engine raced and I jumped again. "That's the gas," he said. I sensed he really wanted to say "that's the gas, stupid," but he didn't. "The other one's the brake." I moved my foot to the other pedal. "That's the one you push when you want to stop the car. The gas is the one that makes it go. Got that?"

I bit my tongue and nodded.

"Now, turn that handle and release the emergency brake." He reached across me to point down to a black plastic handle sticking out from under the dash on the left. I did what he said.

"Okay, now put it in gear. This has an automatic transmission, so you don't have to worry about a clutch." He was getting way too technical. I didn't have a clue as to what a clutch was or why I should care. Nor how to put the car in gear. Impatiently, he jabbed a finger at the lever on the right side of the steering wheel and told me to pull it down until a little indicator pointed to "D" at the base of the steering column. When I did as he said, the car begin to move. "Brake!" he ordered.

"Which brake?" I said, starting to panic as the car picked up speed.

I reached for the emergency brake handle I'd just turned but he snapped, "Not that one! The one under your foot!" I immediately stomped on the pedal as hard as I could and the car slammed to a stop, throwing Larry into the dash and me into the steering wheel where my elbow hit the horn. The blare was deafening. "Christ Almighty!" he exclaimed. He yanked my arm off the horn and shoved the gear shift lever to where it pointed to "P."

"I . . . I'm sorry," I stammered.

Larry gritted his teeth and his eyes bulged with the coming explosion. I braced myself for a blow. Instead, he took a deep, deep breath, held it, and exhaled with a whoosh. "All right, try it again. Put your foot on the brake, put it in gear, give it a little gas and try not to kill me."

I wiped my sweaty palms on my jeans and did as I was told. The car inched forward.

"Steer to the center of the street," he said. I managed to do that, too, swerving back and forth a little, but I didn't hit anything. He told me to drive around the block. Fortunately, there wasn't any traffic on our quiet street, so I got us back home without disaster. When we got there, he said, "Pull over to the curb, put it in 'park' and pull the emergency brake. That's enough for today."

"Uh, thank you," was the only reply I could think of. What I was thankful for was the end of the lesson, but I kept that to myself.

"We're not done yet. Get out and let me show you a couple of other things every man should know."

Now what? We went to the back of the car, where he opened the trunk and lifted out a gray metal toolbox. He knelt and put it on the ground and motioned for me to kneel next to him. He lifted the lid and started jabbing his finger at the things inside. "A man should always have some basic tools in case his car breaks down. A straight screwdriver, a Phillips, two adjustable wrenches, channel lock pliers, a pair of needle-nose pliers, and a ball peen hammer. Got that?"

"That's a good idea," I answered. Left unsaid, of course, was you'd have to know how to use them.

Larry preened a little bit. "And it's a good idea to have a spare key on you all the time, too. I keep a car key and a house key in my wallet." He took the wallet out of his back pocket and showed me the two keys inside. "You never know when your key ring is going to fall into the toilet or something. Har! Har! Har!"

"What's that?" I asked, pointing to a slim foil packet next to the keys in his wallet. I knew very well what it was, but I wanted to hear him explain it.

"Well, uh, every guy needs one of those on hand at all times, too. For protection, you know?"

I started to ask him if Mom knew it was there, but he was getting a little weird, so I chuckled, "Oh yeah! Sure!"

He belched and said, "I need a beer." As he closed the toolbox and we stood up, I noticed Mom watching us from the house. I waved and tried to look happy.

That night, I went to bed knowing Larry would leave for his shift at the firehouse before I got up in the morning so he wouldn't be around to ruin my birthday. I didn't expect much in the way of celebration, but at least he wouldn't be part of it. I had overheard Mom on the telephone whispering to Aunt Mae that afternoon, so I knew they were planning something. I fell asleep feeling loved.

In the middle of the night, Willie screamed.

"Get them off me!" he screeched as I sat up in bed. "Daniel! Daniel! Get them off me!" Scared and confused, I tried to shake off my sleep as his shouts grew louder.

I managed to get out of bed and turn on the light. Willy cowered in the corner of his bed across the room, his little hands slapping at his legs and belly.

"Get them off! Get them off!" he pleaded, but I couldn't see anything on him.

"Where?" I shouted. "What are they?"

"Bugs and snakes! Spiders!" He was trapped in a nightmare, unable to wake up. His arms flailed about his body. His eyes were wide open but he wasn't seeing the real world. I shivered at the otherness of his eyes. His contorted face scared me, but I climbed into his bed and tried to help him brush away the imaginary horrors.

"It's okay," I said over and over. "I'm here."

"You boys shut up in there!" Larry yelled from the other bedroom.

Willy's skin was clammy, his face covered with sweat, his pajamas soaked and clinging to his legs. He had wet himself. "Get me out," he whimpered.

"Out of where, Willy? I don't understand."

"The dark room with the big machines. It wants to cut off my fingers!"

"I said, shut up in there!" Larry hollered again.

The door to the other bedroom opened and Mom rushed to Willy's bed. Larry was behind her but stopped at the doorway.

"Shut that fucking brat up," he ordered. "I have to go work tomorrow."

Mom ignored him and lifted Willy out of my arms. She petted and soothed him until he woke up. "He's okay," she said as much to herself as to me. "He has a fever and it gave him a bad dream."

She rocked him for a minute, then said, "I'm going to give him a bath," She asked me to change the sheets on his bed.

"He ought to sleep in his own piss," Larry snarled as he turned back to his room and slammed the door.

Mom carried Willy into the bathroom. His eyes drooped as she gently washed him and hummed a tender lullaby. He was almost asleep when she toweled him off and carried him back to our room.

"His mattress is wet, Mom," I said. "Better put him in bed with me."

"Good night, Daniel," she said as she left our bedroom. "See if you can get some sleep now. It is all going to be okay."

I knew Mom was wrong. I couldn't erase the sight of Willy quivering in the corner of his bed, eyes wide and seeing things that weren't there. I tried to sleep, but I couldn't escape the knowledge that we were a long way from okay.

~ 15 ~

Is thirteen a lucky number or an unlucky number? It would be hard to tell if you had to judge by all the things that happened on my thirteenth birthday. Some were wonderful and some were terrible, which is maybe why I remember everything about that day. It began like any other Friday, although Mom gave me pancakes for breakfast and hinted there was more good stuff to come. As usual, I pedaled my bike to Bruno's grocery and sorted his bottles. Because I got started late, it was nearly noon when I finished. As he handed me the dime I'd earned, Bruno said, "Your Aunt Mae wants you to go see her." He had a strange little twitch in his lip when he said it, as if he had a secret he was itching to tell me. I would have stopped in to see Aunt Mae anyway, so I didn't think anything about it. When I went across the street to the tavern, I caught her at the grill cooking hamburger patties with a suspicious smile on her face. Something was up, I decided. Something good.

I thought I had the solution in hand when she gave me a silver dollar. "Here's a little present for your birthday, Daniel," she said. "Look at it close." I never had a real silver dollar before and was fascinated by the portrait of Lady Liberty striding across the horizon against the sunrise. When I examined it in more detail, I saw the date it was minted, 1943. "I put that aside the year you were born. I thought I'd give it to you someday when you needed a little extra luck in your life."

"Wow! Thanks! I'll never spend it."

"Don't make promises you can't keep," she chuckled.

She glanced at the Hamm's Beer clock over the bar and started laying silverware and setting condiments on the table.

"What's going on?" I asked. "Can I help?"

Before she could answer, the front door opened and Rusty pushed his bike in and leaned it against the front booth next to mine like he did when we played pinball. Only it wasn't Monday and I didn't remember telling him to meet me. He was smiling like he'd just been elected king of the candy store.

"Happy birthday, boys and girls!" he said. "Where's the party?"

"Right here, you hooligan," Aunt Mae said. "Just like it says on the wall." She pointed to a hand-lettered placard that hung over the cash register and read it out loud. "There ain't no place just like this place anywhere near this place, so this must be the place!"

"I couldn't have said it better myself," Rusty said.

The door opened again and Bruno and his wife came in and then a taxi dropped off Mom and Willy. Mom carried a cake to the table where Aunt Mae was setting out plates and glasses. "It's devil's food, Daniel!" Willy shouted. "Blow out the candles!"

"Not yet, silly," Mom laughed. "I have to light them first."

"And we need some real food, too," Aunt Mae said. "Who wants to eat?" She sat a platter of burgers on the table and the party officially began. Between passing the potato chips and pickles, everybody had a story to tell. Bruno blabbed about the day he caught me stealing bottles. "He okay kid," he added quickly when Mom's eyebrows shot up. Aunt Mae told how I learned to walk in the tavern by lurching from one bar stool to the next and how Mom propped me up on the bar in an empty beer case when I was a newborn and she was waiting tables. "The customers at the bar thought it was a hoot of feed you soda crackers," she said, "Like you were some kind of parrot."

"Maybe that's why you're such a birdbrain," Rusty cracked. Then he told how he tried to juggle a banana, a hard-boiled egg, and a carton of milk at the lunch table at school one time. When the carton split open and drenched his pants, it had made me laugh so hard I snorted milk out of my nose.

Willy almost fell off of his chair laughing at the idea. "Do it now!" he cried.

"Let's have cake instead," Mom said. Aunt Mae lit the candles and singing proceeded. Before I could blow out the candles, Rusty added a verse that said I smelled like a monkey, which set Willy off into gales of giggles yet again. To settle him down, Mom suggested he give me my birthday card. He proudly informed everyone that he had drawn it himself, so it was very, very good. Actually, it wasn't a bad likeness of me in a Willy sort of way.

"This is a great picture," I said. "But why do I have all these red and blue circles on my face?"

He giggled. "I made you a clown! Don't you look funny?"

"That's a perfect likeness," Rusty said. "My present will fit right in." With a big gapped-tooth grin, he put an odd-shaped package on the table in front of me.

Inside was a chrome horn with a black rubber bulb. "What's this for?" I asked.

"Squeeze the bulb, Clarabelle, " he answered. "Even a clown like you should be smart enough to handle that."

I did and the horn squawked just like the one the clown used on "Howdy Doody."

"It goes on your bike, in case you can't tell," Rusty said as I turned it over in my hands. "Or are you really as dumb as you look?"

I laughed and Mom said, "But not your old bike. It's for your new one." Aunt Mae came from the back room pushing a brand new three-speed racer just like Rusty's. "Happy birthday!" everyone shouted.

"This is from your mom and me," Aunt Mae said. "Rusty showed us which one to get at the hardware store where his dad bought his."

"It's incredible!" was all I could say.

My new bike was as fancy as a fully-equipped Ferrari, at least compared to my old clunker. In addition to three speeds, it had hand brakes and skinny tires, a green racing frame and even a rack on the back where I could carry stuff.

Interrupting my inspection, Rusty said, "So let's take it for a spin. I guarantee I'm still faster than you."

"Hah! No way, Jose," I answered. Before I asked Mom if I could go, I had a thought. "Hey, Willy," I said. "Do you want my old bike? I'll teach you to ride it tomorrow."

Willy's eyes almost popped out of his head. "Wowwweee!" he squealed.

I hugged Aunt Mae and Mom and thanked Bruno, then Rusty and I left to see what my new bike could do. Our destination, Krug Park, was about a half hour away on the north side of town. We spent a lot of time there. A pair of stone pillars marked the park entrance. A picturesque pond where people fed the resident ducks lay next to a parking circle. On the far side of the pond was an abandoned formal garden with arbors and paths between once-sculptured boxwoods now grown shapeless from neglect. To the left and above the pond and garden was an Italianate field house on the verge of collapse. Like the rest of St. Joe, Krug Park had seen better days. It was a great place to hang out, though, and had one special feature—a steep, winding road that climbed through the park to the highest elevation in town before returning to the entrance in a precipitous plummet. The road was perfect for daredevil bike racing.

"Now we'll see what you're made of," Rusty shouted over his shoulder with a grin as he stood on his pedals and veered off to go up the steep hill.

"I'll show you!" I called back as I took off after him. It was a real test of manhood to pedal a bike to the top of Krug Park without getting off to walk it up the steep grade. Following Rusty's lead, I switched back and forth up the street to reduce the incline. Rusty finally got off to walk and push his bike after a car came along and we had to stop crisscrossing the street to let it pass. I got back on my bike and kept pedaling, though, determined to make it all the way to the top. The three speeds on my new bike helped a lot. I could never make it all the way on my old one.

I got there—barely—and dropped my bike on the grass to catch my breath while Rusty finished the climb. Below me was a natural amphitheater with a stage at the bottom, the old formal garden and the pond behind it, and quiet city streets in the distance below. It was as if I'd ridden my bike to the top of the world.

Before Rusty came into sight, I heard a motorcycle rumbling up the hill I'd just climbed. It got louder and louder as the rider down-shifted on the turns. I could tell from the roar that it wasn't slowing down. I hoped Rusty didn't switch-back across the street into its path. There weren't any squealing tires, though, and it wasn't long before the motorcycle topped the hill behind me. The rider looked my way as he passed, then circled back as if to make sure I knew he had seen me. He did another U-turn and disappeared at the top of the hill. It must have been one of Mike's gang following me. I heard him roar through the tunnel at the bottom of the park, then fade into the distance. I hoped he was gone.

I shrugged it off as Rusty rolled to a stop beside me and announced, "Okay, you beat me." He panted and fell into the grass. After he caught his breath, he said, "This race isn't over, you know. You ready for the next leg?"

I grinned and answered, "Yeah, I'm ready, but you've got to follow the rules."

"Watch me," he taunted, throwing his leg over his bike and shoving off. I followed him across the crest of the hill to the other side of the park where we stopped to get focused for the challenge of racing down the tallest hill in town.

There was only one rule for the last leg of the race. The road was all downhill from there so you didn't need any effort to build up speed. You could pedal if you wanted, but you could never touch your brakes. Ever! That was the one rule. No brakes! When you obeyed it, the ride really grabbed your guts.

"Brakes are for chickens! Go!" I yelled as I rolled past Rusty and lifted my hands to show I wasn't touching my brake levers. As he kicked off right behind me, I heard the motorcycle circling back up the street to the top of the hill we had just left. In less than a minute the motorcycle was behind us and I was speeding down the hill ahead of Rusty faster than I wanted to go. The deep rumble grew louder and louder as I went faster and faster. I went through a dark underpass and swooshed around a curve where I could see the pond over the tree tops far, far below. It would be death to miss that turn and barrel off the street and down into the trees. The motorcycle passed Rusty and he whooped a warning. Gathering speed, I leaned into the next curve to keep from being thrown off my bike and prayed the wheels wouldn't slip sideways. The motorcycle cut inside me, forcing me toward the edge of the pavement. If I slipped, a rickety wooden guardrail was the only thing to stop my deadly plunge into the tree tops. My stomach burned with adrenaline. The motorcycle swerved in front of me and sped ahead in a cloud of blue exhaust. He disappeared as I hit the final curve just before the tunnel under the field house. The street leveled off inside the tunnel and slowed me down. The sunshine hit me in the face as I came out the other side of the tunnel and turned on one leg to skid the bike to a standstill in the parking lot, Rusty right behind me.

"Man oh man!" was all I could say.

"That guy tried to kill you!" Rusty said.

"Maybe," I gasped as I caught my breath, "Or maybe it was just some kind of warning."

"Yeah, a warning he wants to kill you," Rusty insisted.

"Okay, okay! Let's get out of here before he comes back to finish the job."

~ 16 ~

Remember my dad? He comes in and out of this story right up to the very end, just like he did on my birthday.

Willy met me at the front door when I got home from the bike ride. Somberly, he said, "Dad was here."

"What do you mean? Where is he?" I demanded, pushing past him into the front room. Mom slumped on the sofa, her eyes red and weepy as she told me what happened.

"He's gone. Said he just came by to say goodbye."

"Goodbye?" I cried. "Couldn't he wait for me?"

"I'm sorry, Daniel, but was in a big hurry. He didn't even sit down."

"I haven't seen him for a month. That's not fair!" I realized how childish I sounded and took a breath to bring myself back to the real world. "Where has he been all this time?" I asked.

"Apparently, he's been hiding across the river in Kansas. He said he's pretty sure they found out he where was, so he has to get out of town." She raised her head. "He said to tell you he's real, real sorry." His apology hung in my mind for a moment before I accepted it.

"Did he say where he was going?"

"No. He said it's better if we don't know—at least for now."

"Is he coming back?" I dreaded the answer.

"I don't know," Mom said. She sighed as she added, "He took his fake book. Said he needs it."

That's when I knew Dad wasn't coming back. We wouldn't be playing any duets together on Sunday. Maybe never.

"He left this box, though. Said it was for you and Willy."

She handed me a long, narrow box with an envelope taped to the outside with my name on it. The envelope was thick but not heavy, like it had several pieces of paper in it. I used my pocket knife to slit it open. Inside was "Worried Man Blues" on a page from Dad's fake book and a birthday card with a cartoon drawing of a cake with one big candle on top and "Happy Birthday!" printed inside. The most important thing was the note Dad wrote on the back of the music.

Dear Daniel,

I sure wish I could be there for your birthday. I'm sorry I have to leave town so fast. It is for the best, although you may not believe that. Here's what happened. The radio station fired all the musicians and started playing records so I went to work for a guy. That was dumb. I lost some of his stuff and now I owe him a lot of money. The guy is looking for me, so I have to leave town. I have a really big gig lined up, so I hope I will be back on my feet soon and all this can get straightened out.

You must believe me when I say I love you. I hope you'll think of me when you sing this song. The present inside the box is for Willy. Teach him to play it and take good care of him and your mom. I am very proud of you. I pray we will be together some day when it is safe. In the meantime, I will hold you in my heart and hope you do the same for me.

Love,

Dad

I didn't know what I was supposed to feel, only that I didn't need to cry. He was safe and alive, somewhere, and he was still my dad. I gave the card to Mom to read. She sobbed once, but wiped her eyes and hugged me without breaking down.

"I'm proud of you, too," she said. "It's been hard, but we're getting through it, aren't we?"

With my head against her shoulder, I said, "Sure, Mom, but it's not getting any easier." I was talking about Larry and I think Mom was, too.

"It will," she said. "Sometimes the only thing you can do is toughen up and wait."

"Wait for what?"

"Wait for the bad times to pass. They will, you know. They always do."

"I guess so, but what if somebody gets hurt while you're waiting?" She didn't answer right away. Finally, she pushed us apart so she could look me straight in the eyes.

"Daniel, I know you look out for me and Willy and I love you for it. But you're still a boy with a lot of growing up to do. The most important person you need to take care of right now is yourself."

In my heart, I didn't agree, but I didn't feel like arguing anymore.

I picked up the long box and shook it a little before I handed it to Willy. "This is from Dad. Be careful when you open it." If it was what I thought it was, he was going to go bonkers. He opened the box and yelled.

"Yay! My gitfiddle!"

We ate cold fried chicken and leftover birthday cake for supper. While Mom cleaned up the kitchen, I held Willy on my lap and reached my arms around him to help him strum his gitfiddle like Dad had done. I would have played with him all night, but Mom finally sent us to bed.

I may have just been a kid, but I thought I understood the mess Dad was in. Maybe he'd made some bad business decisions, but it wasn't entirely his fault they didn't work out the way he'd hoped. I guess he was just trying to get ahead and do better for his family the only way he knew how. Besides, it was pretty clear Dad wasn't some kind of superhero. He was just a guy, loving but imperfect. What more could you expect a man to be?

Now, I have to stop right here and warn you that things go from bad to worse at this point in the story. The truth comes out in more ways than one. Remember, though, that the truth may set you free but it can also kill you.

Willy woke up the next day feeling better. After lunch, he reminded me I had promised to teach him to ride my old bike so I rolled it out into the yard and adjusted the seat so he could reach the pedals. The bike was faded red and rusty, with fat tires and a thick steel frame. It only had one speed and a coaster brake that worked when you pedaled backwards. It was a good bike to learn on because you really couldn't break it. It had plastic streamers on the hand grips, too, and a spring-loaded bell that rang despite the dent in it. Willy loved that bell.

Remembering how Dad had taught me to ride, I did the same with Willy. Mom and Dad had taken me to the school playground, which was nice and smooth and had a lot of room to ride big circles on the bike. Dad trotted along beside me holding the back of the seat to keep the bike upright. Mom stood in the center of the circle and cheered us on while we went around and around. When Dad finally let go, he kept running beside me so I wouldn't know I was on my own. Mom clapped and yelled and Dad slowed down until I pedaled away from him. I was riding a bike!

It didn't happen quite that way with Willy. At first he was scared and whimpered some, but I steadied him until he settled down and kept his feet on the pedals while I ran behind pushing and holding him up. After a couple of circles in our neighbor's flat back yard, he was getting the hang of it and even giggling a little bit.

Mom came out of the house to watch. Larry did, too. He had been in the garage all morning doing something to his car and, I suspect, drinking beer. After he watched me guiding Willy around one more turn, Larry scoffed, "He's never going to learn that way." I didn't say anything. Neither did Mom. When Willy and I circled around the neighbor's maple tree, Larry stepped in front of us and grabbed the handlebars. "I'll teach him," he said. Surprised, I stepped back and let go of the bike seat. The bike started to tip, so Willy grabbed the nearby tree trunk.

"Get off the bike," Larry said. Willy shook his head and tightened his grip on the tree. He didn't know what to do. He couldn't get off the bike while holding on to the tree and if he let go, he and the bike would fall over. Mostly, he was scared of Larry. "Get off!" Larry ordered. Willy shook his head again and Larry grabbed his wrists and forcefully peeled his arms away from the tree. The bike fell over as Larry lifted him clear. "Bring the bike, Daniel." I jumped to pull it upright and pushed it behind them as Larry carried Willy to the top of the grassy embankment in our back yard, the one Willy loved to roll down.

"Larry, what are you doing?" Mom asked.

"I'm going to teach him how to ride a bike," he answered. He set Willy on the bike facing down the slope.

Mom saw what he was going to do. "Larry, please," she pleaded.

He ignored her and gave the bike a quick shove to get it started down the hill.

"Pedal!" he yelled as Willy careened down the slope. Panicked, Willy instinctively tried to stop by dragging his feet on the grass. They tangled with the pedals, and he tipped over halfway down. Mom and I ran to see if he was hurt but Larry got there first.

"Get up and stop your crying," he ordered. He picked up the bike with one hand and pulled Willy out of Mom's grasp with the other. Willy wasn't hurt. He sobbed once, mostly from fear, then choked back another one. Larry dragged both him and the bike back to the top of the hill.

"No! Larry! Stop!" Mom cried.

"You treat both your brats like babies," Larry snapped. "He's not hurt." He straddled the bike's rear wheel to hold it upright between his legs and manhandled Willy onto the seat as Mom ran back up the embankment to stop him. "Keep your feet on the pedals and steer straight," he ordered. Before Mom could get to them, he pushed Willy down the slope again. And once again, Willy's feet flew loose and he tumbled off. He lay tangled in the bike, crying at the bottom of the hill.

"You've got to pedal, stupid!" Larry yelled.

Mom wailed and ran to Willy. She was trying to get him untangled from the bike when Larry stomped down the hill and wrenched the bike out of her hands. He yanked it up and the handlebars snapped around to hit her in the thigh. "Ow!" she cried. Willy's foot was wedged between the frame and one of the pedals. He screamed and Larry jerked the bike once more. The handlebar hit Mom's leg again. She pulled the bike away and shouted, "Stop it! You're hurting him."

"What a little baby," Larry snarled. As Mom freed Willy's foot from the frame, Larry turned his back and went to the garage, leaving the rest of us crying. I helped Willy push the bike back to the house to store it next to mine under the eaves.

"Are you okay?" I asked.

Willy sobbed, "I hate him,"

I hated him, too, but more than anything, I hated myself. I wasn't capable of protecting my little brother or my mom against a bully. Dad was the only person I could turn to, and he was gone.

Willy and I came in the house and found Mom collapsed into a chair in the kitchen. She was rubbing her leg where the bike had hit her. I told Willy to go wash up and put on some clean clothes. I sat down across the table from her. She was talking to herself, so distraught she didn't realize I was sitting there.

"I am so tired of fighting all the time," she muttered. "If I wasn't so stupid, I wouldn't have left Johnny. He couldn't pay the bills, but at least he never hurt anybody."

Was it possible she would leave Larry?

"Mom," I said. She looked up and came out of her fog. "Can't you ask Dad to come back? I know he would. He could help us."

"If I knew where he was . . . ." She shook her head. "But I don't. And besides, Larry's right, it's really all my fault." She hung her head and sobbed.

"But Dad . . . ."

"Forget it, Daniel. Your dad is gone.

She dissolved into tears, lost in despair, so I did the only thing I knew to do. I hugged her until she calmed down. When she stopped sobbing, I got her a glass of water. She was wrong. It wasn't her fault. It was Larry's. He was guilty. He had hurt her and Willy. As she drank the water, I stood up, my jaw clenched, and went to the garage.

Larry was at the workbench tinkering with a carburetor clamped in the vice. I know he heard me come in, but he didn't look up. He was a lot bigger than me. Not just taller, but thicker, with a deep chest like a buffalo and biceps built by hours of pounding and bending steel and manhandling heavy air wrenches. His well-earned beer belly was hard, not flabby. On a hot day, he could drink a case of Schlitz. Once, when he made me help him install a rebuilt transmission, he jacked up the car and slid underneath laying on his back on a creeper. As I watched, he manhandled the old transmission onto his chest before wriggling out from under the car with it. It must have weighed two hundred pounds.

I did not care how strong he was. I was blind angry. I stopped an arm's length away and glared at the side of his face. I loosened my jaw enough to say, "You better never do that again!"

He didn't look up from the bench but he glanced at me out of the corner of his eye. "Do what?" he said.

"Hurt my mom. Or my brother."

His fingers moved a screwdriver around the carburetor, but he wasn't really doing anything with it, just pretending to ignore me. Finally, he said, "Nobody got hurt."

That wasn't right. "But they did get hurt," I snapped. "And you're the one who did it. You better say you're sorry."

He turned to face me, surprised that I would try to order him around. He sized me up, calculating just how mad I was. He put the screwdriver down but I didn't back away. I didn't blink, either. His eyes went to a ball peen hammer lying on the bench. He didn't reach for it but he took a step closer to me and I could see he had come to a decision. "Or what?" he said.

"Or . . . Or I'll kill you!"

The threat popped out on its own and surprised even me, but I meant it.

He snorted and turned back to the workbench. Hot, red anger filled me. I pulled out my pocket knife. When I clicked it open, he snorted again. Then he picked up the hammer. My hand quivered as he growled, "You better put that frog-sticker away before I teach you to mind your own business, Bub."

He cocked his muscular arm and raised the hammer. I tried to make myself stab him, but my hand shook so hard the knife slipped out of my sweaty fingers and clattered on the workbench. Larry brought the heavy hammer down on it, shattering the blade. I ran away with his disdainful shout of "Hah! So much for that!" ringing in my ears.

~ 18 ~

That was it. All I could stand. I had to get out of there. Out of town. Out of my life. Unfortunately, your life is like your skin. You're born with it and you can't get out of it. Oh, the top layer dries up and falls off all the time, but new skin grows to replace it so it stays with you whether you like it or not, complete with the scars from the past.

I jumped on my bike and raced to Aunt Mae. The tavern was quiet, with only a couple of guys drinking at the bar and chatting with Jim, the bartender, while Aunt Mae worked at the steam table getting ready for the dinner trade.

"Daniel! What a nice surprise," she said when I came in, but when she saw the desperate look on my face, she hurried around the bar. "What's wrong? Did something happen?"

"Larry . . . Mom . . . he broke my knife . . . Dad gave it to me . . . ."

She put her arm around me and took me to a booth. "Now, take a deep breath and start at the beginning."

I told her about the bike and Mom's bruises and how I threatened to kill Larry. "That's when he smashed my knife with a hammer. Then he laughed at me. I ran away. I don't know what to do now."

"Oh, dear. What a mess," she said. "Did he hit you? Was anybody hurt?"

"No, not me. I ran away. He hurt Mom, though. I mean . . . before he hit her with the bike."

Aunt Mae's lips tightened. "Do you mean another time? How do you know?" When I told her about the bruises on Mom's arms, the ones she claimed she got from the plumbing under the sink, Aunt Mae said, mostly to herself, "I was afraid he was one of those guys. Maybe this will open her eyes."

"What about the police?" I said. "Could you tell them to arrest him? You know some of them, don't you?"

She shook her head sadly. "My word doesn't mean anything. Your mom has to do it. She has to file a complaint. And I know she won't."

"Why not? I mean, he hurt her!"

"Daniel, it's not that simple. He's a fireman and that makes the cops his buddies. Even more, though, your mom's a woman and the cops are men, some of them men like Larry. It would be her word against his and the cops would always suspect she somehow deserved it even if they believed her in the first place. They won't admit it, but that's what she'd be up against. Your mom and Larry aren't married, either, so the first thing the cops would say is she should just leave. Even then, the most they will do is give him a warning."

"That won't do any good! It will just make him mad. They have to lock him up."

"That's right. But they won't. Your mom knows that, too."

"So why doesn't she leave? We can come back and live here, can't we?"

"Of course you can, sweetheart. But your mom isn't going to do that either." When I looked perplexed, she added, "Look, your mom doesn't feel real good about herself right now. She split up with your dad and then she chose Larry. If she leaves him, she thinks that will mean she's failed again." I started to protest, but she cut me off. "Besides, she may have it in her head she can re-form him somehow. Maybe make him a better person. Then she would be a hero, at least to herself."

"That's stupid."

"Now, Daniel, don't be so hard on your mom. She's doing the best she can with what she's got. You know that, don't you?"

"Yeah, I know." I felt like crap. Then I remembered how Mom had said she was sorry for splitting up with Dad. "Dad could help, though. If he knew what was going on, I know he'd come back."

Aunt Mae didn't answer right away. "Maybe, but you can't count on it. Your dad is in serious trouble or he wouldn't have left town. Anyway, you don't know where he is, do you?"

I shook my head. "So what do I do now?"

"I think it's best if you go home. Apologize to Larry. It will be hard, but that's the only thing you can do." Throwing myself on Larry's mercy didn't sound at all like a good idea. I shook my head, but she said, "Daniel, you can't solve this. You're a big help to your mom, but you're not her savior." When I still hesitated, she asked, "Do you want me to call him for you?"

"No, that's okay," I sighed. "I guess you're right."

We got up from the booth and she gave me a hug.

"I love you, Daniel, and so does your mom. It will all work out for the best."

I turned my bike toward home in case she was watching as I rode away. As soon as I was out of her sight, I turned and headed for Rusty's. An apology was not going to happen. And Aunt Mae wasn't going to help me get out of town or go into hiding or whatever I had to do to escape the hell that was life with Larry. Rusty would, though. I knew I could count on him. He was the best friend I ever had. Maybe my only friend.

His mother greeted me at the door like she always did, cheerfully and distracted by whatever she was whipping up in the kitchen, and sent me around to the back yard. I found Rusty sitting at their picnic table playing chess with himself.

"What's up, my man?" he said without looking up from the board.

"I tried to kill Larry," I blurted.

His head snapped up. "Whoa! Are you kidding me?"

"No, I tried to kill him—for real. Only, I screwed up and couldn't get it done."

"I should hope so! I mean, the man's pure scum and deserves to die a horrible death, but you'd end up in prison for sure if you murdered him. Are the cops looking for you?"

"I don't know. Maybe. Probably. It doesn't matter. I'm getting out of here."

"Slow down a minute. Let's think this through. What about your dad? Can he help?"

"He's gone, remember?"

"Oh, yeah. Well, how about your mom? She's not going to let anything happen to you."

At the mention of her name, I remembered mom dejected and crying, sitting at the kitchen table. On the verge of crying myself, I shook my head. "She's afraid of him. Even if she did try to stop him, he'd smack her. I can't let her get hurt just because I'm an idiot."

"So you're running away?"

"Yeah, right now."

Rusty squinted hard at me to see how determined I was. Then he shook his head.

"How? On your bike? If they're looking for you, the cops will run your butt down before you get to the city limits. Besides, where are you going to go?"

"I don't know."

"Well, if you're skipping town, you need two things: transportation and a destination. And your bike is not long-distance transportation. That takes money. You got any?"

"Not much," I said. "I've got some at home, though." I thought about his arguments. I also recalled Mom's slip about her feelings for Dad. "The place I need to go is to find my dad."

"Do you have any idea where he is?"

My voice faltered as I fought back tears. "No. I wish I did."

"Listen, just chill for a minute," Rusty said. "We'll figure this out. And when we do, we'll go together." I started to shake my head, but he added, "You obviously need the trusty Rusty brain to do your thinking for you. Besides, it will be boring around here if I don't have your bacon to pull out of the fire every day."

Before I could answer, his mother came to the door and told me Mom was on the phone.

"See?" Rusty said. "Left to your own incapable devices, you got caught right away. Tell you what. You decide where we're going and I'll figure out how we get there. Deal?"

"Deal."

Mom was concerned but calmer than I expected on the phone, although she may have just been acting that way for my sake. I didn't know what to think about anybody anymore.

"Daniel," she said, "Are you all right?"

"Yes. I mean no. I'm scared."

"Well, you don't need to be. Everything is going to be okay."

"What about Larry?"

"He cooled down. Don't you worry about him. I'll take care of it. I think you'd better stay at Rusty's house tonight, though. I already asked his mother and she said that's fine."

"But what if Larry hits you again? Or Willy?"

"I told you, Larry is not mad. He's not going to hurt any of us. He will be at the firehouse tomorrow, so you and I can talk when you come home, all right?"

I still didn't know what to think or do, but I reluctantly agreed.

After supper, Rusty and I went to his room to figure out a plan. I told him what Mom said about Larry, and added that I couldn't leave without at least hearing what else she had to say.

"Whatever you do," he warned, "Don't tell her you're even thinking about running away. She'll just lock you in your room or chain you to the refrigerator or something."

"Yeah, I know."

"Hey!" he said. "It's Saturday night. Your favorite program is on the radio isn't it?" Rusty had his own radio in his room, so he switched it on and we flopped down on the floor to listen. The *Ozark Jubilee* produced the first hour of its Saturday night show on network radio before adding the television broadcast for the second hour. The studio audience got to see the full two-hour program.

The star of the show, Red Foley, opened the evening with "Salty Dog Rag" backed up by the house band, the Crossroads Boys. Then he introduced a singer from Strafford, Missouri, who played the mandolin in front of a string band with bass, banjo, fiddle and guitar. They did "Lovesick Blues," the last song I played with Dad before he disappeared. Remembering that day and listening to the show in Rusty's room helped push my worries about Larry to the back of my mind. I escaped my troubles by drifting with the music and dreaming about playing in front of that audience someday.

The singer had a "high lonesome" voice and the string band was really good, too. After every verse in the number, each musician played a solo. The banjo player did the first one, then the fiddler. When the guitar player took his turn, his guitar rang out as it could only ring when played by brass finger picks. That caught my attention. When he walked into his chord changes using Dad's signature double-note-harmony licks, my head exploded. That's what Dad had tried to teach me weeks ago! No one else plays that lick. It had to be him! And he was on the stage of the Jewell Theater, clear across the state in Springfield, Missouri. I jumped to my feet, jabbed a finger at the radio, and shouted, "There! That's where we're going!"

"Shhh!" Rusty said. "My folks will hear you!"

It was hard, but I lowered my voice. "There! That's where my dad is!"

"In the radio?" he said. "What are you talking about?"

I got myself under control and explained. "That was my dad playing guitar on the *Ozark Jubilee.* The show is live. He's on the stage in Springfield right this very minute!"

"Springfield, huh?" Rusty asked. "Are you sure it was him?"

"No doubt about it. Dad must have driven down there after he dropped off my birthday card. Let's go to the Greyhound station and catch the next bus. It can't be more than five or six hours away."

Rusty shook his head. "Bad idea. The first place they'll look for us is the bus station. When the agent tells them he sold tickets for Springfield to two knuckleheads, the cops will be there to meet us when we get off the bus. Let the trusty Rusty brain do the heavy thinking, okay? We can't leave until tomorrow night after every-one's asleep. Besides, you want to go to your house to get your gui-tar, don't you?"

"Yeah, I guess you're right." I wanted to talk to Mom, too, and see Willy one last time.

"Okay. Let's assume we go tomorrow night. Didn't you say Larry will be on duty at the firehouse? What time does he go to bed?"

I was puzzled. "What's that got to do with anything?"

"Simple," he answered with his big gapped-tooth grin. "We're going to borrow his car."

~ 19 ~

Remember? I told you there would be felonies. First, I committed assault with a deadly weapon. Then we made plans for grand theft auto. And, you'll see, that was just the beginning.

After sleeping on it, I wasn't sure running away and leaving Mom and Willy behind was the best thing to do, but I was leaning harder in that direction now that I knew where to find Dad. Plus, as I pedaled home the next morning, I began to think that appearing on the *Ozark Jubilee* with Dad wasn't such a crazy dream after all. Mixed up with it all in my overworked mind was Rusty's plan and the many moving parts he explained while we were eating breakfast. His plan wasn't foolproof, but I couldn't think of anything better. The whole scheme depended on several people not noticing me do some things or me lying my way out of it if I got caught. That was probably the weak point in the plan—I couldn't tell a lie worth spit. With all those things swirling around in my head, I felt like I was watching a faulty traffic light randomly flashing red, green, yellow, and sometimes all the colors at once.

At home, I found Mom pacing the kitchen. It was after noon, but she was still in her bathrobe and I don't think she'd combed her hair since the day before. She was red-eyed and sniffly, twisting a Kleenex in her fingers, and the floor was covered with a snowdrift of damp, crumpled tissues from a near-empty box on the table.

She managed to give me a crooked smile when I came to her and took her hands in mine to stop her pacing. Trying to sound calm so she wouldn't get even more agitated, I asked, "Did Larry hurt you again?"

"No, Daniel, I'm fine. He apologized to me last night. He told Willy he was sorry, too. He was real sweet. I think he really meant it."

"What's wrong, then?" I asked again.

"I don't know what to do," she said, her eyes welling up again. "I believe him, but then I don't. He's basically a good guy, but sometimes he doesn't act like one." I had already kicked Larry out of the good guy club, but I kept my mouth shut. She didn't need anyone arguing with her. She was doing enough of that herself. She choked back a sob. "And we need him, Daniel. He owns the house we live in! He puts food on our table! We can't just up and leave."

"Sure we can, Mom. We can go back to Aunt Mae's. We can stay there until Dad comes back. I can go find him...."

Before I could tell her where I knew he was, she cut me off. "You are not going anywhere, young man. Even if you knew where to look, I can't count on him. He ran out on us, he's in big trouble, and I absolutely forbid any wild goose chase. He could be anywhere. Kansas City, St. Louis, Des Moines. Pick a direction!"

"But . . . ."

"No 'buts,' Daniel. Besides, Larry is going to do better. I know it." She lifted my chin to look in my eyes. "Please give Larry one more chance, Daniel. For me. He promised he won't do anything about what you did with the knife." I didn't believe that for an instant.

Seeing my skeptical look, she added, "He even offered to give me a job. He's going to pay me to clean out the cars in his garage."

"You mean crawl inside to vacuum and scrub the carpets and seats, stuff like that?"

"Yes, but he's going to pay me, Daniel. That's good, isn't it?"

I shook my head at her naivete. Mom was tiny but she thought she was tough. Her attitude was unconscious camouflage, though.

She was fooling herself. Her hands were red, her knuckles swollen from washing dishes and waiting tables, but her wrists were thin as a sparrow's ankles. Her shoulders were wiry with ropy muscle from doing the neighbor ladies' ironing to earn a few nickels and dimes, but when I put my arms around her, I felt how delicate she was. Larry knew it, too. Her insistence on playing tough coupled with her fragility drew out the bully in him.

She reached out to take my hands again and the sleeve on her robe rode up. She had a new big blue-purple bruise on her fore-arm.

"What's that?"

She looked at her arm like she got bruises like that all the time. Maybe she did, I realized. This wasn't the first one and maybe there were others hiding under her clothes where I couldn't see them. This one looked fresh. "That's nothing," she said. "That's just where the handlebars on Willy's bike hit me."

I tried to keep my voice steady as my anger rose. "You mean where Larry hit you," I insisted, pulling my hands out of hers. "The bike didn't hit your arm, it hit your leg."

She tugged her sleeve back down. Defensively, she said, "That was an accident, Daniel. He didn't mean to do it. He said he was sorry. Don't you believe him?"

Larry had loosened the ties that bound my mom and me to-gether and now she was lying to protect him. It was going to take more than a speech from me to open her eyes. "Okay, yeah, sure. If you say so." Before she could protest any more, I went to my room.

Now that I had decided to run away to Springfield, I had several things to do. I got my fake book and slid it into the case with my guitar. Then I found a length of rope in the garage and made a sling with it so I could carry the guitar case across my back riding on my bike. I took what little money I had out of the cigar box I used as a bank. I had the two dollars from sanding the car and a pile of change from working for Bruno and Aunt Mae. It wasn't much, but it was all I had aside from the silver dollar Aunt Mae gave me for my birthday. I always kept that in my pocket. I put the change and the two dollar bills in a Mason jar and screwed the lid on tight. The cigar box also held my two birthday cards, one from Dad and one from Willy. I put them in a pillowcase with the Mason jar. It didn't seem like very much stuff to take on a trip that could possibly—hopefully—change the course of my life, but then, I didn't have much else that I could call my own. I hid the pillowcase under my bed. When Mom was out of the kitchen and away from the phone, I called Rusty.

"We're going on the road," I whispered as soon as he answered.

"Got it. See you at midnight."

"I thought of something," I said. "See if your dad has any road maps. We need one we can mark with the route to Nashville."

"I thought we were going to Springfield."

"We are. The map is a red herring."

"Right! Like Sherlock Holmes," he said. I could practically hear his grin.

The most important thing I did that afternoon was spend time with Willy. While Mom was making supper, he and I went outside. "Come on, let's go finish your bike lesson," I said.

"I don't want to," he mumbled. "I'm scared."

"It wasn't the bike's fault, Willy. You'll see. You can do it."

He dragged his feet as he followed me to where his bike leaned against the back of the house and watched apprehensively as I straightened the handlebars. I pushed the bike down to our neighbor's yard and held it while he got on. He clamped his little fingers around my wrist.

"Don't let me fall," he pleaded.

"Don't you worry. Just hold on to the handlebars and don't forget to pedal." I walked alongside, then trotted with him, holding the bike upright until he relaxed a little bit. After a couple of circuits, he was giggling and pedaling like he had done before. It seemed like years ago. When I finally let him go on his own, he wobbled successfully around the neighbor's yard.

After supper, I sat Willy between my legs and helped him play his gitfiddle like Dad had done. My eyes grew moist as I wrapped my arms around his thin shoulders and guided his hands across the strings. I wanted to take him with me, to get him safely away from Larry, but I knew that would never work. I had to remind myself I wasn't deserting him, I was leaving to get help to save him.

Mom tucked Willy into bed and came across the bedroom to give my forehead a goodnight kiss "to seal in sweet dreams" she always said. My stomach churned at the thought of lying to her, but I steeled myself to do what I had to do. "Mom, do you think I'll ever play good enough to be on the Grand Ole Opry in Nashville?"

"When you grow up, you can do anything your heart desires," she said, "but I thought you wanted to be on the *Ozark Jubilee*?"

"I do, but I remember Dad talking about getting lots of gigs in Nashville and I thought maybe he'd be there." The lie came out easier when I told myself it was another necessary red herring.

"God knows where your dad is, Daniel, so pray for him but don't go looking for him in Tennessee or anywhere else. You have to live the life you've got today, not the one in your dreams of the future."

"Okay, but Nashville sounds pretty cool."

Willy went to sleep without any chatter, leaving me to deal with my whirling thoughts. I couldn't help but wonder if it was a mistake to leave Mom and Willy living with a bully while I ran away. Was I really doing it for them or just for myself? That black thought gave me a knot in my chest. At the same time, I had to own up to not being able to protect them anyway. In fact, my open war with Larry may have made things worse. None of that mattered, though, because Mom apparently didn't want to escape. She was unsure, afraid, maybe confused, but clearly not willing to stand up to him. And where did Dad fit in all this? It looked like neither one of my parents was capable of handling the dark side of life. They sure couldn't deal with trouble. Which left me and Willy in the lurch. But, in a way, I was deserting Mom and Willy the same way Dad did. On the other hand, I was trying to straighten out this mess by somehow bringing him home to save the day—a faint hope, but hope nonetheless. I was trading life as I knew it—ugly as it may have been—for an endless stream of unknowns in the future, hoping one of them would swell into a river of happier times. As I listened to Mom go to bed and finally settle down, I stiffened my resolve to go.

Timing was the key to Rusty's plan. I waited in bed until Mom was sound asleep and my alarm clock showed eleven PM. I slid the pillowcase out from under the bed and stood up to get my guitar case in its rope sling from behind the door. Just then, from out of the darkness came Willy's voice, "What are you doing, Daniel?" I almost screamed at the sound, but managed to take a deep breath and whisper, "I'm just going to the bathroom. Go back to sleep." Drowsily, he said "Okay" and turned over. I waited a few seconds until his breathing deepened, then crept out the back door, got on my bike, and headed across town to meet Rusty. The next stop on my crime spree was the firehouse.

$$\sim 20 \sim$$

Sometimes I wonder what would have happened if. You know, if radio stations hadn't fired all the live entertainers and filled the airwaves with recorded music. Or if the drug dealer had refused to do business with Dad. Or if Mom had met a nice guy—somebody other than Larry. These all would have been good "ifs." But there are bad "ifs," too. What if we got caught stealing Larry's car?

"Are they asleep?" I asked Rusty when I got to the firehouse. He was hiding in some bushes waiting for me. There were no lights on upstairs where the firemen slept, but a dim light shone through the windows on the first floor. That's where the firetruck sat, ready to go.

"They turned out the lights about an hour ago," Rusty said. "If they're not sleeping, what else would they be doing in the dark?"

We stashed our bikes and my other things in the bushes and crossed the street hoping no one upstairs was sitting by a window, unable to sleep and staring outside. Rusty slowly pushed open a door on the side of the building. We stopped to listen for any sounds. We heard nothing, so we walked the length of the incredibly shiny fire engine, our reflections wavering on it like images in a fun house mirror. The firemen polished that truck every day, Larry had bragged. I was glad I wasn't around—he would have made me do it.

We found the stairs and I started up. The first stair creaked when I stepped on it and my stomach turned over. Rusty guided me gently toward the wall.

"Step on the side of the stair, not the middle," he whispered.

We made it to the second floor breathing heavily but without making any more noise—or at least any sounds louder than the snores coming from Larry and the other two firemen sleeping at the end of the big room. It was a hot, humid night, and a whirring window fan helped mask the sound of our movements.

"Where are his car keys?" Rusty whispered.

I shrugged and pointed to where Larry lay sleeping in his underwear. There was a small table next to his bed, but we couldn't see anything on it in the dark.

The entire second floor was one big open room so the firemen wouldn't have to navigate doors and other obstacles in the event of an alarm. There was a kitchen and some tables and chairs at the front of the room. The beds were at the other end. A bright brass pole came up through an opening in the floor in the middle, positioned so they could slide down to the truck without using the stairs.

Tucked against the wall opposite us was the only separate space, the bathroom with showers and some lockers. I led the way as we crept across the wooden floor on our toes to lighten the squeaks and creaks. I found a locker with Larry's name on it and pulled the metal door open as quietly as I could. It clanked a little, but the roaring fan helped smother the sound. Larry's trousers hung from a hook inside and I remembered the spare car key he kept in his wallet. I slipped the wallet out of his pants pocket and turned to show it to Rusty.

He was nowhere in sight.

Panicked, I stepped back into the main room and peered about in the darkness. One of the firemen coughed and turned over in bed. I froze. I fought the urge to whisper Rusty's name. I took another tentative step into the dark room, hoping he would appear. My stomach lurched when a shadow moved across the room behind the brass pole. The fireman coughed again. The shadow stepped out from behind the pole. It was Rusty, frantically waving me away toward the stairs.

I ran down the stairs on my tiptoes, keeping next to the wall and holding my breath. As I got to the first floor, Rusty slid down the brass pole and landed lightly on his feet next to the fire engine. His gap-toothed grin stretched from ear to ear.

"I always wanted to do that!" he whispered. I wanted to kill him.

Larry and the other firemen parked their cars on the street behind the firehouse. I got my guitar and pillowcase from the bushes and put them in the trunk of Larry's car, making sure not to slam the lid. I opened the driver's-side door as quietly as I could. No lights came on inside the firehouse. So far, so good. I got behind the wheel and unlocked the passenger door for Rusty.

Now came the potentially disastrous part of the plan. Could I start the car and drive away without waking up anyone? When I put the key into the ignition and turned it the way Larry had shown me, the engine roared and my heart stopped, or so it seemed. I got a grip on myself and pulled the gear shift lever to "Drive" and stepped on the gas. The engine raced, but the car didn't move. "Go! Go! Go!," Rusty urged. I let up on the gas and closed my eyes, trying to remember the things Larry had made me do. The emergency brake! I released it, stepped on the gas again, and looked back at the firehouse as I drove away. No lights. And no regrets.

Despite the debacle of my lesson from Larry, driving wasn't as difficult as I feared. I soon figured out how hard to push on the gas pedal and the brake, and, after swerving from one side of the street to the other a couple of times, I got the hang of the steering wheel. There wasn't any traffic in the wee hours, so I drove down the middle of the street to keep from side-swiping the parked cars.

When I finally felt confident I probably wasn't going to smash into a tree, I relaxed enough to ask Rusty, "Any problems at your house?"

"Nah, I told them we were going on a camping trip with your dad and would be gone for two nights. Said we were leaving tonight so we could get to the lake by morning. Easy-peasy. My old man was snoring like a broken chain saw when I left. My mom sounded even worse."

The firehouse was on a major thoroughfare we needed to avoid, so we crept through the residential neighborhoods where the houses were dark in the midnight hour. Following the route Rusty had laid out on a road map he'd swiped from his dad, I turned cautiously onto Highway 36 just outside town, relieved that we hadn't seen any city cop cars and pretty confident that the state police wouldn't be patrolling the deserted two-lane highway at this time of night.

My death grip on the steering wheel relaxed and I leaned back in the seat, ready to cruise the countryside like the king of the road. Rusty rolled down his window to enjoy the night air. I told him to turn on the radio. As he reached for the knob, a horn blared behind us and high-beam headlights flashed in my rearview mirror. A pickup truck raced around us, the driver calling me everything but a Christian as he roared past just inches from my door. My heart jumped into my throat. Rusty and I both screamed. I cranked the steering wheel first one way and then the other. Our tires squealed on the pavement and the car swerved back and forth until I stepped on the brake pedal and got myself, then the car, under control. We stopped on the shoulder.

"Holy shit! That was close," I huffed, laying my forehead against the steering wheel and closing my eyes.

"That guy was flying!" Rusty said.

"I guess I need to pay more attention."

"You've got to speed it up, too" Rusty said. "We're going to get noticed if we're poking along the highway like a hay wagon. Not to mention, maybe get killed by somebody. Try going the speed limit."

"Right." I took a deep breath to steady myself and pulled back onto the pavement.

"Put the pedal to the metal, good buddy," Rusty said.

Soon we were racing along too fast for me to be comfortable, but fast enough to keep from getting rear-ended by traffic from behind. We drove through the dark Missouri countryside, sensing rather than seeing cornfields on either side of the road and slowing only as we passed through tiny farm towns where lights shone in a very few houses where someone was either sick or couldn't sleep. My veins pumped pure adrenaline. My eyes shifted constantly from the road ahead to the rear-view mirror, down to the speedometer, back to the road where the white lines flashed by in an endless trail. My singular goal was to keep the car between those lines and out of the ditch next to them.

The route Rusty laid out wasn't direct. It took us nowhere near big, bustling Kansas City, south of St. Joe, which is where most runaway kids from our town ended up. Our first destination was instead Columbia, the university town in the middle of the state where we would stage the final diversion to throw off any pursuers. We drove due east for two hours, then turned south at Macon onto Highway 63.

Fifteen minutes later, in the middle of no place, the engine sputtered, raced for a moment, then sputtered again. I jerked the wheel and got the car to the shoulder just as it died completely.

"What happened?" Rusty said.

My hands were clamped on the steering wheel, my shoulders knotted from the stress of running away from home, stealing a car, driving through the black of night straining to stay alive on the highway. I lost it. "How should I know?" I shouted. "I barely know how to drive!"

"Whoa, buddy," he said, raising both hands as if to defend himself. "You're doing fine. Just chill, okay?"

I glared at him before taking a deep, calming breath. I unclenched my hands from the wheel and dropped them into my lap.

"Sorry," I said, cooling down. "It's been a long night."

"Yeah, and it's not over yet. What do you think is wrong with the car?"

I turned the key to "off" then back to "start." The engine turned over, coughed, but wouldn't run. I tried it again with the same result. I looked at the dials on the dash board. The only one I recognized was the gas gauge. It pointed to "E."

"Oh, jeez. Now what?" he said when I told him.

We got out of the car and looked up and down the road. The black night sky was slightly lighter on the horizon but I saw nothing in either direction.

"Didn't we pass a gas station?" I asked.

"I don't remember. If we did, it wasn't open."

"So what do we do now?"

A cow lowed and shuffled its hooves somewhere in the darkness, I turned toward the sound. In the distance beyond it, a single light burned.

"There," I pointed. "Maybe it's a farmhouse. And I bet farmers have gas."

As soon as we stepped off the road, we ran into a barbed wire fence. Rusty held two strands apart and I carefully squeezed through, then did the same for him. The cow lowed again, closer this time. The green smell of freshly-grazed grass rose around us as we made our way across the pasture. The light in the distance grew brighter with every step. Finally, we came to a gate and could make out a small, single-story wood frame house with a pickup truck parked next to it. The light we saw came from a window next to a concrete stoop and a door. We crossed the yard. I heard a voice inside as I knocked on the door.

An outside light came on overhead and an old farmer in overalls and a faded blue shirt opened the door. He squinted into my face, his eyes rheumy, his grizzled chin thrust out. "Who are you?" he demanded.

A movement behind him drew my attention. The room was an unkempt kitchen, dirty plates on the table, a chair overturned next to it. A woman, much younger than the farmer, lifted the chair upright. Her dress was torn, one white shoulder exposed. Beneath her nose was a splotch of red.

"We, uh, I, uh, my name is Daniel," I stammered. "Our car ran out of gas."

"What do you want me to do about it?"

"Can you give us some?"

"Give you some! I ain't Santy Claus." Over his shoulder, he ordered. "Get my breakfast on the table, woman. You got cows to milk."

"We can pay you for some gas," Rusty said. "How much do you want?"

"How much money you got?"

"Well, I could give you a dollar for, say, five gallons?"

Another movement in the kitchen caught my eye. The woman was taking a pan off the stove. It was heavy—maybe cast iron—and she had to lift it with both hands. As she turned to take it to the table, the light caught purple bruises on her arms and what looked like a streak of blood staining her dress. Watching her, I lost track of the haggling between Rusty and the farmer.

"Well, boy, you want gas?" the farmer said. I thought he was talking to me, but before I could answer, he held out his hand to Rusty. "You got the math bass-akwards. It's five dollars for a gallon."

"Five dollars!" Rusty protested.

Something moved behind the farmer.

"Yep. Take it or take a hike."

The pan slammed into the back of the farmer's head with a dull clank. He slumped to the floor, his surprised eyes open but unseeing, a run of spittle on his chin. The woman stood behind him, panting, her own eyes wild.

"My god, lady!" Rusty exclaimed.

She looked at us standing on her stoop as if seeing us for the first time. She lowered the pan and stood with it hanging from her hand by her side. Tonelessly, she said, "Is he dead?"

I didn't want to, but I knelt and put three fingers on his neck to feel for a pulse. "I think he's alive. You better call an ambulance."

She shook her head, "I gotta be gone before he comes to."

"So, you want me to call the ambulance?" I said.

"You can't. He ripped the phone out of the wall last night." She stared at the farmer on the floor. A trickle of blood seeped from beneath his head. When she looked up again, her eyes had lost their wild madness. It had been replaced by desperation. "Please take me with you. Please?" she pleaded.

Rusty looked at me. It was my decision. The only way we could help the farmer was to drive him to a doctor. But I had no idea where to find one and the woman wasn't going to tell us. She needed help herself, but she had tried to kill someone right in front of us. Maybe she even succeeded! Was she sane? Could we trust her? From what we had seen, the man on the floor was mean, rude, crude, a bully. It looked like he had hurt her, but could he have been defending himself before we got there? Was she the victim or the perpetrator? I chased the unanswered questions in my head for seconds that seemed like hours, then realized I was rationalizing the man's abuse the same way the cops would if Mom called them on Larry. I had no choice.

"You can come, but we have to hurry," I said.

"Oh, thank you, thank you! I'll get my stuff." She rushed across the room but turned in the doorway and ran back to kneel and take the farmer's wallet from the pocket of his overalls. "I need money and he never let me have none," she said, embarrassed when she noticed me watching. As she stood up, she added, "He keeps gas for the mower in a can in the shed."

By the time Rusty found the can and we poured the gas into the Chevy, she was in the back seat with a brown carboard suitcase not much bigger than a briefcase. She'd put on a clean dress, too.

"We're going to Columbia, that okay with you?" Rusty asked.

"Can you drop me at the bus station?"

Rusty and I exchanged glances. That was where we were headed, but I said, "Sure." We could figure it out later.

She looked out the back window as we drove away in silence. When the farmhouse disappeared behind us, she said, "I pray to Jesus to forgive me, but I hope he dies. He was a mean, mean man."

As gently as I could, I asked, "Did he hurt you much?"

"That son of a bitch beat me on the night of our honeymoon and every day since."

"Oh, jeez," Rusty said, "Didn't you call the cops?"

She snorted in disgust. "Plenty! In fact, the sheriff come just last night. It was the same as always. Gave him a good scolding. That's all the cops ever did—talk, talk, talk. After the sheriff left, he had his way with me, rough like always, then he gave me this fat lip." She sniffled and her voice turned hard. "This morning, he did this to me." She leaned forward to hold her arm over the front seat and pulled her sleeve up to show an angry red knot the size of a walnut on her elbow. "If I hadn't ducked off my chair, he'd of broke my arm. That was when you boys come to the door."

"Where will you go now?" I asked.

"My boy lives in Kansas City. I can stay there. The son of a bitch will find me, but my boy will chase him off if he comes around."

The bus to Kansas City was loading when we pulled into the station in Columbia. As the woman closed the car door, she said, "I better hurry. Thank you for all you done."

"Be safe, ma'am," Rusty said. Then he turned to me and whispered. "Better drive around the block." By the time we got back, her bus was gone. I parked in front of the station. My hands had been clamped to the steering wheel so tightly I wasn't sure I could straighten my fingers. Rusty stretched his arms and yawned.

I turned to him and said, "Okay, we're here. What's next on the plan?"

His mouth fell open and his eyes bugged out like I'd asked him to marry me. He gulped and whispered, "You gotta sit up real, real tall." I realized he wasn't looking at me, he was looking beyond me. I turned to see what had spooked him.

A cop car sat right next to us. The policeman motioned for me to roll down my window. Petrified, I stared at him. His command didn't register in my brain. All I could think to do was try to look like I wasn't a thirteen-year-old runaway in a stolen car that had helped a murderer flee the scene of her crime not an hour ago. I braced my feet against the floor and pushed myself up as tall as I could in the seat.

"Now roll down your window before he shoots us," Rusty hissed between his teeth, smiling past me at the policeman.

I closed my eyes, waiting for the gunshot.

Rusty poked me in the thigh and I opened my eyes. He gave the cop a friendly wave. "I got this!" he whispered to me. "Roll down your window." Like a robot, I turned the window crank.

"No parking here," the cop said. "Are you boys from the university? You look pretty young. What are you, freshmen?"

"Yes, sir, officer," Rusty answered. "We start next month. We came early to see if we could get a dorm room together. Then my mom got sick and I gotta catch a bus to go home."

"Okay, but hurry it up. It's almost six AM and the next bus will pull through here in a few minutes."

"Yes, sir," Rusty said. "Thanks for the warning." He poked me again. "Get out and open the trunk," he whispered, "and smile at the nice officer while you're doing it."

I did as I was told, although I'm sure my sick smile made me look like a demented car thief. But the cop drove slowly away, watching us in his rear-view mirror. He stopped and waved at me as I got out of the car, then turned the corner and disappeared—I hoped.

I put our things on the curb. There wasn't much, just my pillow case and my guitar. "I'll stay here with the stuff," Rusty said. "Can you handle the car?"

I must have been holding my breath since the police car first appeared. I took a deep gulp of air and said, "As long as I don't see any more cops."

I drove around the corner and found a fire hydrant in the next block. According to Rusty's plan, if we parked illegally, the car was bound to draw attention pretty soon, which is what we wanted. I checked all around to make sure the police were nowhere in sight, got out, and let the air out of the left front tire so it looked like we'd abandoned the car because we had a flat. I started to drop the key down a nearby storm drain, but decided that would be too mean, regardless of how much Larry deserved it. I tossed it onto the front seat on top of the road map Rusty had marked with the route from St. Joe to Nashville—yet another of our red herrings. Then I hurried back to the bus depot.

"Be sure to call me by name," Rusty said as we went inside. The ticket window was on the other end of the small waiting room. "Daniel, are you sure you're ready for the Grand Ole Opry?" he said a trifle too loudly as we walked to the counter.

"Let's hope so, Rusty," I said. I was sure we sounded like blithering idiots, but the ticket agent didn't seem to notice.

"We'd like two tickets on the next bus to Nashville, please," Rusty said.

"Gonna be famous, huh?" the ticket agent said with a knowing smirk.

"Yes sir," I said. "That's the plan."

"You aren't the first ones with that plan," the agent said as he stamped two tickets and pushed them across the counter.

"Daniel Freemont" Rusty said. "Remember that name so you can say you knew him when."

"I'll do that. In the meantime, even Grand Ole Opry stars have to pay the fare. That will be three dollars. The bus leaves in an hour. There's a coffee shop in the next block."

"Pay the man, Daniel," Rusty grinned. "And let's indulge in some breakfast."

I started to get the mason jar out of my pillowcase, then re-membered Larry's wallet. I checked inside and found a small for-tune—a ten dollar bill. I paid for the tickets and stuffed the change back into the wallet. I didn't put the wallet in my pocket, though. Instead I gave it to Rusty when we got outside. "If you're going to be my manager," I said, "you should be handling the money." He didn't argue. We gathered up our things and walked in the di-rection of the coffee shop. The tickets, of course, would never be used, and leaving the stolen car in Columbia with a map marked for Nashville on the front seat was the ultimate red herring to con-firm the ticket agent's memory of two knuckleheads buying tick-ets to stardom. Now, all we had to do was get from Columbia to Springfield and find my dad.

These days, you probably wouldn't do what we did, which was stick out our thumbs and jump in the first car that stopped for us. Maybe back then there weren't as many serial killers and assorted perverts on the loose—I don't know, but we didn't worry about it the way folks do now. As it turned out, though, we should have been a lot more careful.

~ 21 ~

Hitchhiking out of Columbia was easy. Being a university town, it had lots of young folk coming and going all the time, even in summer, and most of them were quite willing to help their fellow travelers. Rusty couldn't pass for a college student because he was short even for a thirteen-year-old, but I was taller and my guitar gave us some credence. Rusty's disarming gap-toothed grin did the rest when we stood on the side of the road and threw out our thumbs.

"Where you headed?" asked a young man who pulled over in a Plymouth that had seen better days.

"South," Rusty said, keeping it vague.

"I'm going to Jefferson City, so I can take you that far."

"That's the right direction," Rusty said as I put my guitar in the back seat and climbed in after it.

I was exhausted after living through the drama of running away from home, not to mention the tension of looking over my shoulder while driving a stolen car all night and watching a woman possibly kill her husband. I quickly fell asleep while Rusty chatted with our driver and didn't wake up until the tires clanked on the metal roadway of a bridge. We were crossing the Missouri River and the sight of boaters on the water below brought back memories of the town we had fled. St. Joe was only a couple of hundred miles upriver. Our driver pulled over a few minutes later. It was right after lunch time.

"Here's where I have to leave you, fellas. Good luck to you."

The dome of the state capitol building was reflected in the dark windows of a bar on the street where we got out of the car. Rusty laughed when he read the sign on the bar, "Art's Liquid Lounge. "We better pick our next ride from somebody going in rather than coming out, don't you think?"

That's exactly what we did, but it turned out to be a big mistake. We should have known something was wrong when a radiantly new maroon Cadillac with whitewalls as wide as my hand on the tires and bumper guards like missiles on the front grill pulled over to the curb in front of us before we even had a chance to put our thumbs in the air.

"You boys looking for a ride?"

"Yes we are," Rusty said without hesitation. "Are you headed south?"

"That's my plan," the man said. "How far are you going?"

"Tulsa," I said, trying not to give our destination to somebody who might repeat it later.

"Well, I'm not going that far, but I can get you to Fair's Grove. That's almost to Springfield."

"Perfect," Rusty said. "I've got dibs on the back seat."

I opened the back door and put my guitar and pillow case behind the driver, then got in the shotgun seat.

"My name's Elrod," the guy said. "What's your handle?"

Rusty answered quickly, "I'm John and he's Jim." At the lie, I whipped around to stare at him. Elrod caught me and snickered.

"Okay, whatever you say, John. You did say 'John' didn't you?"

"Uh, yeah," Rusty muttered. "Listen, don't mind me. I need forty winks." He closed his eyes and left me to deal with any other questions.

"Guess you're buddy's tuckered out," Elrod said. He was a tall guy who barely fit behind the wheel. His head seemed a size too big for his body and his eyes were rimmed in red like a rat's. His hair was slickly combed and his face smooth except for a neatly trimmed mustache. Given the expensive car and a hefty silver pinky ring on his hand, I guessed him to be a local salesman of some kind.

"Yeah, we were on the road all night," I said, then realized I'd just told him something that could be useful in figuring out where we came from. "I mean, we were up all night. I was playing a gig." Another mistake.

"No kidding," the man said. "Where'd you play?"

Now I was in trouble. Rusty would have had a ready answer, truthful or not, but I stumble every time I try to lie.

"I forget," I said. "Some tavern up the road." My answer sounded lame even to me.

"You guys seem kind of young to be entertaining in beer joints. Your folks with you or something?"

"Uh, no. They couldn't make it. That's why we had to hitch a ride home."

"Going home, huh? Where's that? You told me but I forgot."

Now I was in trouble again. And while my brain whirled trying to come up with an answer that wasn't an answer, a warning light flashed in my mind: why did this guy want to know all this? I took a chance and tried to sound like I was kidding while I confronted him. "What are you, some kind of detective or something?"

He chuckled wetly. "No, young man, I don't want to see the police any more than two boys running away from home want to see them. That's what you're doing, am I right?"

I mumbled, "No, we're just going home to Joplin."

"I thought you said you were going to Tulsa."

Damn, I forgot! "I meant in the direction of Tulsa."

He chuckled again, then tapped on the steering wheel with his pinky ring. "Don't you worry, little friend," he said, reaching over to pat me on the thigh. "I'll get you down the road toward wherever it is you're going."

I scrunched against the door away from his touch.

"Now, don't go all scaredy-cat on me," the man cooed. "Just relax. Nobody's going to hurt you."

I didn't feel comfortable but settled back with one eye on the guy and the other eye on the passing countryside. It wasn't long before the flat farmlands we'd been traveling through turned into rolling hills which soon gave way to the forested Ozark Mountains. Our route on Highway 54 angled southwest. The guy lowered the visor to shade his eyes from the sun glaring through the windshield and I followed suit. He was beyond creepy, but he drove in silence and kept his hands to himself. Billboards for motels and restaurants on the Lake of the Ozarks cropped up with increasing frequency along the route. Rusty snored lightly in the seat behind me. More and more signs appeared for boat dealers, fishing guides, tour operators, caves, caverns, and other tourist attractions until they lined the roadside. The man turned off the highway at a sign for someplace called Osage Hills Cabins. The sign had an arrow that pointed down a gravel road that disappeared into the trees.

"Hey, where are you going? Is this where we get out?" I asked. My voice roused Rusty.

"What's up, guys?" he asked, rubbing the sleep from his eyes before stretching his arms and rolling his neck. "Man, I slept like a brick. Where are we?"

"We're going to take a little detour, my friends," Elrod said.

"Oh no we're not!" I said. "You let us out right here. Right now!"

Elrod didn't answer as he stepped on the gas and the Cadillac swerved on the gravel. We plunged ahead, trees thickly lining both sides of the road, the highway out of sight behind us.

"Whoa, buddy," Rusty said. He leaned over the seat and laid his hand on the man's shoulder. "Didn't you hear him? Pull over! We're getting out."

Without taking his eyes off the road, the man backhanded Rusty, knocking him back into his seat.

"Hey!" I yelled. I lunged for the steering wheel and he swiped at me with his fist. I dodged, but his pinky ring caught my forehead just above my eye. Before I could bounce up and try again, the car skidded to a stop. In one motion, the man pulled a switchblade out of nowhere, snapped it open, and pressed the point against my neck.

"Okay, boys, that's enough nonsense. Red, take your stuff and go into that cabin right there. If you try to run away, I'm going to skewer your friend here like a chicken on a spit."

"But . . . ."

Rusty tried to argue, but the man cut him off. "Now git!" Rusty got out of the car with my guitar and pillowcase and went to the cabin door. He turned to protest, but the man raised the knife and said, "We're right behind you." As soon as Rusty went inside, the man got out of the car, came around to my door, and pulled me out. The knife wasn't in my face, but he kept it in sight as he pushed me to the cabin.

It was a tacky one-room shack at the end of a row of six, each one shabbier than the next. The roofs sagged, the windows were broken, the weeds grew unfettered right up to the doorways. Ours was clearly the only one occupied. There would be no witnesses to whatever he was going to do to us.

The man pushed me through the door. An unmade bed stood in the middle of the dark room. Rusty and I exchanged terrified looks, neither one of us able to say anything. The man laid down his car keys and picked up a glass lamp from a table next to the bed and shook it to check for kerosene. Satisfied, he lifted the sooty glass chimney and lit it, filling the room with sick yellow light.

"Put that stuff down," he told Rusty, who put my guitar case on the floor with the pillowcase on top of it. "All right, boys. Just follow my stage directions and everybody will stay healthy." He pointed to me. "You take off all your clothes and get up on that bed." When I hesitated, he waggled his switchblade. "That means now." I slowly started unbuttoning my shirt. He pointed the blade at Rusty. "You, Red, are going to get naked and do the same."

"Then what?" Rusty said. I don't know who was more surprised at the question, the pervert or me.

"Then you're going to play a duet with your musician friend on his skin flute until I join you. Now get your clothes off."

"Okay," Rusty said. "Sounds like fun." I was astonished.

"That's the spirit!" the creep laughed. Rusty stepped away from him and turned his back as if to unzip his jeans. The creep laid the switchblade on the table and unbuckled his own belt. When he noticed I was still dressed, he yelled, "Get with it, boy, or you're going to be sorry!"

Just then, Rusty swung my pillowcase around his head and smashed it into the side of the guy's face. My Mason jar full of coins shattered. The man's nose spouted a gusher of blood. Rusty swung the pillowcase around again and caught him square in the forehead. The cloth ripped, shards of glass and coins exploded, and the creep fell to the floor clawing at his eyes.

I jumped away from the bed, snagged my feet on the sheets, and stumbled against the table. The glass lamp tipped over and burst on the floor, splashing kerosene everywhere. By the time I got myself untangled, flames were rising from the bed sheet that tripped me.

"Let's go!" Rusty urged.

I grabbed my guitar while Rusty snatched Elrod's keys from the table and we dashed to the car. As we sped away in a spray of gravel, the pervert ran screaming from the smoking cabin.

The Cadillac was much bigger than Larry's Chevy, so I skidded all over the gravel road trying to steer it where I wanted to go. I got it more or less under control as I turned onto the highway. The late afternoon traffic on the main drag was like nothing I'd navigated the night before. I dodged station wagons full of tourists and cringed from the trucks barreling along among them. The traffic grew heavier with each passing mile, but it never slowed. I tried desperately to keep up with the stream while staying in my lane, but I lost control when a pickup full of fishermen passed me on a hill and had to cut back in front of me at the crest when a semi came from the other direction. The truck driver laid on his horn, the pickup swerved, and I swung the Cadillac off the road and into a ditch. Rusty's door flew open. He landed face-first in the dirt. I jumped out and ran around the car.

"Are you hurt?" I said, leaning over his inert body.

He moaned and opened his eyes. "Hell yes, I'm hurt, you numb-skull." He sat up and looked around. "Where are we?"

"I don't know," I said. I had a knot rising on my forehead from where the pervert's pinky ring had hit me. Rusty was banged up pretty good, too. His palms and elbows were skinned and the knees of his jeans torn and bloody from impact with the ground. The car wreck was a close call, but it was nothing compared to what that creep was going to do. I still shudder every time I think about his hand on my thigh. And when I remember standing next to his bed, scared witless he was going to hurt me bad if I didn't do what he ordered, I get sick to my stomach. I never took my clothes off, but I felt as naked and ashamed as if I did. Looking back, I imagine that's pretty much how Mom felt when she was with Larry.

I looked at Rusty and asked, "Now what?"

He peered back up the road as if considering a return to Columbia, then shook his head and looked in the other direction. "Where are all these people going?" he asked. I followed his gaze. In addition to the lines of traffic, there were cars parked all along the shoulder and people walking along the highway. All of the pedestrians were headed south. They were turning onto another road not far from us.

"Let's find out," I said. "I think I see something down there."

We walked down the road until we could read the sign at a crossroads where most of the cars were turning west.

"Son of a gun," Rusty grinned. "There's a dam diner on a dam road."

Sure enough, the sign at the intersection said, "Bagnell Dam Motel and Diner" Another sign pointed to "Bagnell Dam Road." We were at the gateway to the Lake of the Ozarks. That meant Springfield--and my dad--wasn't far away.

"I could eat a damn horse if they've got one," Rusty said. "We got any money?"

"Check the wallet. I think there's six dollars left." All I had in my pocket was the silver dollar Aunt Mae gave me for my birthday. The rest of what little money I had was burned up in the cabin fire. Tired and hungry, we trudged along the sidewalk across the top of the colossal dam. The sun pushed our lengthening shadows ahead of us. As the dam curved to stiffen itself against the lake behind it, our shadows crept over the edge until they were cast like silhouettes of giants hung upside down by their heels over the front of the five-story concrete face of the massive dam. Cars full of gawking tourists crept slowly along. Sunburned pedestrians with cameras around their necks and ball caps on their heads gave us a wide berth as they ambled past us on the sidewalk. Not that we scared anybody. Two thirteen-year-olds with a guitar weren't a threat to anyone. But nobody wanted to get involved with my banged up face and Rusty's bloody elbows and ripped jeans.

At the diner on the other side of the dam, we found seats at the counter and asked for burgers and fries. The waitress wrote our order on her pad and said, "You boys look like you rode into town on the wrong end of a hay rake. If you want to clean up, the bathroom's in the back."

My reflection in the chrome napkin holder showed a line of dried blood on my temple and dark smudges under both eyes. Rusty looked worse. "Good idea, Margie," Rusty said, reading the name tag on her uniform. By the time Margie came back with our food, we had taken turns in the bathroom and were almost presentable. The dinner crowd was beginning to fill the booths and tables when we finished our burgers, but we were in no hurry to leave. Rusty checked the pie case and asked, "Margie, what exactly is 'dam pie'?"

The waitress chuckled and said, "It's just apple pie with a wedge of cheese on one side and some ice cream on the other. You want a piece?"

"You bet!" he said. "I'd love some dam pie."

"The damn jokes are getting old," I said.

"What! Did you lose your sense of damn humor?"

"I just thought Margie might not care for your language," I said, checking her reaction out of the corner of my eye.

"Oh honey," she said with a tired smile. "I've heard them all and lots more I can't repeat to nice boys like you."

Margie in her uniform reminded me of Mom waiting tables in Aunt Mae's tavern. I wondered what she had been doing since she found me gone. She was probably frantic and fearful, phoning everyone she could think of and pleading for help to track me down. Less predictable was Larry, who was certain to be crazed about his precious car. It was too soon for the Columbia police to have found it, trace the license plate, and contact him in St. Joe. I tried to make myself believe he wouldn't take it out on Mom. I hated to think about the explosive mix of emotions I had created by running away.

Margie brought the pie and our check, which was nearly double what I had expected. Paying it left us with just three dollars. "Where are we going to sleep?" I whispered to Rusty. It would be dark soon and we had been on the road all night and needed a place to rest. We could probably find a park bench, but I desperately wanted a pillow and blanket.

"Excuse me, ma'am," I said. "How much is a room in the motel?" She saw the troubled look on my face and the trio of bills in my hand.

"More than you've got, sweetheart," she said. "It's tourist season, so everything's high."

Discouraged, I swiveled away from the counter and looked out the front window. A line of waiting customers stretched from the door into the parking lot.

"Come on," I said. "I've got an idea."

I picked up my guitar case and found a spot near the corner of the building not far from the middle of the line of customers in the parking lot. I flipped open the case and left it open on the ground. I hung my guitar around my neck, checked the tuning, and struck a few loud chords to draw attention. Rusty caught on right away, and before I could begin a song, he jumped in front of me and shouted, "Ladies and gentlemen, here's the next big star of the *Ozark Jubilee!*" A spattering of confused applause greeted his announcement as I plunged into an upbeat Hank Williams tune, "Honky Tonkin'." The people in the parking lot were just like the ones in Aunt Mae's tavern—I guessed they'd like a song with a little get-up-and-go.

The line swerved toward us as more people crowded up to see what was going on. A few of them nodded and smiled as I played. Some of them tossed a quarter or two into the case. Somebody in the back said, "That boy's darn good!" Before I could start another song, Rusty jumped up again and announced, "That's just a sample, folks. If you'd like to hear more, please contribute to this future star's career!" He asked a little girl standing in front if he could borrow the snazzy cap she wore. She giggled and asked him what he wanted it for.

When he told her she said, "He just sang one of my favorite songs. Let me help." She took off the cap and walked up the row of people herself with a saucy attitude even Rusty couldn't match. She came back with her cap full of loose change and a couple of dollar bills. When she emptied it into Rusty's hands, there wasn't enough money for a motel room, but it was a start.

"Brenda Lee!" A woman I assumed was her mother scolded, "What do you think you're doing?"

"I'm just helping these nice boys, Mama," she answered. "This boy sings like an angel and picks that guitar hot, hot, hot! They're going to be on the *Ozark Jubilee* just like me!"

Rusty was busy counting the money so he missed that part. My ears perked up, though.

"Hey, kid!" someone from the crowd shouted. "What else you got?"

Before I could answer, Brenda whispered to me, "Do you know 'Jambalaya'?"

"Sure."

"Can I sing it with you?"

I nodded at her and winked at Rusty.

"Give me back your cap," he said with a grin. "This should make a million bucks."

I played the first four bars, nodded to Brenda, and we swung into the song. We doubled up as a duet on the first verse and the chorus, then I let her take the second verse. She looked like she was about eleven years old, but she had a thin, pure voice that she could break huskily like Patsy Cline's at just the right time. We doubled again on the chorus, repeated it, and finished big, holding the last note a full eight beats while I double strummed the final chord with the guitar held high.

The applause rocked me back on my heels. The crowd whistled and hooted and hollered for more while Rusty hustled along the line with the cap. Brenda's eyes sparkled.

"Now, come along, Brenda," her mother said. "We've got to eat some dinner if we're going to make it to Springfield tonight."

Rusty's head snapped up from counting the money. "Did you say you're on your way to Springfield?"

"That's where we're going," Brenda piped up. "I auditioned for Mr. Red Foley when he was touring back home in Georgia and I'm going to be on TV Saturday night on the *Ozark Jubilee*! He said I was dynamite!"

"Why, that's where we're going!" Rusty said. "Daniel's going to play on the *Ozark Jubilee*, too." I tried to say that I only hoped I could be on the show someday, but Rusty cut me off. "Could you give us a lift?" he said. "We had a little complication in our travel arrangements."

A man with Brenda and her mother narrowed his eyes. "Is that so?" he said. "You boys travelling alone?" I was suddenly conscious of the knot on my forehead. I'm sure he suspected I didn't get it bobbing for apples in Sunday School.

"Yes, sir," Rusty answered, building steam. "We've been visiting our mom and now we're going home to our dad in Springfield. We made a mistake and spent all our money on the wrong bus ticket, so we've been hitching rides with kind, good folks like yourself. Could you help us out?"

"Funny, you two sure don't look like brothers," the man said, ignoring Rusty's heavy-handed plea but pointedly staring at his red hair.

"We're stepbrothers," I said, trying to be helpful. "Different fathers. Rusty's dad is my stepdad."

"A stepdad just like you, Daddy Jay," Brenda said. "Please, can't we give the boys a ride?

"I'm not buying any of their bullshit," the man said. "They smell like nothing but trouble and they look like they just lost a bar fight. And I don't see any luggage, do you? It's most likely they're on the run—probably from home if not the police. We're sure not giving a ride to two bums that ought to be home with their mamas."

The man was saying more truth than he knew. I saw another spell of standing on the side of the road with our thumbs out in our near future, so I was delighted when Brenda's mother said, "Jay, let's talk about it while we eat our dinner. You boys wait here and we'll let you know." Brenda gave me a big wink and went into the diner.

"What do you think?" I asked when the door closed behind them.

"I think that little girl wants to marry you," Rusty grinned. "and I'm pretty sure we got the mother's vote. So we win two to one."

The line of customers thinned out as dinner time came and went. I played three more songs, but the tips got smaller with each one without Brenda to fire up the crowd. When the audience finally disappeared, I packed up my guitar and sat down on the case while Rusty counted our money. I was too tired to care how much it was. It had been a very long day, not to mention a night that was little more than a blur of highway signs and dotted white lines illuminated by the lights of a stolen car. We were so close, yet so far from our destination. I wondered what would happen once we got there—if we ever got there.

~ 23 ~

Did you ever find your sorry self in a strange town at midnight with no car, no map, no idea where you were going to sleep? I've had that experience a couple of times and it's no fun. Just imagine, if you will, what it would be like to live that way every day. That's one reason I always drop a few coins in a busker's cup or a homeless person's outstretched hand. There but for the grace of God, and so forth. Of course, when Rusty and I hit Springfield, it wasn't quite that bad. Even though we were young and stupid and had a couple of dollars, it was all still an adventure. We had no idea what was in store.

As Rusty predicted, we won Brenda's vote and her mom's, so we got a ride to Springfield. Brenda's stepdad mumbled and grumbled as he made space for us in the back seat of their car, but her mom hissed at him once, making it clear he better get used to the notion if he knew what was good for him. Rusty and I took the back seat with my guitar between us. Brenda sat up front between her parents, jumping up and turning around every few minutes to chatter about singing on the *Ozark Jubilee*. Her head didn't even reach the top of the car's seat and she had to get up on her knees to look at us. Which is what she did.

"Did you send an audition tape to Mr. Foley?" she asked. Without waiting for an answer, she said. "That's what my Daddy Jay did. I was singing at the Bell Auditorium down in Augusta and Mr. Foley was on the show, too, and he got all hepped up about my number and said I was 'Little Miss Dynamite' and everything so Daddy Jay got a tape from Mr. Peanut at the radio station and . . . ."

"Brenda Lee! You turn around here and put a cork in it," her stepdad ordered.

"Well, you did!" she protested as she turned around and sat back down. In the moment it took for Rusty to look at me and grin, she popped back up.

"You sure play that guitar good. That crowd went hog wild! What's your name? You're cute, too. Do you think I'm cute?"

"Brenda!" huffed her mother.

A hot blush crept up my neck and my mouth went dry. "I'm Daniel," I managed to say. I did indeed think she was cute, too, but could only sputter, "Yeah . . . I guess . . . I mean . . . I kind of like your hair." Rusty was holding in a laugh so hard his eyes bugged out.

"Why, thank you, Daniel," Brenda chirped. "Wait until you see how my mama fixes it up for the show. She puts it up in pin curls and . . . ."

"Brenda!" her stepdad snapped. "Get your butt back in this here seat and leave those boys alone!" Brenda blew me a kiss and flopped around to sit down again. Daddy Jay twisted his head around to me and warned, "Don't you get no ideas, you hear me?"

"Yes, sir. I mean, no sir," I answered. The stepdad glared at Rusty for good measure and turned his eyes back to the road. Rusty had both hands over his mouth and was rolling in the seat. I reached over the guitar case and punched him in the arm.

Two chatty hours later, Brenda's stepfather navigated off the highway into downtown Springfield and pulled up in front of the grand doors of the Colonial Hotel. The Jewell Theater, home to the *Ozark Jubilee*, was across the street. The building was dark, but the marquee shone like a beacon to me.

"Okay, this is as far as we go," the stepdad announced.

"Jay, it's pretty late. Don't you think we should take them to their daddy's house?" Brenda's mother said.

Before the man could answer and ask something embarrassing about where Dad lived, Rusty said, "Oh, that's not necessary. Our dad's place is just up the street."

"Yeah, we don't mind walking," I said. "Thanks for the ride."

Rusty and I hurried to slide out of the car to avoid any more uncomfortable questions.

The passenger door swung open and Brenda scrambled across her mother's lap and onto the sidewalk. Before I knew what was happening, she jumped up onto her toes and kissed me right on the mouth.

"Brenda!" her mother and stepdad protested in unison.

"Come on, Romeo," Rusty said, pulling me away. Brenda jumped up and down in a fit of giggles.

"See you at rehearsal!" she shouted.

I waved. "You bet."

We hustled up the sidewalk as Brenda's mother corralled her and her stepdad dealt with the bellhop who materialized from the hotel. As soon as we turned the corner and were out of sight, I asked Rusty where we were going.

"I don't have any idea," he said, "but let's get out of here before Brenda decides to come and marry you right here on the sidewalk. She's a sweetheart but we don't need to add kidnapping to our rap sheet. I don't know if you noticed, but Daddy Jay is looking for any excuse to turn us in to the cops."

It was nearly midnight and it had been a long, long time since my head had been on a pillow. We stopped at the next corner and saw nothing that looked like a place to spend the night. We knew the hotel was not an option, even with the money we'd collected at the diner. Across the street were nothing but office buildings and darkened storefronts. Straight ahead, the streetlights petered out as the business district came to an end a few blocks away.

"My gut says we go that way," Rusty said.

"Are you sure?"

"Have I ever led you wrong?"

"Don't get me started," I answered. "But one way's as good as the next. Let's go."

We followed Rusty's nose for three blocks past empty parking lots, miscellaneous stores closed for the night, office buildings that would be bustling in the morning but were dark now, and intersections where traffic lights blinked through the night without cars to direct. We passed a bank with a clock over its door that read twelve thirty. We had been on the run for twenty-four hours. It seemed like twenty-four days.

After a few blocks, we stumbled across a house with a porch light burning over a small sign that read "Boarding House – Vacancy."

"Home sweet home," Rusty said.

The bricks on the foundation were weathered and worn. The white paint on the door was cracked and peeling. But none of the windows were broken and the porch looked like it was swept clean every day. The place may not have been very fancy, but it looked secure enough. Besides, it had to be better than sleeping on a park bench. I rang the doorbell, assuming the porch light was an invitation even though it was the middle of the night.

Rusty pushed the bell again. Before it stopped ringing, the door swung open and we were greeted by a behemoth with curlers in her hair. She sized us up, then coughed and got right down to business. "Seven bucks a week in advance, breakfast and dinner included if you get to the table on time. I got one room with one bed, so you better be good friends. If the cops show up looking for you, you told me your parents were coming right behind you. Can you remember all that?"

"Yes ma'am," I said. Somehow, she made me feel safe by checking us out and laying down some rules. I was pretty sure she would brook no nonsense from us or anyone else. I picked up my guitar and moved toward the door.

"You a musician?" She shook her head. "Of course, you're all musicians. That's why I keep the light on all night. And you're going to be famous someday, aren't you? Well, you still can't play that thing in your room. Any time, day or night? Got that?"

"Yes ma'am," I answered again.

"I'll keep an eye on him for you," Rusty added.

She squinted at him and said, "What are you, his keeper?"

"Yep, that's my job!" he said. "I'm his manager."

She let a little smile play across her stern face, then wiped it off. "If you're the manager, then you're the guy who pays the bills, right?" She said, holding out her hand.

"Yes, ma'am, Mrs . . . uh," Rusty said as he counted out the rent into her meaty palm.

"Stamey, Lois Stamey," she said, filling in the blank for him. "Everybody calls me 'Ma'. And who are you? I need your names—your real names. This place may not be the Waldorf Astoria, but I keep a respectable house."

"I'm Daniel Freemont and he is Rusty James," I said. "Thanks for letting us stay here, Mrs. Stamey."

"There's no missus about it. Like I said, call me 'Ma'." As we followed her up the stairs, she said, "That's Rusty James like Jesse James?"

"Yes, ma'am" Rusty answered.

She snorted. "Figures you'd be the manager."

The room was small, but big enough for the two of us and my guitar. It had a chair and a wooden table with one leg propped up by a brick. There was no closet, which didn't matter since we didn't have any clothes to hang in one anyway. The double bed had seen better days, but we didn't care. As soon as our heads hit the pillows, we were out.

Ma had told us breakfast was at eight the next morning and we almost slept right through it. The sun glaring through the window in our room finally woke me up and I climbed over Rusty to go down the hall to the bathroom. I saw a little dried blood near my hairline and washed it off. The goose egg on my forehead was smaller, about the size of a grape instead of an egg, and had turned pale purple. When I came back, Rusty was pulling on his torn jeans, wincing as they went over his scabbed knees.

"How are we going to find your dad?" he asked.

"We'll start where they stage the *Ozark Jubilee*, at the Jewell Theater," I said with confidence I didn't feel. "I heard him on the radio, so somebody around the show must know him."

"We need to find him pretty soon if we want to eat," Rusty said. "The first week's rent just about wiped us out."

I was surprised no one else was at the breakfast table except Ma. Her curlers had been replaced by a hair net and she wore a faded dress that was so large it may have had a previous life as a sofa cover. She grunted "good morning," gave us each a bowl of cornflakes and a glass of milk, then sat back down herself with a cup of coffee and a cigarette.

"Where is everybody?" I asked, mainly to make conversation.

"Most of my tenants are musicians. They don't get up much before noon," she said. "The guys and gals with real jobs ate already and are on their way to work."

That made sense. I remembered how late Dad used to sleep the morning after a gig and how Mom would keep me and Willy quiet so he could get some rest. The memory of those happy times weighed on me and I lowered my head over my cornflakes and made myself eat.

Rusty slurped the last of his cereal straight out of the bowl. He wiped the milk mustache off his freckled face and said "Dee-licious. That hit the spot!"

"You want some more?" Ma asked. From the twinkle in her eye, it was clear Rusty had somehow touched a soft spot.

"No thank you," Rusty said. I thanked her, too, and we stood up to go.

"Sit back down a minute," she said. As soon as we sat, she leaned forward in her chair and asked, "You boys look kind of beat up. You running from some kind of trouble? Tell me straight."

Before I could answer, Rusty said, "Kind of. Our stepdad whipped us pretty good the other day so we ran away."

"You look like somebody beat you up all right. Where are you from?"

I started to answer, but Rusty gave me a quick look to tell me to keep my mouth shut. "Kansas City," he said.

"So if I call the long-distance operator in Kansas City to find your mother, do I ask for Mrs. Freemont or Mrs. James?"

"What do you mean?" Rusty said.

"I mean you don't look like brothers and you don't have the same last name, but those are the names you gave me last night. Now, what's going on here? Tell me true!"

"It's true!" Rusty exclaimed. "We have different dads but the same mom! We're really half-brothers. And mom married again and again, and he's our stepdad and he's the one who beat us up. Honest, Ma."

"Still sounds fishy to me," she said, squinting at Rusty, then at me. "So what are you doing in Springfield?"

"We ran away to come live with my real dad," I said, jumping in before Rusty could make up more lies we'd have to remember. "He lives here in Springfield. He's on the *Ozark Jubilee*."

"Oh for crying out loud, another musician!" Ma said, throwing her hands up in the air. "And I guess he wasn't home, which is why you ended up ringing my doorbell at midnight."

I said, "Not exactly . . . ." But Rusty took over.

"That's right. He didn't know we were coming and he must have left on tour. His landlady wasn't as nice as you and she wouldn't let us stay in his room. She turned us out on the street. Wasn't that mean?" He gave Ma the sweetest, most wide-eyed innocent look I'd ever seen on his freckled face. I just hoped she wouldn't ask us where dad lived. She didn't, but I could tell she didn't believe any of Rusty's malarkey. She looked us over pretty carefully then gave me an encouraging nod.

"Well, you boys are dressed like you lost a fight with a pack of pit bulls. You got any clean clothes?" I looked down at my soiled, sweaty shirt and found a blood stain on the sleeve. Rusty's jeans were an absolute mess, both legs ripped open and sagging to show his scabbed knees underneath.

"No, ma'am," I said. I realized we needed to clean up if we wanted to avoid the bum's rush when we went to the Jewell Theater.

"Come on downstairs," she said. "My boy is grown and gone, but I've still got some of his things. There ought to be something to fit you."

We followed Ma into the basement. It doubled as her laundry room, so it was brightly lit, clean, and dry. She pulled a wooden crate from a shelf and set it on the floor between us. "Help yourselves," she said. "These duds aren't doing anybody any good sitting in a box waiting to rot." We rummaged through it looking for things that might fit. Her son was evidently a little bigger than Rusty but not quite as tall as me, but we couldn't be picky.

"Where's your son now?" I asked before I caught myself. "Sorry, I don't mean to pry."

"He's out on the road with his pa," she answered. "They're playing with some rock-a-billy band in Texas, last I heard."

"Musicians, huh?" Rusty said.

"You got it," she snorted. "One of them is more worthless than the other. Think only about themselves and their damn licks and

riffs and such. All I ever get from them is a postcard now and then."
She sounded so bitter I thought she was about to spit on the floor.
I wondered if I also fit into that description somehow. I was a musician, or at least working on being one, and had abandoned my
mom, too. It wasn't a happy thought.

"Hey, look! These fit perfect," Rusty said, breaking the mood. He
wrapped the waistband of a pair of jeans against his own waist and
stood up. "What do you think?"

"Those will do," Ma said, brightening as she looked him over.
"You might have to cuff them up a couple of times, but go on and
take them." She pulled a shirt out of the box and handed it to him.
"Here, you need this, too." I found a clean shirt and another pair
of jeans for me. "Now go on, you two," she said. "I got work to do.
This place don't run itself." We thanked her and went upstairs to
change. It was time to go looking for Dad.

~ 24 ~

Springfield wasn't exactly Hollywood, but it was pretty much the center of country music television in the 1950s because it was the home of the *Ozark Jubilee*. Oh, the Grand Ole Opry was a big deal, too, but it was more successful on radio than it ever was on TV. In fact, when the *Ozark Jubilee* started its television program on the ABC network, Red Foley quit his job as emcee of the Opry to come to Springfield. Bet that was something you didn't know.

Of course, the only thing that mattered to me at the time was that I heard my dad on the *Ozark Jubilee*—the radio version that aired along with the TV show—so we were in the right place to start looking for him.

As we came down the boarding house steps, someone was picking a lively version of "Turkey in the Straw" on a strange instrument in the backyard. It had to be some type of gitfiddle. I wildly hoped for a minute that it was Dad, but when I went to the back door to see, it was a man I didn't know. I started to go outside to ask him if he knew Dad, but Rusty took my arm and dragged me toward the sidewalk. He insisted, rightly enough, that wandering around in the Springfield summer heat asking strangers if they knew a guitar player from St. Joe wasn't the best part of our plan.

"Focus, Daniel, focus!" he commanded. "Let's go find the *Ozark Jubilee* office and see if your dad is there."

"Right. Let's go."

"And we'll sign you up to play while we're at it."

Rusty really loved being a manager. Unfortunately, he didn't have any idea of how to go about it. I didn't have the heart to tell him I couldn't just simply show up and go on stage. I knew I'd need to audition. I also knew Dad had played at the Jewell Theater Saturday night, but he wouldn't be sleeping there. I hoped someone could tell me how to get in touch with him wherever he was living.

We had seen the Jewell Theater across the street as Brenda's stepdad parked the car at the hotel, so we retraced our footsteps from the night before back downtown. The theater's two-story façade had fancy columns and a big banner on the second floor, while a giant neon marquee jutted out over the sidewalk. My heart raced as I walked under the big black letters that spelled "*Ozark Jubilee – Saturday Night*" and for a moment I imagined my name up there, too. I came down to earth, though, when we discovered all the doors across the front of the building were locked. Even the box office window was closed and a "Sold Out" sign hung behind the glass. Rusty rattled each of the doors again, working his way down the line. As he got to the end, the last door opened and a security guard stepped out.

"Move along," he said. "Can't you see the theater is closed?"

"We are here to see Mr. Red Foley," Rusty announced. "Will you please tell him we've arrived?"

"I'm not telling anybody anything about anyone, especially a smartass like you," the guard snorted. "You want to talk to somebody who gives a shit, go to the office. It's around back."

I thanked him despite his nasty attitude and we found our way around the building to an unmarked door that someone had propped ajar with an empty pop bottle. I gave Rusty a questioning look. He shrugged and opened the door. We stepped into a dark hallway, where we were blind after our walk in the brilliant afternoon sun. A crack of light showed under a door a few steps down the hall. I knocked and a woman said to come in.

A young lady with bright red lipstick and lusciously-bobbed blond hair looked up from behind a desk in the reception area as we came in. Chairs lined the walls in front of her and there was a closed door behind. A plaque on her desk said she was "Emily Harris." Efficient but friendly, she asked, "Can I help you?"

"Yes ma'am," Rusty said. "We'd like to see Mr. Red Foley."

She tried to keep a straight face so as to let him down easy. "Sweetheart, you need an appointment just to get an appointment with Red. Besides, he's not here today."

"Can you tell me when we can see him?" Rusty pressed. "My man, Daniel, came here to play on the show."

"Oh he's here to play on national television, is he?" she laughed.

"Excuse my ignorant friend, Miss Harris," I interrupted. "He's not usually this obnoxious." She thought that was pretty funny, too. "I would like to audition, but I'm actually here looking for one of the musicians on the show, John Freemont. He's my dad. He's a guitar player and I heard him on the show Saturday night. Can you maybe tell me where to find him?"

She frowned and shook her head. "I don't recognize the name. You say he was on Saturday's show?" She riffled through a stack of papers on her desk, then took another pile out of a basket behind her. "Here's the cast rundown," she said, pulling several pages stapled together out of the pile. She looked through them carefully, turning the pages slowly and moving her finger down each one line by line. "No, sorry. This was for Saturday night, and there's no John Freemont on it. I checked each of the bands and even the square dance troupe." I was too emotionally drained to cry, but she must have seen the despair playing across my face.

Rusty saw it, too. "Then we'll just keep looking for him," he said. "But in the meantime, can Daniel get an audition? He's a really, really good singer and guitar picker."

"I'm sure he is, honey. But the audition list is full through Christmas." She turned to me and said, "You can sign up for then if you want. Or, if you've got a tape, you can leave it for us. Otherwise, I'm sorry. I can't help you."

Coming on top of my disappointment about Dad, this news hit as if someone had slammed a door on my dreams. I wasn't really expecting an immediate audition, but deep inside, I hoped for one. I didn't have an audition tape or any way to make one and I certainly couldn't sign up now and wait around until December. Who was I kidding? I was never going to be on the *Ozark Jubilee.* I was nothing but a high school freshman who was probably going to get arrested for grand theft auto—or worse—by dinner time.

Most importantly, though, we had reached a dead end in the search for my dad. The only thing we could do now was wander around the streets of Springfield hoping to get lucky and stumble across him. Dejected, I mumbled my thanks and turned to leave.

"Wait a minute," Miss Harris said, "I'll tell you what. The office is closed for the next couple of days, but you come back Friday and I'll check the lineups for the last few weeks. Maybe his name will be on one of them."

Rusty saw that I was about to break down, so he thanked her for both of us. "That's really great," he said. "We sure appreciate it. You're so nice! We'll see you Friday."

"Rehearsals start at noon, so be here before then, okay?"

Miss Harris is one of those people who don't think twice about helping somebody else. She didn't do it to get any awards or earn a place in heaven or anything like that. She helped people because it was the right thing to do. That's a pretty rare quality. It's folks like her that make it possible to forget the assholes all around who are just the opposite. I'm not going to name any names, but you know who they are.

~ 25 ~

Waiting is one of the hardest things in the world because, when it comes to the sands of time, you can't push them through the hourglass any faster than the laws of physics allow them to go. To this day, I can't kill time worth squat. Always have to be doing something productive—or at least something that lets me think I'm accomplishing something other than twiddling my thumbs. I always hated that feeling of helplessness, of just sitting and waiting, but never more so than when I had to kill those two days without knowing if I still had a chance to find my dad. I fiddled around doing nothing until after lunch the next day, but finally couldn't stand it. I dragged Rusty out of the boardinghouse to go with me to see if Dad had played any of the bars and beer joints downtown.

I was so impatient to go that we were nearly a block from the boardinghouse before I remembered my guitar. I turned to go back.

"What do you need it for?" Rusty asked.

"I don't know. I just don't like leaving it in the room. I trust Ma Stamey, but we don't know any of the other roomers." As it turned out later, some of those roomers became real compadres.

After I ran back and retrieved it, Rusty suggested we head back to the theater. "There ought to be places to eat and drink around there," he said. We started in that block, but didn't have any luck. There were restaurants and bars, but the ones that offered live music hadn't heard of Dad.

"Guitar pickers come and go," one bartender said. "But you might try Lindberg's Tavern. They've been around since forever. They have music almost every night."

Lindberg's Tavern was across town and my guitar got heavier and heavier the longer we walked. It was a cloudless day, too, so the sun beat down on us the entire way. By the time we opened the tavern's heavy wooden door, I was beat and my shoulders ached from carrying my guitar. It was a relief to step into the cool, dimly lit tavern. The place made Aunt Mae's look almost shabby by comparison. The booths were sturdy oak instead of plywood. The well-polished bar was oak, too, complete with a brass foot rail and stools with leather seats. The classic stamped-tin ceiling was smoke-tinted and high enough to allow ceiling fans with wooden blades to circulate the summer air. I was impressed by the elevated stage that occupied the far end of the room. I could imagine my dad and me performing together under the spot lights that hung from the ceiling. That dream evaporated when the bartender said he'd never heard of Dad, nor did he remember ever seeing any guitar player use brass finger picks the way I told him Dad did. Discouraged, I told Rusty it was time to call it a day.

We stepped out of the tavern into the glaring afternoon sun and I groaned as I shifted my guitar from one tired hand to the other

"What me to haul that load for a while?" Rusty asked.

"Yeah, thanks. I'll spell you along the way."

"Hey boys, I'll be glad to do you one better," a voice said. It came from a red Ford pickup truck idling at the curb in front of the tavern. "You look like you could use a lift."

"Well . . . ." I hesitated, a vision of the pervert who picked us up last time flashing through my head. Rusty didn't blink.

"That would be great," he said. "I'm bushed."

"Hop in, friends," the guy said. "Where to?"

"Do you know Stamey's boarding house?" Rusty asked.

"Why sure! If you're living there, you guys must be musicians. I am, too. I stayed at Ma's when I first came to town. Throw your guitar in the back."

I laid my guitar case in the bed of the pickup and got in the seat between Rusty and the driver.

"My name's Stan," the guy said. "What's your moniker?"

"I'm Daniel and he's Rusty," I said.

"Pleased to make your acquaintance." He was a tall guy with hands so big they made the steering wheel look tiny. He wore a yellow cowboy-style shirt with two pockets with pointed flaps and white pearl snaps instead of buttons. There was a bolo tie around his neck with a turquoise slide that matched the hat band on a black Stetson hat so tall it almost touched the roof of the truck cab.

"So did you find what you were looking for in the Lindberg?"

"What do you mean?" I said.

"Well, as I was leaving, I saw you come in and talk to the bartender, but you didn't stay long. Figured you were looking for something. That's all. I'm just making small talk. Didn't mean to stick my nose in your business."

I was tired, but my antennae were still up and alert to trouble. There was something about Stan that didn't ring true. For some reason, I didn't know whether to believe him or not. On the other hand, maybe I was being oversensitive. "That's okay. Are you really a musician?"

"Yessireebob. In fact, I'm on my way home right now from an audition for a spot on the Opry."

"In Nashville?"

"That's the one!" he grinned and added, "I see you're a six-string guy like me," he said, jerking his thumb over his shoulder pointing to my guitar in the back seat. "What's in the case?"

"It's a Martin D-18," I answered, unable to keep the pride out of my voice.

"No kidding? You know, that's what Elvis played in his last session at Sun Records this year. That's quite a box for a youngster like yourself. Worth a pretty penny."

"My dad gave it to me. He's a really good . . . ." I caught myself fading into a funk over my fruitless search for Dad. To change the subject, I said, "What kind of guitar do you play?"

"I'm a Gibson man, myself."

"Cool."

He turned on the radio and asked, "WSM okay with you?" When I nodded, he pushed one of the buttons and Sonny James came through the speakers singing "Young Love." I felt a bit more comfortable with the situation and settled back to enjoy the ride. It felt good to be off my feet. Rusty snored lightly beside me, his head against the window. Sonny James was followed by Marty Robbins, Carl Perkins, and Ray Price, although every other song seemed to come from Elvis.

Not long after we passed the Colonial Hotel, Stan said, "I need to make a stop. I think there's a filling station up around the corner." He found it and turned in. The change in motion woke up Rusty, who yawned and asked if we were there already. "No, just stopping for some gas," Stan said as he pulled up next to a pump displaying the red Conoco triangle. We all got out of the truck to stretch. A slow-moving teenager came out of a garage next to the station wiping his hands on a red rag. Stan asked him to check the oil. "I'll pump the gas myself," he said. "I don't mind." The boy shrugged and opened the hood.

"I gotta pee," Rusty said and headed for the building.

"The key's hanging by the door of the office," the boy called after him.

"I could go for a cold Coca-Cola," Stan said. "How about you?" He handed me three nickels. "See if there's a machine inside and get one for you and—what's his name?—oh yeah, Rusty."

I found the red Coke cooler where it hummed against the back wall of the station office. I lifted the insulated steel lid and slid the first frosty bottle along the rack to the gate at the end where it hung by its glass neck. I put in the first nickel, the gate opened, and I pulled the bottle out. I held it against my cheek for a moment to enjoy the cold before repeating the purchase for two more bottles. Rusty came in as I hooked a bottle under the opener on the side of the cooler and popped the cap. When I handed the bottle to him, he took a long swig. "Ah, the pause that refreshes," he said when he came up for air. He went outside as I opened the other two bottles.

The door slammed and Rusty shouted, "Hey! Where are you going!" I rushed outside only to see the pickup pulling away from the pump and heading for the road.

"Wait for us!" I yelled. Stan's head turned briefly in our direction, but he stepped on the gas. The pickup swerved and the tires squealed and Rusty threw his pop bottle. It spun through the air spewing Coke but shattered harmlessly on the pavement. Rusty took off running.

I hollered "Stop! Wait! My guitar!" and dashed after Rusty. My guitar was in the back of the truck, alone and vulnerable. It was my only tangible connection to home and Dad, my refuge in times of trouble, perhaps the ticket to my future, a future that was dark and bleak without it. What would I do if it was lost? How could I be so gullible? Angry with myself, I stretched my stride and caught up to Rusty as the pickup reached the end of the driveway and turned onto the street.

The tires smoked and Stan swerved to dodge a police car turning into the gas station from the opposite direction. The patrol car barely missed Rusty, who dove out of its way and landed on his hands and knees on the pavement. The cop jumped out just as I got to him.

"How bad are you hurt?" I said, reaching down to help Rusty up. His palms were bloody and he wiped them on his jeans.

"Bad enough, but I'll live. Did that bastard get away?"

"What bastard?" the policeman said.

"That guy in the pickup. He stole my guitar! Can you catch him?" I pleaded.

"The one that almost hit me?"

Agitated, Rusty said, "Yeah, that one. Come on, let's go catch him." He dashed over to the patrol car and opened the passenger door.

"Hold on, there, buster!" the cop commanded.

"Please, please, please!" I cried. "He's getting away!"

He looked into my frantic eyes. "Okay. But you two ride in the back. Regulations. Get in."

He jumped behind the wheel and, as soon as I closed our door, put the car into a spin that sprayed gravel all over the gas station before it straightened out and sped down the road. He reached under the dash and flipped a couple of switches. The siren wailed.

"Now tell me what happened," the cop said without taking his eyes off the road.

"He was giving us a ride, but he dumped us and took off." Rusty answered.

"Why'd you get in his car? Were you buying something from him?"

That's a strange question, I thought. "No sir, he was just giving us a ride home."

"You sure he wasn't selling you a little weed?"

"No way!" Rusty exclaimed. "We were just going home to Ma Stamey's."

The cop looked puzzled. "Why do you live in a boardinghouse?"

Rusty didn't miss a beat. "We have to. But just until our Mom gets out of the hospital. She's real sick."

"Okay," the cop said. I couldn't tell if he was buying Rusty's story or not. It didn't matter as long as he kept going.

"He took my guitar," I added. "It's worth a lot of money. Can you catch him?"

"One way or another," he answered. He took a microphone off a hook on the dash. "All cars, this is Unit 2. I need backup at Little Eddie's. On my way to investigate a possible theft by a person residing there. You know the drill for that address. Approach with caution. Over."

The radio squawked. "This is Unit 3, Sarge. We're on our way. ETA five minutes."

"Ten-Four Unit 3."

"Wow," Rusty said. "Just like on TV. So you're a sergeant? "

The cop didn't smile as put the microphone back on its hook. "Yep, something like that."

"The guy said his name was Stan and he was heading home from Nashville," I said. I realized as I spoke that probably none of that was true and resolved to never again believe someone I don't know.

The cop sped back through downtown, past the Colonial Hotel and Jewell Theater, then through neighborhoods with more homes than storefronts. Without slowing, he turned off his flashing lights and siren. A few blocks later, he turned on to a street that parallelled railroad tracks lined with weeds. A single house stood at the end of the street. The red Ford pickup was parked in front. He pulled to a stop directly behind it.

"We got him!" I crowed. I yanked the door handle but it didn't budge.

"Just relax, you two," Sarge said as he opened his door. "Passengers in the back of a patrol car can't get out until I let them out." A second patrol car pulled up behind us and two other cops got out. "I'll be back in a minute."

The cops strolled up the walk like they were trying to be casual, although I noticed the last one kept his hand on his holster. They climbed three steps to a wide porch that stretched across the front of the house. A handful of men loitering on the porch parted as the cops walked between them. Locked in the back of the car, I couldn't hear them, but a couple of the men said something and Sarge snarled back at them. The men took another step back and the cops went in the front door without knocking.

"Man, I don't like this," Rusty said.

"Scared?" I said, only half paying attention to him. I was fuming about being locked in the back of the car and itching to get my hands on my guitar.

"Kinda. Something's not right. They just walked in the front door. No search warrant or guns out or nothing! Broderick Crawford would never do that."

Before I answered, Sarge came out to get us.

"Stan is here, all right," he said. "And he has a guitar in a case. Says it's his. Bought it off some guy passing through town that needed the money."

I exploded. "What! that lying sack of . . . ."

"Hold on, fella," the cop said. "Come on inside and we'll straighten this out with Little Eddie."

"Who's that?" Rusty said.

"I don't care," I said before the cop could answer. "As long as he can give me back my guitar."

The men on the porch let us pass but one of them snickered as we went through the door. Rusty's head swiveled as if to respond, but before he could, Sarge told the guy to shut up. He guided us into a room to the right just inside the front door. A man not much taller than me was waiting for us. Stan stood behind him. My guitar case lay unopened on the floor.

"Good afternoon, gentlemen," the short man said with a smile that revealed teeth the same shade of yellow as his t-shirt. "Let's see if we can clear up this little misunderstanding."

The cop said, "Yep, somebody's not telling the truth, Eddie, and I am more inclined to believe these boys here than I am your man, Stan."

"I'll grant these are trustworthy-looking fellas, Sergeant Riley," Eddie answered. I didn't miss the familiar way he called the cop by name. "Stan tells me you're musicians staying at Ma Stamey's until your sick mama can come and get you, or something like that. I can identify with your predicament. My own mama died when I was about your age and my worthless daddy disappeared right away. I was left to tend to myself." He paused to give us a sly smile. "Sometimes I had to do some things a little, shall we say, 'clever', to get along. You know what I mean?

I didn't see how accusing Stan of stealing my guitar was "clever" and told him so.

He chuckled. "Let's say maybe you need a little cash. And you saw this guitar when Stan gave you a lift to the gas station out of the goodness of his heart."

"What!" Rusty shouted. "That creep left us in the dust! He stole that guitar!"

"All right, that's enough," Sarge said. "Let's just see who owns what here. Stan, what kind of guitar is in that case?"

Smugly, Stan said, "That there is a Martin D-18. I checked it out before I paid good money for it."

"Is that what it is?" the cop asked me.

"Yes. But I told him that when he picked us up!" I panicked. It was my word against his.

"Ask him what else is in the case," Rusty demanded.

The cop shrugged and looked at Stan. "Well?" he said.

Stan looked uncertain, but brightened after a moment. "There's some guitar picks and a capo in there. In the compartment under the neck." He knew that was a safe guess.

"What kind of picks?" Rusty asked.

"What do you mean? Picks is picks," Stan said.

"Okay, if you say so. But what else is in the case?" Rusty said with a knowing smile.

"That's a trick question! There ain't room for nothing else in there."

"Daniel?" Rusty said with his best gap-toothed grin. I knew we had him now.

"He's wrong about the picks. I use brass finger picks," I said. "They are in the compartment."

"And?" Rusty said, grinning bigger than ever.

Now I was confused. What was he getting at? Guitar, picks, what else? Then I remembered.

"Oh yeah! My fake book." I said with relief. "My name is in it. Daniel Freemont."

Stan turned white. The cop opened the guitar case and lifted out the guitar. My fake book lay beneath it. He flipped it open.

"There, inside the cover," I said.

"Daniel Freemont," the cop read aloud. "Just like you said." He held up the book and turned to Eddie. "Unless the guy he bought it from has the same name as this boy here, this is not Stan's guitar."

Stan dashed past Little Eddie, around the startled cops, and through the door before anyone could stop him. Shouts of "Go Stan!" mixed with guffaws from the men on the porch. An engine roared and Stan's pickup flashed past the window.

"Go!" Sarge ordered. The two other cops pushed their way through the laughing men on the porch and ran to their car. I was dumbstruck by it all. Rusty, for a change, had no words either.

Shaking his head, Sarge turned to Little Eddie and said, "Now, what are you going to do about this?"

"Well, Sergeant Riley, the first thing is, we're going to give this young man this guitar, since it is unquestionably his." Little Eddie obviously didn't care what might happen to Stan. "Then I'm going to apologize for Stan's unfriendly actions. Daniel, I hope you won't hold it against me. Like I said, I've been in the same boat as you and I'm sorry one of my associates rocked yours."

He carefully put my guitar back in its case, closed the lid, and set it on its side in front of me. "Friends?" he asked, holding out his hand.

I was beyond confused by the whole mess. Sarge and Little Eddie apparently had known each other for quite some time. Still, I had my guitar, and that was all that mattered at the moment. Little Eddie extended his hand farther and I shook it.

"Good boy," he said. "Listen, I owe you one for all this hassle. You ever need anything, or anybody in this town gives you any trouble, you just say the word and I'll take care of it. Deal?"

"Sure," I muttered as I picked up my guitar.

"Hey, what about the thief?" Rusty said.

"I guarantee you that Sergeant Riley will bring him to justice, isn't that right?" Little Eddie said.

"Yeah, as soon as we catch him," Sarge said. "Come on, boys, I'll take you back to Ma Stamey's."

~ 26 ~

We were in our room at the boardinghouse Thursday afternoon when someone started playing the gitfiddle I'd heard the day before. It had the plucky bounce of a banjo but was more resonant and sweeter, almost like a guitar. Whoever was playing it was pretty good, too. It wasn't very loud but the notes were clear and sure, the chords were solid. I was going stir crazy in our room, so I grabbed my guitar and headed downstairs with Rusty right behind me.

By the time we got there, a small group was tuning up. There was a fiddle, a mandolin, a banjo and the unknown instrument that somehow sounded like two or three of the others. All the players went silent when Rusty and I came out the back door.

"Looks like we got ourselves a guitar man," the mandolin player said.

"Welcome, son," the fiddler added. They were all old enough to call me son or even grandson.

"Hi," I said with an uncertain smile. "I didn't come to play. I just don't like to leave my guitar in the room."

"Got to watch out for the moneymaker, don't you?" the banjo player smiled back.

"Yes, sir."

"What's your name, young man?" someone asked.

"I'm Daniel," I answered. "I heard someone playing a few minutes ago. Is that what I heard?" I pointed to the unusual instrument. It had the body of a viola but the fretted neck of a banjo.

"This, Daniel, is my gitfiddle," the man held it up so I could see it better. "My name is Joe. I had this one made out of an old viola with a broken neck and a tenor banjo I found on a junk pile because the drum head was busted. There's an old boy up in the hills made it for me."

"Yeah, it takes a hillbilly to make one and another hillbilly named Joe to play one," the fiddler added. Everybody laughed.

"Would you like to try it?" Joe said.

"Sure!" I answered, but when I reached for it, he pulled it back with a grin.

"First, you've got to sing for your supper. Limber up that guitar of yours and play a tune with us. Our guitar thumper left for parts unknown and we need a box to round out our sound."

I didn't mind at all. I got out my guitar and checked my tuning with theirs. As I slipped on my thumb and finger picks, the git-fiddler and the mandolin player exchanged surprised glances, but nobody said anything until the fiddler said, "'Mountain Dew' in G, boys. One-two, one-two-three-four." They chased into the tune like they'd been playing together all their lives—maybe they had been. They were good, definitely pros, but I kept up by not trying anything fancy on the guitar and singing only on the chorus when everybody joined in. Rusty clapped and whistled when the song came to its rollicking end.

"Whew! You sure tore it up, boy!" the fiddler said. "Where'd you learn to play like that?"

"From my dad." I smiled and blushed.

"You sound real good. I only heard one other guy play guitar with brass finger picks," Joe said.

My throat tightened. Did he know Dad? "What . . . what's his name?" I asked, trying to keep the tremble out of my voice.

"Let me think," he said. "There was something funny about his name." He looked up into the sky trying to remember. "What was it?" I wanted to grab him by the throat and shake it out of him, but

I could see he wasn't teasing me. "Oh yeah! Now I remember. He said his name was the same as his guitar! Martin. His name is Chris Martin and he plays a big Martin guitar just like yours."

My spirits sank. Thousands of people—pros and amateurs alike—played Martin guitars. And "Chris Martin" sure wasn't my dad's name.

Rusty thought of something else, though. "Did he play on the *Ozark Jubilee* last Saturday?"

The gitfiddler shook his head. "I don't know about that. I never been on that stage. I played with him at a church dance, must have been a week or so ago. He stayed here at Ma's one night and said he was only in town for a couple of days and had to go home, wherever that was. He could have come back to be on the *Ozark Jubilee* last weekend, I guess. We were playing down in Branson, so I didn't hear the show." It seemed like every time I got a lead on Dad's whereabouts, it turned into a dead end.

The back door opened and Ma came out. "You sound pretty good for a bunch of reprobates." All the men laughed. "I'll make some lemonade if you play 'You Are My Sunshine' for me." Frosty lemonade sounded like a fine idea in the afternoon heat.

"You got it, Ma," the mandolin player said. Can you sing it in C, Daniel?" I nodded and he said, "Then it's all yours."

When the song ended, Ma lifted the hem of her apron and dabbed her eyes.

"Hey, Ma," the gitfiddler said. "Do you remember a guy name of Chris Martin? He plays guitar just like Daniel."

Ma straightened up with a stern look. "Chris Martin? I certainly do remember him. He stiffed me for a night's rent." She looked hard at me. "You related to him?"

"I, uh, I don't think so," I stuttered. I wasn't sure, although aside from his name, the guy sure sounded like my dad. I tried my hardest not to get my hopes up.

~ 27 ~

By the time we left the boarding house the next day, I was ready to explode. I really needed to find Dad, but the trail was anything but hot. Still, I refused to admit we were at a dead end, since there was still some hope for whoever this Chris Martin guy might be. Meanwhile, Mom and Willy were home—unprotected—with Larry—and the cops were probably looking all over the state for Rusty and me. The only light at the end of the tunnel was coming from the *Ozark Jubilee.*

Friday morning, Rusty and I walked to the theater but found the office door locked. We were too early. We stood around helplessly for what seemed like an hour, but nobody came. We walked a complete circle around the theater and found some other unmarked doors, but they were locked, too. Rusty saw a shady spot under a tree on the other side of the parking lot, so we went to sit on the curb and wait. And wait. And wait. I had my guitar, of course, since I could never let it out of my sight again, so I tried to keep busy learning a new lick I'd heard Joe the gitfiddler play. But I couldn't concentrate and gave it up after a half dozen tries.

At last, a long, green Buick Roadmaster with a driver in front and a man in the back pulled up near the building. The passenger, a man in a coat and tie, got out, unlocked the theater door, and went inside. We jumped up from the curb and ran across the parking lot, but the car was gone by the time we got there and the man had apparently locked the door behind him. Rusty pounded on the door, but nobody came.

"Who was that guy?" he said.

"Might have been Red Foley," I answered. "But I couldn't see what color his hair was."

"Who else would have a chauffeur to drive him around?" Rusty said. He rattled the knob and knocked again, but got no answer.

"We better wait here," I said. "I'm pretty sure Miss Harris will come sooner or later."

The sun was high and hot by the time she came. Disheveled and breathless, she dashed around the corner and rushed right between us to stick her key in the door.

"Miss Harris!" I said as she opened the door. "It's me, Daniel Freemont. You said to come back today and you'd help me find my dad?"

"Oh, gosh," she said. "I'm sorry. I'm so late today." She looked through the door and down the dark hall as if checking to see if someone was waiting to berate her for being late. "I've got to get rehearsal organized right now, but come on in. Just give me a few minutes."

When we got to her office, I heard a man talking on the telephone in the room behind her desk. "Wait over there, please," she said, pointing to the chairs along the wall. She opened the door behind her and the man's voice got louder. The only part of him I could see was one cowboy boot propped up on his desk. Miss Harris laid some papers next to his boot and closed the door as she came back out.

She gave me a quick smile as she sat down and dialed the telephone on her desk. "Good morning," she said into the handset. "This is Emily Harris in Mr. Foley's office. Can you please check the payroll records for the last four shows? I'm looking for a musician named John Freemont who was on the show. Yes, I can hold."

Miss Harris crimped her shoulder to hold the phone against her ear so she could use both hands to work on some of the papers on her desk. The wait seemed as long as the one we'd had under the tree in the parking lot. Finally, she raised her eyes from her paperwork as someone came on the other end of the line. Miss Harris said, "Are you sure? All right. Thank you."

She shook her head as she hung up the telephone. "I'm sorry, Daniel, but there's no record of your father playing on the show. There would be pay stubs for him if he had, but the accounting department didn't find any paperwork with that name."

The letdown crushed me. I slumped over until my elbows rested on my knees and my head hung down. I stared at the floor between my feet. I was absolutely sure it was Dad I heard playing on the radio. The double-note walking chord changes I heard were his, they had to be! And the sound of his guitar with the brass finger picks was distinctive. No one else played the guitar that way. Except . . . .

"Miss Harris, could you check another name?" I asked. "I promise we won't bother you again. The name is Chris Martin. Can you check your files?"

Her blue eyes smiled as she said, "I don't have to check the files. I remember that name from Saturday's line up. Is that your father?"

"Maybe!" I said, wishful thinking giving rise to hope. Then a solution came to me. "Maybe he's using a stage name. Can you give us his address?"

"Accounting will have that," she said as she dialed the telephone again. When they answered, she asked and nodded before she hung up. "They will look it up and call me back."

I wanted to jump out of my chair and hug her. I still hadn't seen his face, but I latched onto the idea that Chris Martin was John Freemont. He had to be. Rusty saw me fidgeting in my seat and gave me a big grin and a thumbs up.

A moment later, the door swung open and Brenda Lee marched into the office with her parents close behind her. She let out an ear-splitting squeal when she saw me.

"Oh boy! Daniel! Oh boy!" she shouted. "Are you going to be on the *Ozark Jubilee* with me? Won't that be fun!" She squealed again and threw her arms around my neck.

The door behind Miss Harris opened and Red Foley came out smiling. He wasn't as tall as I expected, yet he easily took command of the room with a beaming smile and the air of a star performer.

"Why, that sounds like Little Miss Dynamite," he said. "She sounds awful glad to see me." Then I stood up with Brenda hanging from me and he added wryly, "Or happy to see someone."

"Good afternoon, Red," Brenda's stepfather said. "Don't pay any attention to Brenda and her little friend. Do you have a contract for me to sign?"

Brenda noticed my guitar case and released my neck with another squeal. "Come on, Daniel, let's show Mr. Foley how good we sound together. Mr. Foley, Daniel is the best guitar player there is and he's going to sing with me on the show. I hope that's okay!"

Foley's smile didn't dim but he looked to Miss Harris for help. "Uh, Brenda, I think your number is already set. Isn't that so, Miss Harris?" The secretary glanced at the rundown on her desk and nodded. Foley said, "I'm sorry, but we can't change the lineup the day before the broadcast."

"But Daniel is real, real good! If he can't sing with me, then I'll sing on his number, too. What are you going to play, Daniel? I hope it's a song I know."

Embarrassed to be put on the spot in front of Red Foley, I said, "I'm, uh, I'm not on the show."

"We can't even get an audition!" Rusty blurted. I wanted to crawl in a hole. Then he added, "How do you like that, Brenda?"

"Oh yes you can!" she proclaimed. She put her hands on her hips and stamped her foot. "Mr. Foley, you just have to listen to Daniel right now this minute! Daniel, you get that guitar out of that case and play 'Honkey Tonkin' for Mr. Foley. Right now!"

No one wanted to stand up to the little budding superstar, especially me, so I did as ordered. I tried not to look at Red Foley while I nervously fixed my guitar strap around my neck and put the picks on my shaking fingers. Sweat popped out on my palms and my throat wanted to close up in the worst way. I pushed myself to strum an intro and plunge into the tune. As soon as I did, I lost track of everything except the song. I finally looked up when I got to the chorus. Red Foley was watching me with one eye while keeping the other one on Brenda. Everyone else in the office was doing the same, except Rusty, who motioned for me to step up the tempo. Brenda gave me a huge encouraging smile, so I focused on her hazel eyes and sang to her as if she were the only audience that mattered. She was eating up my song, so I fed it to her. When I sang the final "we'll go honky tonkin' round this town" she jumped up and down and squealed. "See, Mr. Foley! Didn't I tell you he is just the best!"

"Why, yes he is," Foley said. He put his hand on my shoulder and looked me straight in the eye. "Daniel, do you think you can sing that song in front of twelve million people?"

My mouth stopped working. My brain lost its connection to my lips and tongue. Words wouldn't come out, breath wouldn't go in. All I could do was nod like an idiot. What was he saying? Was he asking me to appear on the *Ozark Jubilee*? I looked at Rusty and even he was speechless, probably for the first time in his life. Finally, I managed a weak, "Really?"

"Miss Harris," Foley said with a smile and wink to me, "would you please check the program rundown for next week and find a spot for this young man? And organize his paperwork, of course. And as for you, Little Miss Dynamite, I need you to step into my office with your stepdaddy and mama so we can sign this contract. That is, if that's all right with you."

"Yes sir, Mr. Foley!" Brenda chirped. She gave me a long hug and a smacking kiss on the lips before running into Foley's office after her parents.

I was tongue-tied and frozen in place, my guitar still around my neck, one hand clamped around the fingerboard, the other poised over the sound hole as if ready to play another tune. Did I just audition for the *Ozark Jubilee*? Did Red Foley just hire me?

Rusty clapped me on the back to bring me back to reality. "I don't care what her stepdaddy says, you're going to marry that little girl!" he grinned. "She just made you a TV star."

Miss Harris smiled sweetly. "Congratulations, Daniel. Now, there are a few things you need to know. You have to be at tech rehearsal next Friday—that's a week from today—to work out your number with the house band. Then there's a dress rehearsal Saturday afternoon before the show that evening. There's a dinner break in between." She paused to look me over from head to toe. "I'm guessing you might need a little wardrobe enhancement, too, so let's you and I go shopping Monday." Before I could tell her I had no money to buy new clothes, she read my mind and said, "The show will pay for them, so don't worry about that." She made a note to herself on her calendar as her phone rang.

It was the accounting department. She wrote down what they told her and handed the note to me. It was an address. "One more thing. You're not old enough, so your mother or father will have to sign a contract for you to appear. Will that be a problem?"

I was speechless, fixated on Chris Martin's address, but Rusty answered for me in his best managerial manner. "Not at all."

"Good. Now I have to get this rehearsal moving."

I finally remembered how to talk. I gushed, "Yes ma'am! Thanks for everything!" The only thing that would make this day any better would be to find Dad at the address on the paper in my hand.

~ 28 ~

Life has its ups and downs, as the song says. When we left the theater, I was up more than I was down, riding on a whirlwind of dreams coming true and things going right for a change. But to quote another song, what goes up must come down.

We left the Jewell Theater office with wings on our feet. As we rushed across the parking lot, Rusty said, "Hey, superstar, do you know where we're going?"

I stopped in my tracks and looked at the address. I didn't have any idea. "Wherever this is."

There was no one handy to ask, so rather than bother Miss Harris again, we went back around the building to the main doors. Musicians were killing time outside waiting for their slot in the rehearsal. I resisted an urge to tell them I was one of them, that I belonged there. We asked a couple of performers if they recognized the address, but they were both from out of town and couldn't help. Eventually, we worked our way through the small crowd until we found the guard. When I showed him the note, he gave a low whistle. "Man alive! You boys got no business wandering around in that neighborhood."

"Is it rough?" Rusty asked.

"Rough?" he scoffed. "It's so rough most of the cops won't go there except in pairs—and they won't go at all after dark. It's on the edge of town, too. Isolated, you might say. If you get in any trouble out there, won't nobody hear you scream. You best stay away."

"Thanks for the warning," I said, "but I've got to find the guy who lives at this address. It's important. Can you give us directions?"

He pointed us in the opposite direction from Ma Stamey's boarding house. "You go about a dozen blocks that way. When you get to the railroad tracks, you'll be on this street here." He pointed to the address on the note. "When you run out of street at the railroad tracks, take a right. It's the only house out there. I'm telling you, kid, don't hang around there after dark."

I thanked him and we started walking. The guard's description was scary, but it made me even more determined to see if my dad was there. I didn't like the thought, but the place sounded like the kind of cheap lodging where he would need to stay.

As we followed the guard's directions, the street we were on seemed familiar. By the time we reached the railroad tracks and turned right, I knew exactly where we were going. It was Little Eddie's house. This time, though, Stan's Ford pickup wasn't parked outside. Could Dad be living here? There was no sign to indicate it was a boardinghouse, but the men on the porch were hanging around like they lived inside. I took a deep breath of steamy summer air and approached the porch.

"You back again?" one of them said.

"Uh, yessir," I said, trying to not show any fear. "Does Chris Martin live here?"

"Why do you want to know?" one of the men asked

"We need to see him about some family business," Rusty said.

"Child support, I reckon," another man said.

The first man spat over the porch rail and said, "Nah, they send the sheriff for that."

"Did old Chris get your sister in a family way?" yet a third man asked. They all laughed.

Undaunted, Rusty said, "So you know him?"

"Boy, you're starting to bother me. You want to know so bad, you go inside and find Little Eddie. He'll tell you what's what."

"Thanks," I said before Rusty could irritate them even more. The men shuffled aside as Rusty and I walked across the porch and through the door.

The place didn't have any curtains or shades on the windows, so it was light enough to see where we were going. The small foyer led to a hallway that ran through the house and looked like it ended in the kitchen. There was a staircase on the left. To the right was the room where we'd gone the last time we were here. I hadn't noticed much then, but now I looked around. It had probably been a parlor at one time, but now it was like somebody's messy bedroom. I jumped when a raspy voice said, "Come on in, my young friends. I'm delighted to see you again." I scanned the room until I spotted the short thin-haired man shoving something into a wood stove in the far corner of the room. When he closed the stove door and stood up, I remembered why he was called "Little" Eddie. He walked over and sat down in a ratty wing chair by a window looking out onto the porch. His face and arms were pale like he hadn't been in the sun—ever. His yellow shirt had been white once upon a time and faded khaki trousers hung on his short legs. He didn't invite us to sit down.

"Let me guess. You boys came back for some wacky tobacky, didn't you? I might be able to help you out."

Rusty and I exchanged looks and Little Eddie chuckled.

"I kind of thought that was how you first met my associate, Stan, but I guess I was mistaken. I'm glad to see you're still in possession of that fine guitar."

"Yes sir," I said. I gave a quick look behind me to make sure Stan wasn't lurking in the shadows, then turned back to Little Eddie. "We're looking for a man named Chris Martin. The guy outside said you could tell us if he lives here."

"He's correct, I can."

He offered nothing more, so I asked, "And does he live here?"

"At the moment."

What did that mean? I brushed aside his enigmatic answer and persisted. "Is he here now?"

"He is not."

I was growing exasperated but tried not to let it show. "Do you know when he's coming back?"

For some reason, Little Eddie relented and said, "He's got a gig at a club in Hot Springs this week. I expect he'll be back Thursday by noon." That was almost a week from now! My high spirits sank and my face showed it. He noticed my reaction. "Sorry, kid, that's the best I can do. He some relation of yours?"

"He's probably my dad."

"That's an unusual way to put it," Little Eddie said. "Don't you know?"

I almost told him about "Chris Martin" actually being a stage name for John Freemont and the how I found him through the *Ozark Jubilee* and everything, but held back. If Dad was hiding under an assumed name, Little Eddie probably didn't know it, I thought, and I didn't want to give him away.

"Say, young man, how well do you play that guitar?" Little Eddie pointed a crooked finger at my case. When he raised his arm, the handgrip of a pistol showed in the waistband of his pants. Pretending I didn't see the gun, I shrugged. Little Eddie said, "I bet you know lots of kids in school, or even other musicians. How would you like to make some money selling a few things for me?"

"Daniel doesn't need any job, mister," Rusty protested. "He's going to be a big star."

Little Eddie smirked. "Sure he is."

"You watch the *Ozark Jubilee* a week from tomorrow and you'll see!"

"I'll do that," Little Eddie said.

"Come on, Rusty, we've got to go." I couldn't get the pistol out of my mind. "Little Eddie looks real busy."

Little Eddie nodded to me, "You think about my proposition, young man. We can talk it over when you come back to see if Chris Martin is your dad. And remember, if you need a little something to get you through the day, you come see me anytime."

I trudged along the street by the railroad tracks in a funk. The ups and downs of the day had taken their toll on me and not finding Dad knocked me off the high from my encounter with Red Foley and Brenda Lee.

As we turned the corner to head back downtown, a motorcycle cruised up the street past us going in the opposite direction. It rolled along slowly as if the rider were looking for something. My stomach lurched when he glanced our way, but he didn't stop and I probably only imagined he slowed down as he passed. I couldn't see his face in the shadow of his helmet, but I noticed his hairy arms were covered by tattoos. I forced myself to calm down. I couldn't see if one of them was a skull-headed snake, so I told myself there were probably thousands of motorcycles in Missouri and their riders all probably had tattoos.

~ 29 ~

Summer is slow. You can't hurry it along any because it takes time to grow good corn, time to ripen sweet apples on the trees, time to let babies get up on their feet and learn to walk. You can't rush stuff like that. If you try, you just get all sweaty and frustrated. That summer in Springfield, I had to do a lot of waiting, which doesn't come naturally to me. Fortunately, I had music to help me pass the time.

Sunday afternoon was a typical Missouri sweatbox with humidity so high it drove the blue right out of the sky and the hard rays of the white sun raked across your skin. The heat drove everybody out of the boarding house in search of a breeze and a place to sit in the shade. Ma Stamey's backyard had a big sycamore tree where Rusty and I and the other boarders sat on chairs we'd dragged from the house. It was too steamy to play, so the musicians sat and made desultory small talk that alternated between complaints about the weather and stories about bad gigs they had played or good ones they hoped to play. Rusty and I kept quiet and drank it in. Ma sat in the deepest shade with her house dress hiked up around her chubby knees and waved a palm-frond fan around various parts of her ample body trying to find relief.

Joe announced he'd wrangled a spot sitting in for someone in the house band next week on the *Ozark Jubilee.* "They told me they'd have to see if my gitfiddle is loud enough for the auditorium. If not, I may have to put a pickup for an amplifier into it."

"Wow, that's great!" Rusty said. "Daniel's going to be on the show next week, too!"

"Really?" Joe asked, turning to me with a grin. "Or is that just another dipper full from Rusty's bucket of bullshit?"

I smiled shyly. "He's not pulling your leg. I'm on the show next Saturday."

"Hey, man, that's fantastic! Congratulations!" the banjo player said amid a rousing round of "wow" and "way-to-go" from the rest of the boarders. "How did you pull that off?" someone asked. Reluctant to tell the story, I ducked my head. Rusty didn't hesitate. He told about meeting Brenda Lee on the road, going to the Jewell Theater looking for my dad, then running into her in Red Foley's office.

Somberly, Ma said, "But it sounds like you didn't find your dad, did you, Daniel?"

"No, not yet," I answered.

"But we think we're getting closer," Rusty blurted. "We followed a lead to a boarding house near the railroad tracks."

Sharply, Ma asked. "Is it a dump with a bunch of tough guys hanging around?"

"Yes," I said. "And a creepy guy inside."

"That's bad news all around," Joe said, looking sideways at Ma. "That's Little Eddie."

"You boys got no business getting mixed up with that degenerate," Ma said.

Rusty said, "That's what we thought when. . ." I coughed to get his attention before he could tell her we'd already come face to face with Little Eddie—not once but twice. I didn't want Ma to mark us as trouble makers. Rusty caught himself and finished ". . . I mean, no ma'am. We got no business there."

"Little Eddie sucks the life out of everybody he meets," Joe added with a snarl like he wanted to chew the man's face off. "He's six kinds of trouble. He's into all kinds of ugly stuff with drugs and girls and anything else he can make a buck off of."

"That includes musicians," Ma said. "He gives desperate gals and guys a place to stay for nothing and says he can line up gigs for a cut of their pay, just like a real agent. Then he offers them a little weed to pick up their spirits and before they know it, they're looking for something stronger, which he provides. It doesn't take long before they're hooked and giving him every dime they can earn or steal just to get another hit. More than a few of them end up pushing dope for him to their friends." She swallowed and paused to collect herself before saying, "I just thank the Lord my husband took our boy on the road before Little Eddie got his hooks into him."

Rusty and I exchanged solemn glances. "We'll be careful," I promised.

When the sun finally took its bow behind the hills, we went inside for a supper of cold ham and leftover potato salad. By the time we finished eating, the steam box day had melted to a westerly breeze. It was still too hot to stay inside, but it was cool in the yard.

One by one, we brought our instruments out. We played a few tunes, then the cicadas cranked up and Joe found a three-quarter beat in their rackety rhythm. He eased into the "Tennessee Waltz" on his gitfiddle while I softly chorded along on my guitar and the tree peepers added a top line of froggy "ribbetts." The fiddle, mandolin, and banjo joined in, too, and the popular lament ended the day on a perfect note.

As we went back inside to go to bed, Ma pulled Rusty and me aside. "Since you're going to play in the *Ozark Jubilee* Saturday night, I guess you'll be staying another week. Am I right?" Her tone was business-like but not unkind.

"Yes ma'am," I said. "If you'll have us."

"You're welcome to stay, but you'll owe another week's rent come Wednesday."

I gave Rusty an inquiring look, but he just gave her his biggest gap-toothed grin and said, "Our credit's good, isn't it Ma? With Daniel being a big TV star and everything?"

Ma smiled back. "Rusty, your credit in this establishment is just as good as Red Foley's. That is to say, not at all. If you want to crash here, you pay cash here."

Never daunted, Rusty said, "Got it, Ma! Wednesday morning you'll add our cash to your stash."

We went upstairs and, as soon as our door closed behind us, I asked him how he expected to pay the rent. "Aw, that's a whole three days away," he said. "Lots of things can happen between then and now. No need to worry about it tonight!"

A few minutes later, a soft knock came on our door and Joe came in.

"Listen, guys, you really should stay away from Little Eddie. Word on the street is there's a gang connected to the mob in Kansas City moving in on him. Somebody's going to get hurt before it's over and you don't want to be hanging around when the shit hits the fan."

I remembered the motorcycle that passed by us. "Yeah, got the message. Thanks."

"There's one other thing," he said. "I didn't mean to snoop, but I overheard Ma dunning you for the rent. You got enough to pay her?"

I shook my head.

"Well, me and the boys figured that might be the situation, so we all chipped in to cover it for you." He handed me seven dollars.

"I don't know what to say," I said.

"Us pickers and grinners got to look out for each other," he said. "Someday maybe you'll do the same for me."

"You know it."

"By the way, if you want to pick up a few more bucks, we're playing a wedding at the American Legion hall Wednesday night and we'd be happy to have you sit in if you're game."

"Count me in!" I answered.

Monday afternoon, we met Miss Harris at the theater office and she walked us three blocks to Heer's Department Store to find me something other than hand-me-down jeans and t-shirts to wear on the *Ozark Jubilee* stage. The closer we got to the ornate seven-story building, the smaller I felt. I'd never been in a store like that, even just window shopping with Mom. She always said those kind of stores were for folks who ate prime rib and pheasant, not beans and ham hocks. I remember her telling me once that Townsend's, the big department store in downtown St. Joe, had a detective that followed you around if you looked like you couldn't afford to buy anything. At Heer's, I lagged back as Miss Harris went through the revolving door without a moment's thought with Rusty right behind her. As soon as she realized I hadn't followed them, she sent him out to get me. I tried to pretend I had stopped to tie my shoe, but I don't think I fooled her.

Miss Harris didn't say anything, though. All she asked was what style of outfit I wanted to wear on stage. When I looked at her like she was speaking Greek, Rusty translated. "Do you want to look like Merle Travis with spangles on your cowboy suit or Carl Perkins with a sport coat and blue suede shoes?"

I visualized the outfits of the two stars, but the images of myself I conjured up in their clothes seemed downright silly. I looked to Miss Harris, who asked, "How about something simple. Do you like Pat Boone?"

I nodded eagerly. He was on the show quite a bit because he was married to Red Foley's daughter and, besides, he had a great voice.

Best of all, he dressed like a normal person. Neat and well-to-do, not like a Hollywood cowboy.

Miss Harris led us onto the elevator and to the fourth floor men's wear department. We were greeted by a salesman she obviously knew. "Jerry, this young man needs a nice single-breasted two-button blazer, moderate notched lapels, gray twill with a single vent. Some pleated navy slacks, no cuff, and a shirt with a flared collar—light blue like we use on stage. We want him to look respectable but stylish. A high-class gentleman, but not a banker. Oh, and he'll need a black Western bow tie like Red wears." She looked me up and down like she was deciding whether to kick me or kiss me, then added, "While you're at it, pack up some socks and underwear." Then she glanced at Rusty and said, "Make that two sets."

"Yes, ma'am," Jerry said. "Young man, if you'll step over here please."

Trying on clothes in the dressing room lined with full-length mirrors was nothing like pawing through racks in the Salvation Army second-hand store looking for pants that didn't have patches on the knees. The salesman stood me on a platform and stretched a tape measure along every line of my body, talking to himself and making notes on a little pad. The most Mom usually did was hold a shirt across my shoulders to see if it would fit. Miss Harris waited outside the dressing room, but I was still embarrassed by the whole rigamarole. Rusty didn't help. He sat on the floor watching and giggling when the salesman asked me to hold one end of the tape in my crotch while he measured my inseam.

I liked the clothes Jerry selected. Miss Harris and I agreed a cowboy hat was a bad idea, but she insisted I'd like boots if I tried some that didn't have pointy toes and high heels. She was right. I wore the boots out of the store to break them in.

Spending time with Miss Harris wasn't the same as being with my mother, but as we walked around, I sensed Mom behind every display in the store and around every street corner when Rusty and I went back to the boarding house. Guilt over leaving and worry about her swelled in my heart with every step I took. I thought about Willy, too, and the promise I made to him. Someday, I pledged to myself, I would go back to them.

The guys in the band insisted I wear my new *Ozark Jubilee* duds when I played at the dance Wednesday night. I must admit I felt pretty special when I put the clothes on and even more special when I stood on stage and started playing under the lights. The crowd seemed to enjoy our performance of all the tried-and-true dance numbers they heard on the radio. I knew most of the tunes from playing along with Dad or the radio, but just to make sure, I asked Joe to give me the keys to play in so I could fake it if I had to. I silently thanked Dad for teaching me how to play a song by ear and make it work even if I'd never heard it before.

As the wedding party thinned out in the ballroom, local customers from the American Legion bar in the next room filtered in to listen to the music and watch the dancers. They were mostly regulars, army or navy veterans who dropped by for a couple of beers on their way home from work. They were polite and stayed to themselves near the ballroom doorway, although they didn't hide how much they enjoyed eyeing the girls on the dance floor. When Joe announced the band was going to take a short break, most of the vets went back to the bar as the folks from the wedding milled around to visit with each other or left the dance floor to take a bathroom break themselves. I noticed two men strolling casually around the edges of the wedding party even though they obviously weren't part of it. They kept their hands in their pockets and looked into the faces of some of the men on the dance floor as they went, occasionally drawing a nod from one of them. When one of the men turned his head, I recognized him as Stan, the guitar thief. He was whispering with one of the wedding guests and didn't notice me. Joe saw my intense stare.

"Stay away from those guys," he said, barely loud enough for me to hear him. I put my guitar in its case so I could make a trip to the bathroom.

"Why? What are they doing?"

"They sell dope for Little Eddie."

Rusty craned his neck to get a better look and I knew from his wide-eyed expression that he recognized Stan, too.

"Don't let them catch you watching," Joe hissed. "They don't like witnesses."

"Sorry," Rusty said.

"And don't go outside, either, especially in the back. That's where the money will change hands."

"Got it," I said. "Is the bathroom okay?"

Joe chuckled. "Yeah, I think it's safe. There's a crowd in there now. You two better stick together, though."

Thinking of Stan, I asked, "Can I leave my guitar here?"

"Sure," Joe said. "I'll be here until you get back."

"Come on, I gotta pee like a race horse," Rusty said, pulling me away from Joe. When we were out of earshot, he said, "What are we going to do about that creep Stan?"

I glanced back to the ballroom. "I don't see him now. We better not say anything. I don't want to mess up the gig, you know? Maybe we can call the cops after the dance."

"Okay, I guess," Rusty said. "Let's go, I wasn't exaggerating about needing the bathroom."

There was a short line outside the men's room, mostly wedding guests. As we waited our turn, one of them said he liked our music, so Rusty told him about Saturday's appearance on the *Ozark Jubilee*.

"No kidding!" the guy said. "Can I have your autograph?"

The request threw me for a loop. "Gee, I, uh," I mumbled.

"Sure, pal," Rusty piped up. "Got a pen and paper?"

The man patted his pockets until he found his wedding invitation and a ball point pen. Rusty turned his back to me so I could use it as a writing desk. When I hesitated, he whispered, "This is when you sign your name, stupid." I got a grip on myself and signed the invitation in the best cursive script I could manage. My hand shook a little as I handed it back.

"Thanks!" the man said with a big grin. "Now I can say I knew you when!"

Embarrassed, I ducked my head as the line moved and we went into the bathroom.

Rusty punched me in the arm and laughed as we stepped up to the urinals. "For a minute there, I thought you were going to ask me how to spell your name! See how much you need a manager like me?"

After the show, we loaded our instruments into the banjo player's car and stood around enjoying the cool night air as we waited for the parking lot traffic to clear. Joe said, "Daniel, did you . . . ."

A loud pop sounded from the other side of the building, followed by a shout of distress and more pops. Rusty looked wide-eyed at Joe. "Are those gunshots?" Before Joe could answer, Stan ran around the corner. Another man came right behind him, stopped to aim, and shot him in the back. Stan fell face down and the gunman disappeared back around the corner.

"Let's git outta here!" Joe yelled.

Roaring motorcycles drowned out everything as four bikers sped across the parking lot to the highway while Rusty and I crouched behind the car.

~ 30 ~

et me ask you something. When did you find out your mom and dad weren't perfect? No, not when you realized they aren't gods. That happens about the time you go to kindergarten and see how discombobulated they can be about things like setting the alarm clock and packing your lunch and getting you off to school on time and stuff. No, I mean when you find out they're not only mere mortals, they're flawed human beings—sometimes flawed deep down to their core. I'm not saying my mom is like that, but I began to wonder about her the night she brought home that jerk, Larry, and took him to her bedroom. As you may remember, I could hear everything that went on in there and they weren't holding no prayer service.

Sorry, my train of thought got diverted to the wrong track. What I meant to tell you about was when I found Dad at Little Eddie's. As I found out that day, his flaws ran pretty deep.

Rusty made me cool my heels and wait all Thursday morning before we went back to Little Eddie's house to see if Chris Martin was really my dad. Little Eddie had said he expected whoever the guy was to return from Little Rock about noon, so there wasn't any reason to get there earlier. We were reluctant to hang around the place after our close call with the drug pushers and motorcycle gang the night before, not to mention everything Joe and Ma had told us about Little Eddie. Still, I needed to see Chris Martin to satisfy the longing in my heart.

I killed time after breakfast working on the song I planned to sing on TV Saturday. By twelve o'clock, I couldn't wait any longer.

I made Rusty almost run the dozen blocks to Little Eddie's. We pulled up short on the sidewalk in front of the house, though, when we saw his goons standing like sentries at each corner. Rusty nudged me and pointed to one lying prone on the roof. These guys weren't just hanging around shucking and jiving. Several of them held rifles or shotguns and the others had pistols. Little Eddie sat in a chair tilted back against the wall on the porch next to the door.

"Looks like the war started last night." I whispered.

"They're not playing cowboys and Indians with cap pistols," Rusty answered. "We going in?"

I had to know if my dad was here. I didn't have a choice. Before I could answer, Little Eddie motioned to us. I took a quick look around for motorcycles and we headed for the house.

When we stepped onto the porch, Little Eddie looked like he hadn't changed clothes since we last saw him. This time, though, he wasn't making any effort to hide the gun under his yellowed shirt. He kept his eyes on the street as he waved us inside. "Upstairs, first door on the left," he said. "I told him somebody might be looking for him."

We dashed upstairs and I knocked hard on the door. "Who's there?" a frightened voice called out.

"Dad! It's me!" I cried. I turned the knob and tried to open the door, but it was locked. I heard Dad move a piece of furniture.

"Dad, it's me, Daniel!" I said again, pounding on the door.

When it opened, I jumped into his arms. He hugged me like I'd dreamed about being hugged ever since he left. After a long embrace, we backed apart to get a better look at each other. He was pale and haggard, thinner than I ever remember him. With sunken cheeks and black circles under his eyes, he looked like someone who had been locked in a dark cell for months.

"Dad, are you okay?"

"Sure, Daniel, sure. I'm fine. Just tired from the road trip. We drove all night and didn't get here until this morning." He straightened up and brushed his hair back off his face. He needed a haircut, too. "How did you find me?"

The question threw me off. Didn't he want to know about Mom and Willy? And how I was doing?

"I heard you on the radio on the *Ozark Jubilee*. I could tell it was you! So Rusty and I came down here and we went to the Jewell Theater and they gave me this address." I figured I'd have plenty of time to fill in all the details later. "Little Eddie told us to come back today."

Dad went to the door and listened for a moment, then opened it and looked both ways up and down the hall. He closed the door and held a finger up to his lips "Speak low, okay?" he whispered. "Did you use my real name?"

"No. I told Little Eddie that Chris Martin is my dad. Was that all right?" Concern for him roiled my stomach. "Are you sure you're okay?"

He pulled me to his chest again and hugged me longer and harder this time. "You did good using that name. And I'm fine, son. I've just gone through a bit of a rough patch. It's all going to be okay, though." He sat down on the side of the bed and hung his head. His long, greasy hair hung over the side of his face as he mumbled, "I'm going to get clean, I promise." I could barely hear him.

"What do you mean . . . ." I tried to ask.

"I'm sorry, son, but . . . well, I'm . . . ." He looked up with a desperate look. "But I'm working on it . . . really . . . and I'm going to get straight."

"Straight?" I said. "I don't understand."

"Clean." He hung his head and whispered. "I'm afraid I got hooked on some bad stuff."

The world collapsed around me. My dad had always been my hero, at least until he ran away. Even then, I sort of understood why he had to leave. But then, I thought, maybe I didn't know the real reason. Tentatively, I asked, "Did you use it at home?"

He shook his head. "Oh no, no! Well, maybe just a little sometimes, but I was always clean when I was with you and your mom. But when things went bad for me and I came south, I was pretty down and Little Eddie . . . . Well, I got hooked." He put his hands on my shoulders and stared into my eyes. "But I'm going to beat this. I promise."

"Promise for sure?"

"For sure." He pulled me to him and his shoulders shook against me. When he finally let me go, he sniffed and wiped his eyes with the back of his hand. "So how are things at home? Really." he asked.

I told him about Mom and Larry and what happened in the garage and what I did with the knife and how I didn't want to abandon her and how Willy needed someone to look out for him but I just had to leave before I did something else terrible. "Mostly, I needed to find you," I added, "so you can come back and help us get away from Larry." After it all poured out of me, I paused for breath and saw the dismay in his eyes.

"I'm so sorry I left you in a hard spot like that."

"I know, Dad. I was mad at you for a long time—but I'm not now. Let's go home, okay?"

He shook his head sadly. "I can't just yet, Daniel." With deep resignation, he added, "I can't even use my real name. If I go back to St. Joe right now, there are people there who will kill me."

It made sense now. The deal gone bad was connected to drugs. I was crushed. With trepidation, I asked, "The motorcycle gang, right? Mike and those guys?"

"Yes. I owe them a lot of money."

When I realized it could have been the same gang that shot up the dance, I pushed my despair into the background. "They might be here," I said. "There was a guy on a big motorcycle sneaking around here when we were here the other day. And last night there was a bunch of them that shot a guy at the American Legion."

"I heard about that. Wait! Were you there?"

"Yeah, I played a gig with a band there last night. The motorcycle guys came and started a big fight after the dance. Joe said they're trying to take over from Little Eddie."

Dad looked totally baffled by the jumbled details of my story. "Wait," he said. "You played a gig with a band? What band? And who is Joe?" Before I could answer, he started firing more questions. "Are you sure it's Mike's gang? How did you say you found me? You heard me play on the *Ozark Jubilee*?"

"Let me start over from the beginning," I said. "Yes, I heard you on the radio, so Rusty and I came down here to find you. And a gitfiddle player we met at Ma Stamey's heard me playing the guitar with brass finger picks and said the only other guy he knew who played like that was named Chris Martin."

"A gitfiddle player, huh? That would be Joe. He's a good guy."

"Yeah, I like him. So after the gig, one of Eddie's guys got shot. There were four guys on motorcycles, but I don't know if they're Mike's gang or not.

"It doesn't sound like they're looking for me," Dad said. "At least not yet." He took a deep breath and the tension left his face as he focused on me. "And you played a real gig with Joe and the boys?"

"That's nothing," Rusty jumped in. "Daniel's going to sing on the *Ozark Jubilee* Saturday night."

"Are you kidding me?" Dad exclaimed.

"That reminds me, Miss Harris said you need to sign this contract because Daniel's not old enough." Rusty dug into his pocket and unfolded the paper Miss Harris had given him.

Dad took the paper and studied it thoughtfully. His face fell. "It says your name is Daniel Freemont." He stared out the window for a minute. "Did you tell them my real name, too? It's okay if you did," he sighed. "I just need to know."

I mentally went back over what I had said when we got to the office. "Yes, I guess I did. I asked for John Freemont the first time. I told them I was looking for my dad. They said there wasn't anybody by that name in their records. That's when I asked about Chris Martin."

Dad nodded. "Well, it was bound to happen sooner or later. I can't deny you this opportunity, Daniel." He signed the contract and handed it to me. He'd signed "John Freemont" on the bottom.

"I guess I'm all set," I said.

"My boy is going to be a real star," he said proudly but with a strangely sad smile. "What are you going to sing?"

"I know what I want to sing, but I have to try it out at rehearsal tomorrow afternoon. Can you come and watch? Maybe help with the arrangement?"

"The music director will handle the arranging and work it all out with the band," he said. "That's what rehearsal is for." When he saw how much I wanted him to be with me, he added, "But I wouldn't miss it for the world. I'll be there!"

"Super!" I said. Then I had an idea. "We could even practice together tonight. Like we used to. The guys at Ma Stamey's would probably help us out, too."

Dad laughed ruefully. "I don't think I'm welcome at Ma's anymore. At least, not without a few dollars in my hand. Besides, as much as I'd like to play with you, there's something I need to do tonight."

"That's okay. As long as you're coming tomorrow."

"You can count on it." A strange, crafty look came over his face. "Say, I just thought of something. Would you guys help me out?"

Rusty and I both nodded.

Little Eddie stood up from his chair on the porch when Rusty and I came out.

"I guess that's your dad, huh?" he said.

I made sure to walk past him before answering. I wanted him to turn his back was to the door.

"Yeah, that's him," I said. I moved toward the front steps and turned around to face him. "Last time we were here, didn't you say something about a job for me and Rusty?"

"I believe I did," he said, perking up. "Interested?"

"Maybe. I kind of need some money. What would we have to do?"

"Well, you sign on with me to be your agent, just like your dad. I line up gigs for you and you play your guitar."

As Little Eddie warmed to his spiel, Dad came down the stairs inside the house behind his back. He caught my eye and gave me a thumbs up as he slipped into Little Eddie's room.

"What about Rusty?" I asked to keep Little Eddie's attention.

"Hmmm," he said as he scratched his chin and gave Rusty the once-over. "What is it you do, little man? Play the kazoo or something?"

"Kazoo nothing," Rusty bristled, "I'm his manager."

"No kidding?" Little Eddie said with a smirk.

"Yep, so I'm in charge of the money," Rusty said. "Which brings up a question: what's your cut in this deal?"

"That's the best part for you guys," Little Eddie said. "I don't charge an agent's fee. In fact, I pay you. You get a commission for selling a few things for me at the events I line up. Or at other places if you want."

"What are we supposed to sell?" I asked. Dad seemed to be taking forever in Little Eddie's room.

"Oh, whatever the customers want. They're going to mostly be other musicians. They like a little weed to take the edge off. Sometimes a little horse to forget their troubles. You know, just like your dad."

My heart sank at that cold description, but I ignored it to focus on what I had to accomplish at that moment.

"I don't know," I said, trying to stall but running out of ways to do it. "What do you think, Rusty?"

"Tell you what," Little Eddie said before Rusty could chime in. "Why don't you take a few samples and ask around. See how easy it is. The stuff sells itself. Let me get some for you." He started to turn back into the house. Dad was still in his room!

"Hey!" Rusty yelled. "Look! Over there!" He grabbed Little Eddie by the arm and dragged him to the porch rail and pointed down the street.

"What? What's there?" Little Eddie said. The guys standing guard on the porch turned as one to peer in the direction of Rusty's finger.

"I saw a guy on a motorcycle!" Rusty exclaimed. "And he had a machine gun!"

"Where?" Little Eddie demanded. He pulled the pistol from the waistband of his pants. "Where is it?"

"He must have gone around the corner," Rusty said.

Little Eddie's eyes narrowed. "I didn't hear any motorcycle." He asked the guards if they had seen or heard anything. They all shrugged and shook their heads. The pistol still in his hand, Little Eddie turned to Rusty.

Rusty backed toward the front steps and held his hands in the air. "I swear it was one of those guys from the dance."

Inside the house, Dad finally came out of Little Eddie's room. He circled his finger and thumb "OK" to me and went back up the stairs. He carried a package just like the one Little Eddie had stuck in his wood stove the first time we were there.

"False alarm," I said. I needed to stall until Dad was in his room. "Let's talk about the money. How much can we make?"

Little Eddie lowered his gun. "That all depends on how much you sell." His lips tight, he glared at Rusty and his voice went steely as he added, "Although I deduct for bullshit, you got me?" He glared at me and demanded an answer. "You in or out?"

"Yeah, maybe. I mean, probably," I stammered. "Let me think about it, okay?"

"Christ on a crutch!" Little Eddie exploded. "Get out of here. Come back when you grow a pair."

Before I could say anything else, Rusty nudged me out of the way. "I've already got a pair twice the size of yours," he smirked.

"If you want to keep them, kid, you better hit the road," Little Eddie snarled. "You need to learn to respect your elders." He turned his back on us and went into the house.

~ 31 ~

The felonies in my story just keep stacking up, don't they? A couple of car thefts, attempted murder two or three times, arson—and now I was involved in some kind of drug heist. None of that mattered to me at the time, though. I only had one question on my mind. What was Dad going to do with Little Eddie's dope? I could only pray he wasn't going to use it to feed his own addiction. That summer, my stomach spent a lot of time in knots.

As usual, Rusty and I were the only boarders who ate Ma's cornflakes Friday morning. The others, musicians all, essentially worked nights, so they slept in most days. Someday, I thought, that will be my life. The dream of making music all night and sleeping all day was a sweet refuge from the drama around me.

"You having any luck finding your dad?" Ma said when we finished eating.

"No ma'am, not yet," I said. I was getting better at lying without thinking about it beforehand. I couldn't tell her we had just seen him the night before because she would figure out Chris Martin was really my dad. The fewer people who knew that, the lower the chance that word of his whereabouts would get back to St. Joe.

"I just hope when you find him that he's not tied up with Little Eddie," she said.

I almost choked on my cornflakes.

"Uh, what's the story behind Little Eddie, anyway?" Rusty quickly asked to cover for me.

"Like I told you before, Little Eddie is nobody to mess with," Ma said. "He came to town from Kansas City before the war. He was in the mob up there, from what I understand. For some reason, he split from them and came down here to set up shop. He knew how the game is played in the big city. He roughed up the nickel-and-dime Springfield boys and took over their rackets. The rumor is he buried a couple of the local yokels by the railroad tracks out behind his house.

"Can't the police do anything about him?"

"Hah! That's a laugh," Ma snorted. "Half of them are in business with him and the other half are scared to death. Besides, you've got to have witnesses to put a guy like that in jail where he belongs. And everybody's too afraid to speak up." She gave me, then Rusty, a hard, serious look. "You two are perfect targets for that creep. You're young and tender, no parents in sight, and wandering around like the world is one big Sunday school. Give Little Eddie half a chance, he'll slip you a Mickey Finn and you'll be sorry you ever saw him. Got that?"

We answered in unison, "Yes, ma'am."

Later, as I took a break from practicing my song under the sycamore tree in the backyard, I asked Rusty, "What's a Mickey Finn?"

"That's a drink spiked with knockout drops," he said. "I heard about it on 'Dragnet' one time." He grew real quiet and turned his face away. "My old man and I watched 'Dragnet' every Thursday night. At the beginning of the show, Dad always recited along with the announcer, 'The story you are about to see is true. Only the names have been changed to protect the innocent.' Then he would point at me. 'But the guilty are all named Rusty!' He broke me up every time." Rusty choked back a sob and tried to cover it with a laugh.

"You homesick?" I asked.

"Yeah, a little, I guess."

"Me, too. I miss Mom and Willy." So much had happened in the last couple of days, this was the first time I'd had to think about them. It wasn't a good feeling. "Do you want to go home?"

"Not really," he said with a wry smile. "I just wish I didn't have to share a bed with a fart machine like you."

"Look who's talking," I said and went back to work on my song. After a few minutes, I asked, "Anything else bothering you? Are you scared of Little Eddie?"

Rusty scoffed, "Hah. If he tries to give me a Mickey Finn, I'll pour it all over his pointy-toed shoes."

That made me laugh until I remembered Little Eddie's pistol. Trying to keep it light, I said, "And then you take off like Speedy Gonzales."

"*¡Ándale! ¡Ándale! ¡Arriba! ¡Arriba!*" Rusty chirped like the cartoon mouse.

"Speaking of running," I said, "we better get over to the tech rehearsal."

The security guard at the theater remembered Rusty right away but still checked his roster for our names. As he let us through the door, I asked him to please add Chris Martin to the list. Inside, the house band was tuning up and ruffling through stacks of sheet music while the performers and several dozen other people milled around in front of the stage. Brenda Lee and her stepdad were among them. She waved as soon as she spotted us but her stepdad grabbed her by the collar before she could make a run for me across the room.

As I waved back, Miss Harris greeted us and checked a clipboard. "You'll rehearse your number with the band in about an hour." She lowered her voice and winked. "Between you and me, the regulars go first and leave as soon as they're done. I'll call you when it's your turn and Bill Wimberly will take you through your number. He's the music director." She pointed to a man chatting with Red Foley near the piano. "Then the floor director will show you where to go on stage and you'll do your song."

"Thanks, Miss Harris," I said. "My dad is going to come later. Is it okay if he watches?"

"Yes, that will be fine. Which reminds me, do you have that contract I gave you?"

"You betcha," Rusty said. She glanced at the paper he handed her, probably to check if Rusty had tried to sign it himself. Dad's signature must have looked authentic enough. Then I remembered he had signed his real name. I started to ask if anybody else would see the contract, but she slipped it into a file folder with a bunch of other papers.

"Okay, you're good to go," she said with a sweet smile. "Break a leg!"

Near the stage, Brenda was talking with the music director and Red Foley. When they finished, the floor director called her over and showed her where to stand. The band played a short intro and Brenda jumped into "Dynamite," a hot number by Tom Glaser. Everybody in the theater stopped to listen as she bopped in place belting out the tune. As soon as she hit the last note, the music director raised his hand with a big "okay" and she jumped off the stage. Her stepdad reached for her, but she scooted away from him and made a beeline to me.

"Hey, Daniel!" she squealed. "How'd you like my song?" Before I could answer, she jumped up to wrap her legs around my waist and threw her arms around my neck. She was short for her age and I was tall for mine, so that was the only way she could get her lips to my face. "That's really our song, Daniel! You're my dynamite!"

I laughed. "Not me, Brenda. You're the hot one." She gave me another kiss, this one lingering a bit.

"Daniel, let's get married," she growled like she did in the song, somehow sounding more like a femme fatale than a sixth-grader.

"Whoa!" I said.

"Brenda Lee, you quit crawling on that boy!" her stepdad yelled as he pushed his way through the performers waiting for their turn on stage.

"See, you're going to get us both in trouble," I said.

She slipped down to the floor and turned to face her rapidly-approaching stepdad. She stomped her foot and planted her hands on her hips. "Daddy Jay, you leave Daniel alone!" she said. "Him and me are going to get married."

I threw up my hands to proclaim my innocence but couldn't stop grinning.

"Ooooh, can I be your best man?" Rusty crooned.

Brenda's stepdad snatched her bodily off the floor and stomped off. Rusty bent over laughing so hard he fell out of his chair.

Once Brenda was gone and the tumult died down, I turned my attention back to the rehearsal. Each performer ran through their songs a couple of times. After a few changes in tempo or instrumental solos were agreed on, that performer made way for the next one. It was straight forward and moved along pretty quickly because the regular stars knew exactly what to do. I listened closely while they were singing, but every time they stopped to confer, I turned around to see if Dad had come in. The longer the rehearsal went without him, the more worried I became. By the time Miss Harris waved for me to come on stage, all I wanted was to go searching for him. Rusty saw my sagging shoulders and knew what bothered me. "Get your butt up there," he ordered. "This is your big chance, so you better make the most of it!"

I dragged myself over to the music director and shook his hand.

"You doing okay, Daniel?" he said.

"Yes, sir. I'm just a little nervous, I guess."

"No need for that, son. We're all here to help you look good. Now, let's get started. Is this your song?" He held up a sheet of music and I nodded. "Good. Give it all you got, okay?"

I nodded again and followed the floor director to a spot on the stage marked with tape in front of a canvas backdrop with a painted haystack and barn. As I went, I reached into my pocket to get my finger picks and touched the only money I carried, the silver dollar Aunt Mae had given to me. It reminded me of what she told me one time: "Your Dad's problems are his own. You have your own life to live." She also said, "If you want to play music for a living, you have to do your job—whether you feel like it or not." Her words helped me focus. I resisted the urge to check the audience one more time to see if Dad had shown up and pushed everything out of my mind except the music. I waited for my cue, then played my heart out. When I struck the last chord, I looked at the music director.

"Good job," he said, "Did it work okay for you singing with the band?"

"Yes, sir," I answered. I saw Joe in the second row with his gitfiddle. He gave me a thumbs up.

Red Foley wanted to hear my song a couple more times and had some questions about why I'd chosen such an old standard rather than a newer number you would expect a kid my age to sing. After I stumbled through an answer, he nodded agreement with my choice and made a suggestion about how I could introduce it. His idea sounded kind of corny at first, but once I'd tried the little speech in my own words, I saw how it would both express my feelings and grab the audience.

"Get a good night's sleep," the music director said. "And don't forget the dress rehearsal tomorrow afternoon."

As I walked off the stage, I looked into the auditorium seats one last time to see if Dad was there. At this point, I didn't really expect to see him, but I still had a sliver of hope. My desire battled with the grim reality of his absence. He'd made a sincere promise to come, but it wasn't the first promise he'd broken. Then there was the dope. Did it mean more to him than I did? Or maybe I was blaming him for something that wasn't his fault. Maybe Little Eddie caught him with his stash. Or maybe the guys on the motorcycles came looking for him. I had to know. I found Rusty and told him I needed to go back to Little Eddie's. It was the last thing I wanted to do but I had to know what happened to Dad, no matter how bad it hurt.

The sun was sliding behind the hills west of town by the time we reached the corner on Little Eddie's street. I was preoccupied with dread of what we might find at the house when Rusty hissed, "Listen! Do you hear that?"

A rumble rose from far down the street behind us. It grew louder as we turned to see what it was and became a roar as a string of motorcycles came into view. Rusty tried to pull me off the sidewalk but I was frozen to the spot. The roar was deafening when the first rider rolled by me. He glanced in my direction, took a second look, and grinned. He had a skull-headed snake tattoo wrapped around his arm. It was Mike. He pointed at me, a warning I'm sure, but didn't stop. Five of his greasy buddies rode behind him. They accelerated as they turned the corner onto the street toward Little Eddie's house. For once in my life, I prayed Dad had disappeared.

We ran after them but stopped as soon as the house came into view. Rusty pulled me down into a ditch along the street. "Stay low until we see what's what," he ordered. "You can't help your dad if you're dead."

Gunshots sounded above the roar of the motorcycles. I stuck my head up to see what was going on. The bikers circled the house like Indians attacking a wagon train while Little Eddie's guys shot at them from the porch and the roof. The bikers fired back. One of the men on the porch took a bullet and fell over the porch rail. A biker got knocked off his motorcycle. He rolled on the ground while his bike skidded on its side into the weeds. I couldn't be sure, but I thought the shot that hit the biker came from Little Eddie firing from the front window.

Mike zoomed around from the back of the house to the front. He raised his arm to signal his men to follow, then swerved into a sharp turn, hit the gas, and charged right up the porch steps. Little Eddie's men scattered, some jumping off the porch, others scrambling through the front door into the house. Little Eddie disappeared from the window as Mike's gang jumped off their bikes and rushed in. Gunshots came in volleys, then stopped. Someone inside the house cried "Please! No!" The plea was answered by a single shot.

In the sudden silence, Rusty gulped. "Now what?" he whispered.

I didn't know. I was too scared to think. "I guess we wait," I said. We couldn't charge into the middle of a gunfight. But I couldn't run away not knowing if Dad was alive or dead.

"Where are the cops, that's what I want to know," Rusty said. "Somebody must have reported gunshots."

"Look around," I answered. "See any neighbors?"

A movement on the other side of the railroad tracks beyond the house caught my eye. Someone was creeping away in the weeds in the dark. Was it Dad? I jumped up to see but Rusty pulled me back down as Mike came out of the house. He stood on the porch looking around, then whistled sharply. The gang came behind him and mounted their bikes. Mike called out an order and everyone circled the house slowly, obviously looking for someone. He pointed down the tracks and one of the men cruised that way. Whomever I had seen in the weeds was either gone or well-hidden, because the biker circled back and joined the gang as they rode away from the house. Rusty and I ducked to the bottom of the ditch as they went by. When the rumble had faded, I stood up.

"Come on," I said. "Dad might be in there." I hoped he wasn't, but I had to know.

The house faced east, so the ramshackle front porch was in deep shadows. We passed the dead biker and his crumpled motorcycle. One of Little Eddie's guys lay dead on the ground in front of the porch and another next to the front door. The wood siding was splattered with bullet holes, the porch railings splintered. We stopped at the bottom of the steps to listen. The quiet was eerie, more of a warning than a welcome. I imagined Little Eddie lurking inside like a crocodile waiting to pull us under the slimy water of his putrid pond.

"I think the goon squad is gone," Rusty said, trying to sound like he wasn't afraid.

"Come on, let's get on with it," I said. I shifted my guitar case from my right to my left hand, gathered my courage, and climbed the porch steps. I tried not to look at the dead man we had to step past to go through the front door.

Inside, the house was dark and silent. The door to Little Eddie's room was closed. I tapped on it in case someone was in there, but no one answered. I put my ear to the door but didn't hear any sounds except my own heartbeat. I swung it open but couldn't see anything until I switched on the light. The room had been ransacked, the furniture overturned, the upholstery on Little Eddie's overstuffed chair slashed. In what must have been a monstrous effort, the wood stove had been tipped over. The chimney pipe hung loose from the wall and ashes coated everything in that end of the room.

"Wow," Rusty said. "It's like Godzilla threw a tantrum."

"Come on, let's check Dad's room."

The light from Little Eddie's room illuminated part of the hallway. A trail of blood led to another body splayed in the shadows at the far end. The last light of day showed through the back door of the house, which hung by one hinge across the doorway.

We crept upstairs to Dad's room and flipped the light switch. The door was open, the room a total mess as if a tornado had struck just before we got there. The mattress was half off the bed and ripped open. Every drawer in the dresser had been pulled out and upended on the floor. Even the closet door was sprung from its hinges. Dad's guitar was gone and I didn't see any of his clothes in the mess. I looked for blood, too, but there wasn't any.

"I guess he got out before the shooting started," I said, more to reassure myself than anything else. I was relieved to not find his body. Still, my heart felt like the room, wrecked and deserted.

"Maybe he'll come get you at Ma's," Rusty said. I wanted to believe that, but I suspected it was at best a long shot. Dad had recruited us to keep Little Eddie busy so he could steal some dope. He wouldn't stick around. It was too dangerous. He probably skipped town as soon as he could. He was on the run again.

Night had fallen and it was dark outside. We needed to get home. The hall was dim, lit only by the light from Dad's room. "Let's go," I said. Rusty was right behind me as I stepped out of the room.

I almost walked right into Little Eddie.

He stood at the top of the stairs outside Dad's room. He raised his pistol and said, "You're not going anywhere." One of his goons was on the stairs behind him.

Little Eddie came by his name naturally, but with the gun in his hand he was ten feet tall. I lurched back and instinctively lifted my guitar case between us as a shield. Rusty's shoulder bumped it as he brushed past to see what was going on.

"Get out of the way," he ordered when he saw Little Eddie.

"Shut your pie hole," the gangster snarled, pointing the pistol at Rusty, who took a step away. Little Eddie swung the pistol back to me. "Where's your old man?" he demanded.

"You tell me," I blurted. "I came here looking for him."

"Or you came back to steal something else for him. Is that what you're up to?"

"I don't know what you're talking about," I said.

"Yeah, you're not making any sense," Rusty chimed in.

"I told you to shut your trap," Little Eddie snapped, swinging the pistol back to him.

"Why do you want my dad?" I said, hoping to distract him from Rusty—and hoping Rusty would shut up.

"He took something that belongs to me. Come to think of it, you two were in on it, weren't you? All that bullshit you pulled yesterday. Distracted me with make-believe motorcycles, that's what you did." He pushed the pistol toward my face.

"I'd say they were pretty real motorcycles," Rusty said, "Unless those are imaginary dead guys on your porch."

"I told you to shut up, you little twerp," he snapped.

Rusty tried to step toward him, but I pushed him back.

"I bet you and your old man are in cahoots with them, too," Little Eddie snarled. "I ought to kill you right now." It was all I could do to keep from peeing my pants. "Did I hear you say you're living at Stamey's?" He didn't wait for an answer. He turned to the goon behind him and told him to go to Ma's and then to the Jewell Theater. "Spread the word that if Chris Martin ever wants to see his kid alive again, he better bring my package back." The guy hurried down the stairs.

"You're not so tough, you little pipsqueak," Rusty said as the front door closed behind the man. "You better let us go."

"I'm going to keep this junior guitar player here as bait," Little Eddie said with a sneer, his voice rising. "But I don't need you and

I'm getting tired of your lip, you red-headed rug rat." I saw what was about to happen and pushed my guitar case at him just as he raised his gun and pulled the trigger. The pistol sounded like a cannon in the tight hallway. My shove knocked Little Eddie back. His foot slipped over the edge of the top step and he tumbled backward head over heels down the wooden stairs until he landed hard in a heap at the bottom. He didn't move.

"Run!" I yelled.

Rusty didn't answer. I spun around and found him sprawled on the floor in a pool of blood.

$$\sim 32 \sim$$

This was the closest I ever came to combat in my life, for which I am very thankful. I was too young to be sent to Korea and too old to be drafted for Vietnam, although I honestly don't know that I would have gone if they had called me for that. Korea, probably, but Vietnam just never made sense to anybody but the politicians, and even they knew it was bogus. The shootout at Little Eddie's was enough for me. There was way too much blood there and blood isn't my favorite thing. I don't like to see it, mine or anybody else's, but especially when it's from someone I love.

"Rusty!" I cried. I fell to my knees and rolled him over onto his back. His eyes were closed, his face covered in blood. I shook him until his head lolled back and forth, but got no response. "Oh God, Rusty, don't die," I moaned. I put my ear to his mouth and felt a faint breath. I laid my head on his chest and heard his heart beating. "You can't die!" I sobbed. "Please wake up." As I lifted my head, a tear fell on his shirt. I shook him again and then again.

His lips parted—barely—and he groaned.

"Rusty, can you hear me?" I shook him again.

"Stop," he mumbled. One of his eyes opened. The other was covered with blood.

"Stop what?" I asked.

"Stop shaking me, you idiot," he answered. He tried to sit up but fell back with a groan. "My head hurts. What happened?"

"Don't move!" I ordered. "You got shot." I ran to the bathroom and came back with a wet towel. I wiped the blood off his face until I found a wound below the hairline on the side of his forehead. It wasn't a hole in his head as much as it was a crease in his skin, but it was still bleeding. He tried to sit up again and made it this time.

"Where is that asshole?" he asked, wincing as he turned his head to look for Little Eddie.

"He fell down the stairs," I said. I realized I didn't know if he was alive or dead from the fall, so he could be coming back up the steps behind us at that very minute. "We've got to get out of here. Can you stand up?" I helped him struggle to his feet. He swayed and I thought he was going to fall back down, but he threw his arm around my neck and steadied himself against me. We made our way to the top of the stairs. Little Eddie still lay at the bottom where he had landed. The wound in Rusty's head gushed blood again.

"Hold on," I said. I dragged him back into Dad's room and sat him on the torn mattress. I ripped a bandage from a crumpled bed sheet and wrapped it around his head. It immediately turned red, but the blood stopped blooming through it after a minute. Then I remembered Little Eddie's goon. He might be coming back to report to him.

I pulled Rusty to his feet again. He was steadier but he still leaned against me. With him on one side and my guitar case in my other hand, we made our way slowly down the stairs. At the bottom, we carefully stepped around Little Eddie. I couldn't tell if he was breathing or not but we didn't stop to find out. Rusty glanced down as he passed and said, "You're a pimple on the ass of society, you little creep. And a lousy shot, too." I spotted Little Eddie's pistol on the floor near the door and set my guitar down long enough to put it in my pocket. If he came to, he wouldn't have it to use on us again.

We picked up the pace once we got onto the sidewalk and Rusty didn't have to navigate any more stairs. After a block or so, he let go of my arm and walked on his own. I stayed close just in case.

"Where are we going?" he asked when I turned to lead him down another street.

"To a hospital," I said. "We need to make sure the trusty Rusty brain doesn't have a bullet in it."

"Nah, I'd feel worse than this if it did. I think I got nicked by a ricochet or something. Really, it doesn't even hurt much now. Besides, we go to the hospital with a gunshot wound, they'll call the cops. Do you really want to explain what we were doing there? And how Little Eddie got his neck broke or whatever? Let's just go back to the boarding house and get cleaned up." He turned on his own toward Ma Stamey's and I reluctantly followed.

When we got to the boarding house, we wanted to slip in through the back door, but Joe was in the backyard strumming his gitfiddle. We tried to sneak by, but he called out, "Hey, boys, did you know Little Eddie is looking for Chris Martin? One of his goons was here earlier." Then Joe noticed the bloody bandage on Rusty's head. "Whoa!" he cried, standing up to get a better look. "What happened to you?"

Ma heard the commotion and turned on a light as she came out the back door. She gasped at the blood all over Rusty's shirt. "You get yourself into the kitchen so I can see better," she ordered. She sat Rusty in a chair and took off the improvised bandage. "This looks like somebody's dirty laundry," she said. "You'll be lucky if you don't get lock jaw." She used clean water to wash off the dried blood covering the wound. "It doesn't look too bad. Just a scratch, really," she muttered to herself, then looked at me. "I'm almost afraid to ask, but how did this happen?"

I opened my mouth to explain, but Rusty jumped in. "It was all my fault, Ma. I was practicing my trick shot routine, you know, the one I'm going to do on 'Arthur Godfrey's Talent Scouts.' I mean, the one I WANT to do on the show. Anyway, I twirled the pistol into the air like a baton, caught it perfectly in my left hand, tossed it to my right, then aimed backwards over my shoulder with a mirror." He waved his hands and arms as if he were demonstrating something that really happened. "I did it all in one smooth motion—very tricky. But the mirror was dirty and I didn't notice and so my aim was off and I shot an iron pole instead of the target on the tree and the bullet ricocheted back and grazed my head when I turned like this." He whipped his head around to look over his shoulder, then turned back to gaze sincerely into Ma's eyes. "Do you think that trick is too dangerous to do on 'Arthur Godfrey's show?'"

Ma Stamey stared at him as if he'd lost his senses, a thought that crossed my mind as well. Joe buckled over holding his sides in laughter. Ma knitted her eyebrows and bent forward until her nose almost bumped Rusty's. Grimly, she asked, "So where is your famous pistol?"

Rusty blinked, but then grinned and said, "I think the bullet ricocheted off my gun first, then hit my head. The gun flew out of my hand and landed on the railroad tracks and a train ran over it and smashed it. I need a new one for Arthur Godfrey." He took a breath and added, "I shot my own gun out of my own hand! Did you ever hear of such a thing?"

Even Ma couldn't hold in the laughter after that whopper. I laughed, too, more as a release of tension than anything else. Shaking her head, Ma dabbed Rusty's wound with iodine and put a clean bandage on it. When she finished, she turned to me and said, "Now, what really happened?"

I told her the whole story—most of it, anyway. How Chris Martin was actually my dad and how he didn't show up for the tech rehearsal, so we went to Little Eddie's house to find out why. How the motorcycle gang shot it out with Little Eddie's gang. How Dad was gone, but Little Eddie trapped us and tried to shoot Rusty so I hit him with my guitar case. "He fell down the stairs and we ran like the dickens."

"What happened to Little Eddie?" Ma asked.

"I don't know. He went down the stairs pretty hard. He wasn't moving when we left, but we didn't get close enough to check if he was alive."

"Was anybody else there?"

"Just me and Rusty."

"Sounds like no witnesses," Joe said, exchanging meaningful looks with Ma.

"If anybody asks how you hurt your head," she said, "you stick with Rusty's cock-and-bull story. You were never anywhere near Little Eddie's tonight. You don't know from nothing about motorcycle gangs and drug dealers. Got that?"

We both nodded.

Her fierce look softened. "I suppose you're going to keep looking for your dad, aren't you?"

"I've got to," I answered.

"Well, give that a rest for a while. There's going to be an uproar over the shootout and somebody might connect him to it. He may be gone, but plenty of folks knew he lived there and it looks kind of suspicious that he disappeared just before all hell broke loose. Don't go asking around about him until it all blows over. You understand?"

I didn't know if I would keep the promise for more than a couple of days, but I said I would.

Joe held up my guitar case and said, "Looks like the bullet went right through here." He pointed to a hole near the bottom edge of the case.

"No!" I said. My Martin guitar was the most precious thing my dad ever gave me! I grabbed the case and opened it, afraid I'd find it destroyed inside. Instead, there was nothing more than a perfectly round hole in the spruce face of the guitar near the bottom and another one through the mahogany back. The bullet must have come out the back because there were a few splinters around that hole. I carefully scraped them away with my thumb, turned the guitar over, and tentatively touched the strings. Aside from being out of tune, it sounded just fine.

Joe pointed to a matching hole in the back of the case. "This is where it came out before it hit Rusty. By then, it didn't have much force. Guess you and your guitar saved him."

All the talk about guns and bullets reminded me I had Little Eddie's pistol. I touched my pocket to be sure, then Rusty and I went to our room. While he was down the hall in the bathroom, I wrapped the gun in a t-shirt and stashed it in my guitar case.

$$\sim\ 33\ \sim$$

I went back and played a gig at the Jewell Theater years after my debut on the *Ozark Jubilee*. I gotta tell you, the theater wasn't the same. You know, that auditorium had been built to seat a thousand folks for live shows, everything from opera to vaudeville. You probably could have heard some blowhard reciting Shakespeare, too, at least in the early days when folks would go to plays like that just to say they'd been. Couldn't understand a word of it, of course, being hillbillies and all, but they'd go and swear they loved it.

Anyway, when I went back there, it was the late sixties and the place had pretty much gone to seed and was staying alive on picture shows. They'd turned the stage into one big movie screen and part of the balcony into a projection booth. The night before we played there, they were showing *Midnight Cowboy*, I seem to recall.

When my band went on stage, we had to cram our gear between the ratty old curtain and the edge of the stage where the orchestra pit used to be. We got 'er done, but only because it was just me and a standup bass player and a rhythm guitar thumper. The audience was crammed in there, too, basically all into the middle section of the orchestra seats. There was only a few dozen of them, so it didn't much matter.

We didn't make significant money from the gig, which wasn't any surprise. The only reason I did it was because we were in the area, playing at Silver Dollar City down around Branson and we had an open night. Of course, I was also remembering the theater and the way it changed my life, not to mention Rusty's close call. Not to mention my own brush with death the next day.

Rusty's head was bruised and sore Saturday morning, but the wound had stopped bleeding and it didn't start again when Ma changed the bandage. She found another of her son's shirts for him, a bright blue one, so he would have something to wear to the show. I told him he looked like he was going to march in a parade. The blue shirt, white bandage, and red hair made him look like a walking Stars and Stripes.

"That's me," he said. "Leader of the parade!"

Ma snorted. "Your place in the parade will be behind the elephants. And you'll be carrying a big shovel." Rusty stuck his tongue out at her but laughed along with the rest of us. Ma had a ticket for the show tonight and promised to meet me backstage to tie my tie.

We set out for the theater after lunch. I carried my bullet-scarred guitar and Rusty brought the stage clothes Miss Harris had bought for me. It was going to be a long day stretching well into the evening. There was a full dress rehearsal in the afternoon because everything had to be perfect for the real thing, a live broadcast on coast-to-coast national television. This might be the best day in my life, I thought. I was going to perform on the biggest country music show on television—and get paid for it—making me a real professional musician just like my dad. I'd wished for this moment forever, it seemed, but especially over the last few months when dreaming of it helped me escape reality. My heart ached that Dad wouldn't be there to see me, but I hoped he was somewhere out of harm's way. Mom and Willy wouldn't be in the audience either, although they might be watching on Larry's television. Boy, wouldn't they be surprised! Then the impact of a national broadcast struck home.

"Hey Rusty," I said. "I just thought of something."

"How many times do I have to tell you, you just play your guitar and the trusty Rusty brain will do all the thinking, okay?"

"Well, did the trusty Rusty brain realize that millions of television viewers will know exactly where we are when Red Foley introduces me tonight? Like my mom and your parents? Larry and probably a million cops, too. And Mike and his motorcycle gang. Maybe even Little Eddie if he's still alive."

"Yipes! You're right," he said. "You better change your name!"

"It's a little late for that, don't you think? Besides, I can't very well change my face."

"That's unfortunately true for several reasons."

"You're no help." I slugged him in the arm.

"You sure you want to go through with this?" he asked. "We could skip town right now."

I shook my head. "I'll never have a chance like this again. Besides, I want to do it for Dad. And the money will be a help to Mom if I can get it to her someday."

"Okay, then be quiet and let me think this through."

"You better think quick. We're here."

The Jewell Theater buzzed with *Ozark Jubilee* activity. Unlike the tech rehearsal the day before, all the performers were here at the same time and the pre-show excitement was building. Nearly all the stars had performed hundreds if not thousands of times on radio programs or stage shows, but this was television—national network television, no less—and millions of people would be watching. Not every home in America had a television set back in those years—or one in every room like today—but plenty of folks gathered in the homes of their more fortunate friends to watch the top shows.

Miss Harris greeted us backstage and asked Rusty what happened to his head. He said something about bumping it in the shower, which seemed to satisfy her curiosity. She showed me to a dressing room I would share with some other musicians and told me I could leave my regular clothes there until it was time to change back into them after the dress rehearsal. After dinner, I would put my stage clothes back on for the live broadcast. Then she showed me where to wait for my cue and told me there wouldn't be any stops and starts because this was a full-run dress rehearsal. Afterward, there would be a break for dinner—Miss Harris suggested I eat something very light at one of the restaurants in the neighborhood—before the actual broadcast.

Just as Miss Harris finished, Brenda Lee bounced up to us. "Hey Daniel! Hey Rusty! You ready to rock and roll?" She wriggled her tiny hips and hopped up and down like a frog on a hot griddle. "What happened to your head?" she said, pointing to Rusty's bandage between bounces.

"I got ambushed by some cattle rustlers," Rusty proclaimed. Before I could cut him off, he added, "I was helping the Lone Ranger this morning because Tonto was sick. The rustlers had rifles and a cannon. I shot back, though. I got three of them and the rest ran away."

Brenda's eyebrows shot up and her mouth dropped open before she stopped bouncing long enough to giggle, "You're a cutie, but that's the biggest bunch of horse hockey I ever heard!" She blew me a kiss. "Break a leg, Daniel," she sang as she skipped back to her place.

"Looks like you've got yourself an eleven-year-old fiancé," Rusty said. "Isn't there a law against that?"

My emotions must have been jazzed up from everything going on around me because I answered, "She is pretty cute. Maybe when she grows up . . . ."

"Oh, fine, Romeo! Better keep that idea to yourself or her stepdaddy will be after us, too."

The house lights went down, the stage lights came up, the band pitched into a lively tune, and the square dance troupe took the stage to kick off the show. The announcer intoned the familiar introduction, "From the Jewell Theater in Springfield, Missouri, it's time for the *Ozark Jubilee*, starring America's favorite country gentleman, Red Foley!" The headliner came out to sing his opening number and the dress rehearsal went into full swing.

My song came two spots after Brenda's. Miss Harris had said, "Sing it just like this is the real show. You never know who might be checking you out." I poured my heart into it. My fingers flew up and down the neck of my guitar and my voice held true without breaking. When I finished, Bill Wimbley gave me a smile and a nod. As I made my way offstage, several of the performers did the same. A pair of country comedians took my place on the set and the show went on as I put my guitar in its case. I'd felt an incredible rush while I was performing on stage but I wanted to collapse once it was over. I hoped I'd get that surge of energy back for the real show in just a couple of hours.

I looked around for Rusty to see what he thought of my song, but he wasn't there.

I searched everywhere backstage but couldn't find him. Brenda giggled when I mentioned his name, but said she hadn't seen him. I finally found the harried Miss Harris, who told me the guard from the front door was looking for Rusty and me. She didn't know why. Red Foley was on stage doing his closing number in the rehearsal, so she told me I could find Rusty and leave. "I'll put your guitar in Red's office for safe keeping. Just be sure to be back in an hour. Red wants to talk to you."

Everyone else in the show had gone to dinner, so I rushed through the theater building calling Rusty's name. Finally, I gave up and went to the dressing room to change clothes. That's where

I found him. He was there, all right, with Ma Stamey and Joe the gitfiddle player, all lined up in front of the cluttered dressing tables and mirrors that lined the brick wall. Little Eddie held them all at gunpoint. I should have known he would have more than one pistol. He leaned heavily on a crutch but was very much in charge.

"Well, the headliner has arrived," he smirked. "Now the show can begin."

"Wha . . . what are you doing here?" I stammered, stunned at seeing him alive.

"Guess you thought you left me for dead, huh?"

"You sure looked dead," I said.

"You smelled pretty dead, too," Rusty said. "Like a dead skunk my dog dug up one time."

"I'm going to give you something that smells even worse than that, buster," Little Eddie said with a sneer as he motioned with his pistol for me to stand next to Rusty. "I've been asking them where your dad went but they don't seem to know. You know, though. And I am sure one of you will tell me when I stick this gun in your ear and count to three."

Little Eddie had a crutch under one arm, but he managed to pinch it in his armpit and lean on it so he could free his hand to grab me. I squirmed helplessly as the gangster pushed the pistol barrel into my ear. "You better start talking, headliner," he said to me. "All you have to do is answer my question. The count starts now. One."

"Don't hurt him!" Rusty cried.

"Where did your dad go with my dope?" he demanded. "Is he working for Mike?"

"That's two questions, you moron," Rusty said.

Little Eddie pinched my ear and I squealed.

"I don't know! I don't know!" I shouted.

"Two," Little Eddie said. "Where is he!"

His fists clenched, Rusty said, "If he knew where his dad was, don't you think he'd be with him?"

"He's right!" I said. "I'm looking for him, too!"

"That's bullshit," Little Eddie growled. "If you know, you better tell me because I could care less about blowing your brains out all over that wall. Three! One last chance." He shoved the gun hard against my ear.

Rusty lunged at him.

The move surprised Little Eddie and he swung the gun toward him. He shouldn't have done that. I kicked him viciously in the bad leg and Little Eddie screamed. I clamped both hands around his wrist and jerked the pistol upward. The shot was deafening, but it went wild into the ceiling.

Joe jumped in and swung his gitfiddle into Little Eddie's face. Rusty knocked the crutch out from under his shoulder and Little Eddie collapsed to the floor. I wrenched his wrist as he fell and his gun flew out of his hand. With a roar, he tried to scramble for the pistol but Ma kicked it away, swirled around, and sat down on him, pinning his wriggling body to the floor under her hefty backside.

A security guard crashed through the dressing room door. "I heard a gunshot! What's going on in here?"

"This clown tried to kill me, but he missed—again," Rusty said. "He's a really, really bad shot."

"Is anybody hurt?"

"Just that sawed-off creep Ma's sitting on," Rusty answered.

"Call the police," Ma said. "I'll hold him till they get here."

Miss Harris crowded into the room and looked around wide-eyed. "What happened here?" she said.

"It's under control, Miss Harris," the security guard said. "Nobody got hurt. I'm calling the police right now."

Bewildered, Miss Harris looked at Ma, scowled at Little Eddie whimpering on the floor, and turned to me with a dozen questions in her eyes.

"Are you boys okay? Are you sure nobody has been injured?"

"Yes, ma'am," I said.

"Thank goodness. Boys, come with me, please. There are people here who want to see you."

~ 34 ~

Some folks think that women bring bad things on themselves. If they'd only stay in their place, do their little jobs like God intended, everyone would be lots happier. You can guess what I think about those folks. Plenty of people say that such tripe used to be the attitude, but it's better now because we're all enlightened about equality and everything. That's dead wrong. Lots of folks of both sexes still think women are second class citizens. It's just that their sick attitude is hidden now. It's kind of like old, dried dog shit kicked under the rug. You can't see it, but it still smells. My mom wouldn't face anything different today than she did back then. The cards were stacked against her no matter how you cut them.

We followed Miss Harris through the theater auditorium to the lobby. Rusty's mother and father stood inside next to the front door. With Willy! And . . . .

"Mom!" I cried.

Mom threw open her arms. I sprang into them. Willy clutched my waist. None of us spoke. We just wept and hugged tighter and tighter. Rusty and his parents were doing the same.

Willy finally let loose and yelled, "Daniel! We found you!"

I grinned through my tears. "You did, buddy. And I'm sure glad." I leaned back in Mom's embrace to get a good look at her. Her makeup had obviously been put on at the last minute, probably in the car. Her hair was disheveled but she had pinned it back. She wore a scarf around her neck. I asked how she found us.

"Your dad called the tavern this morning," she answered. "He told me you and Rusty were here and would be on the show tonight. I called Mr. James and we drove all day to get here." She paused to kiss me. "Your dad said a lot more, too, but I'll tell you all that later. We've got a lot to talk about."

"I think I have a few minutes. Come on over here," I said, pulling her and Willy to a corner where we could have some privacy. "Am I in trouble, Mom?"

She shook her head and smiled. "I should kill you, but I'm too happy to see you alive."

"What about Larry's car?"

"The St. Joe cops put out a bulletin about you two and the missing car. They found it in Columbia a couple of days after you left, so Larry got one of his firefighter buddies to drive him down there to get it. He was plenty mad, but there wasn't any damage. He finally shut up about it when I told him I was coming here to get you." She didn't need to add that he was undoubtedly plotting his revenge for when she brought me home.

I was sorry she found me, but glad, too. I realized I'd missed her and Willy more than I let myself admit. As she talked, I couldn't stop looking at her. The last two weeks had been hard on her. Her eyes were red-rimmed, her skin pale. There was something else...

"Mom, what's this mark on your neck?" Her scarf had slid down when she threw her arms around me. "How did you get this bruise?"

"Oh, that's nothing. My silly feet got tangled up and I slipped in the bathroom. I fell against the towel rack. Really, it's nothing."

She tried to move my hand, but I pushed the scarf down on the other side of her neck. "There's another bruise on this side," I said. "Did Larry . . . ."

"No!" she exclaimed. "He didn't do it on purpose. I mean . . . he was only . . . he's just strong and doesn't know he's hurting me sometimes . . . I . . . ."

"That's bullshit! Mom, you've got to get out of there. Or go to the cops. Do something!"

She turned her head away from the frustration in my eyes. "It's not that easy, Daniel. Besides, he's not a bad guy." Her voice was flat as if she were reciting a well-worn excuse she no longer believed. "He can be real sweet and I know he loves me." Her words had no meaning. They were nothing more than the echoes of her sad life.

"If he loves you so much, why did he try to kill you?"

"Don't be ridiculous, Daniel. Larry didn't try to kill me. It was a mistake . . . a little misunderstanding." She still wouldn't look me in the eye.

"Maybe not this time, but what about next time?" Willy was watching wide-eyed by her side, his chin quivering, tears welling up. "And what about Willy?"

Her head shot up. "Hush! Don't you even think something like that!"

"One of us has to."

She hung her head again. "We need you at home, Daniel."

Before I could answer, Miss Harris came for me.

"It's time to dress for the show," she said. "Mrs. Freemont, please come with me. I have seats for everyone right up front." As I turned to go, Miss Harris added, "Daniel, Red would like to see you and your mother in his office right after the show, so don't leave until you talk to him, okay?"

Let me tell you this: you never forget your first time on stage in front of a thousand people. Even with the spot lights glaring into your eyes, you can see their faces—at least some of them. They all stare at you, some grinning, some scowling, most of them hoping you're going to do something to please them, a couple dozen of them betting that you're going to make them look stupid for paying good money to watch you go down like the Hindenburg. It's been a long time ago, but I still get an adrenaline burn in my stomach when I remember my debut. That night, though, stage fright wasn't the only thing that set my belly on fire.

When the stage manager gave the signal, I found my mark on the stage floor and faced the audience of a thousand *Ozark Jubilee* fans seated before me in the Jewell Theater. More of them stood in the back of the auditorium and even more hung over the railings in the balcony. The crowd was excited and jocular, many of them carrying signs with the names of their home towns, everyone full of light-hearted chatter as I came on stage during the break for a television commercial. As the house band raised their instruments waiting for their cue, applause rose through the theater and I tried to hide my troubles. I felt no fear, no anxiety about my performance, but a cloud lay over me, a cloud of doubt about the decisions I soon had to make about my future.

Willy squirmed in his seat next to Mom. When I ran away, I broke my promise to him. I'd told him I would always take care of him, then I disappeared. From the delight shining from his face as he watched me on stage, though, it looked like he'd already forgiven me. Someday he will understand that a promise is sometimes nothing more than words. It may be sincerely meant when it's said, but it can't always be kept.

Mom smiled crookedly and gave me a little wave of encouragement like she did the time I sang at Aunt Mae's. She looked frightened, too. What should I do? What could I do about her and Willy? The summer had been filled with uncertainty and chaos, and soon I would have to make perhaps the most important decision of my life. Maybe her life, too.

I was sure Dad was taking a break from a gig in a tavern somewhere to tune in the show or huddled around a television in the parlor of a boarding house in whatever town he was hiding in now. I remembered how Dad told me one time that he went into some kind of trance when he performed. Not always, but often enough. It was as if his brain stopped actively thinking while his fingers flew and his voice soared, music feeding his soul, its energy giving him life. It was an actual, physical high—an addictive one he pursued every chance he got. Sometimes it came when he was on stage in front of paying customers, but it could come just as easily when he was jamming with his buddies in somebody's back yard while they waited for the grill to heat up and the beer to get cold. What I didn't realize, and maybe he didn't know either, was that achieving that high wasn't the same as earning a living or feeding his family or putting a roof over their head. Making music, to him, was an addiction, not a money-making profession. Artists have always been that way, I guess. They revel in the creative process, few of them earning more than a monetary pittance while they drown in the dopamine of making art. That's fine and dandy—wonderful, even—when the only body that depends on the artist for food is his own. It's a whole different story when it's their kids and family. I don't know if my dad ever figured that out. Looking at the crowd waiting for me to perform, I tried not to think about him nodding on the floor of some flophouse with a needle in his arm. I resolved to follow Aunt Mae's advice that I had to attend to my own life before I tried to help him or anyone else.

Ma Stamey smiled in the front row where she sat with Joe. I made a silent promise to find his hillbilly luthier and get him another gitfiddle. Rusty and his parents were there, too. Earlier, when Rusty's father asked him how he hurt his head, Rusty had said he tripped over a big bag of money in Red Foley's office and smacked his head on Porter Wagoner's guitar. That made his father laugh.

As I stood on the stage waiting for my cue, I found myself probing the bullet hole in my guitar with my finger. I decided I wouldn't get it fixed. I'd keep it to remind me of this moment and all that led up to it. Aunt Mae's words rang in my head and I put my troubles to one side. I focused on my job. Play the guitar. Sing the song. Don't try to solve the world's problems until you're off the stage. The television camera swung in my direction, the red light came on, and millions of eyes were on me. I guess I should have been afraid, but I wasn't.

Red Foley introduced me as a "bright young man from up St. Joe way." Then he asked me who taught me to play the guitar.

"My dad," I said. "He taught me everything."

"He must be pretty proud of you, Daniel. Why don't you give us a tune and let's see what you learned."

I looked straight into the camera. "This song is for you, Mom, and especially for you, Dad, wherever you are tonight. I hope you're watching." I struck a loud, ringing G chord to tell the audience to get ready to listen. "Here's an old song called the 'Worried Man Blues'," I said. "My dad taught it to me. I hope he takes it to heart."

"It takes a worried man to sing a worried song," I sang. The lines summed up not just my life, but my family's, too. At times, we'd been beyond worried—we'd been desperate and we'd done desperate things. When I got to the verse that goes "Life has its ups and downs, I'm down more than I'm up," I poured my own desperation into it. There had been times this summer when I felt like I was looking up from within a bottomless barrel. I know Mom did, too, and so did Dad. As the song ended, I realized I had known all along what I had to do. I slowed the tempo as I ended the song.

"I'm worried now, but I won't be worried long."

~ 36 ~

You know, life is all about decisions. And it seems like, at the time you have to make one, it's always a matter of life and death. They're not, most of the time at least, but sometimes they really are. The hard part is, at the moment you have to make the decision, you don't know which is which.

Mom and everybody found me after the show among all the pandemonium backstage. Relieved of tension, the performers celebrated with hugs and back slaps while the band packed up their instruments and stagehands carried props through the milling crowd.

"Wowee, Daniel!" Willy shouted. "You done good!" Joe shook my hand and Rusty slugged me in the arm. Mom wrapped her arms around me and squeezed me tight.

"I'm so proud of you," she said.

I spotted Miss Harris showing a clipboard to Red Foley on the other side of the stage in front of a stack of hay bales.

"We've got to go to Mr. Foley's office, Mom. We can talk after."

Ma Stamey overheard me and offered to take care of Willy. She motioned to Rusty and his dad. "We'll wait for you in the lobby."

Before we went into Foley's office, Mom kissed my forehead and whispered, "I think you're angry with me. Please don't be. We need you."

"I know," I answered. I looked into her frightened eyes, not sure how I could tell her I had decided to stay in Springfield. It would be up to her to deal with Larry.

I took her hand and led her into Red Foley's cluttered office. He asked us to make ourselves comfortable, then leaned against the front of his desk and clasped his hands in front of himself like he did on stage.

"You've had a pretty exciting couple of days," he said. "How are you doing?"

"I'm fine, sir."

"And all the trouble is behind you?"

"Yes, sir," I said, hoping I was telling the truth.

"Good. I'm very glad," he smiled and nodded. "Let me say, Daniel, I've heard you perform several times in the last couple of days and you're a darn good musician."

"Thanks, Mr. Foley." Despite his smile, I was suddenly afraid he was letting me down easy and everything was about to come to an end.

"How would you like to join the *Ozark Jubilee*?"

My jaw dropped. I couldn't do anything but gape at him. I had been so preoccupied with everything else that the only music I cared about was the song I sang on the show. Even before Springfield, even before Dad disappeared and Mom met Larry, my dreams of becoming a musician had always been as vague as dreams can be. They took place in some neverland auditorium where spotlights swept across crowds of worshipful fans and I picked my guitar and sang to their raucous applause. But all that happened someday in the future and somewhere else, not here, not now. Red Foley had just made that dream come true. He didn't know it, but he had also given me a way to save Mom and Willy from Larry.

Mom sat speechless as well. Her lips trembled ever so slightly as she watched me weigh my answer. She needed me and so did Willy.

I took a deep breath to stiffen my resolve. "You bet I would, Mr. Foley," I said. Mom gasped. "Can I talk to Mom outside for a minute?"

"Of course," he said. "I'll draw up your contract in the meantime. Your mother can sign it when you're done."

We sat down in the outer office and I took both of Mom's hands in mine.

"Please don't do this," she pleaded. "You've got to come home."

"No, Mom," I said. "I have to do this. Not just for myself, but for you and Willy, too. This is our big chance."

"But you'll have to live here, not in St. Joe. I want us to be together. We're a family!"

"But Larry isn't family, Mom, He's a bully and a jerk. We can't live with him."

"I know, but . . . ."

Before she could repeat all her excuses, I said, "You have to leave him. That's the only way. And then we can be a family together here in Springfield."

"What?"

"Don't you see? With me making money on the show, we can all live together down here. Get a house maybe . . . ."

"He'll never let me do that!" she cried. "He'll never let me go! He'll lock me in the house!"

"Now, Mom," I said softly, trying to calm her. "You don't even have to go back. Just stay here. I bet Ma Stamey would make room for us until we got our feet on the ground."

"No. I mean it! He knows I'm here. He'll come and get me." I had a vision of Larry storming into Ma Stamey's house. Of me confronting him on the stairs like I did with Little Eddie. Of how that ended. Mom thought I was wavering. "You can't stay here alone, either, Daniel. I won't allow it. You aren't old enough to live on your own. I am your mother and . . . and I won't give my permission." She tightened her lips and thrust out her chin. "I won't sign the contract."

She may not have looked like it, but there were times when Mom could fight like a badger. She caught me off guard, but I didn't lash back. I dropped her hands and sat back in my chair. The last few months had made me tough, too. "Maybe you can drag me home, but you'll have to keep me tied up. Larry will have to sleep with one eye open, no matter what he does to me. I promise I will run away again. And next time, I'll make sure no one ever finds me."

Mom's defiance evaporated and tears welled up. "How could you hurt me like that?" she sobbed. "What about Willy? You're his hero, Daniel. You'll break his heart."

My gut twisted. I missed his squeals and giggles, but if I gave in, Willy and Mom would still be under Larry's heavy thumb—or worse. And so would I. I gave her one more chance.

"Mom, this isn't on my shoulders. You have to choose. Me or Larry. Either he goes or I go." I tried hard to keep the fear out of my face. What kind of kid backs his mom into a corner? What if it drives her off the deep end? What if she picks Larry?

She slumped back in her chair with a broken sigh. We stared silently at each other for a minute that seemed like an hour. Finally, she said. "Okay, you win. But on one condition. You have to come home and promise to never run away again."

"And you'll leave Larry?"

"Yes, we'll move back in with Mae."

I felt relief but no triumph. Mom made a hard, hard choice and so did I. The *Ozark Jubilee* had turned back into a dream that didn't come true.

"All right," I said. "I'll come home." I didn't doubt Mom would keep her word, but I knew it wouldn't be easy. "Let's go back and tell Mr. Foley I changed my mind."

"I'm awful proud you asked me, and I really want to be part of the *Ozark Jubilee*, but I'm sorry, Mr. Foley, I have to go home."

He frowned and I watched my life as a musician swirl down the drain. Red Foley was a big man in country music—maybe the biggest. He was someone who made careers happen. Someone not used to hearing "no."

"Are you sure, Daniel?" he said. "Not many guys get a chance like this."

I gulped. "Yes, sir. I am sure. My mom needs me. My brother, too."

He stopped frowning, but he didn't smile. He picked up my contract, looked at it for a minute in silence, then put it down. He moved a pen on his desk from one side to the other.

"I . . . Well, I'm sorry, Mr. Foley."

"I understand. Family comes first." He looked at me thoughtfully for a minute, then at Mom. "Mrs. Freemont, you raised a fine young man here. Could I borrow him from time to time?"

"I don't know what you mean," Mom said.

"Well, St. Joe's not all that far away. Daniel could ride the bus down here to Springfield every once in a while to be on the show. Maybe once a month? He'd have to get here in time for Friday's tech rehearsal, but we'd put him up in the hotel for a couple of nights and send him back home the day after the broadcast. Would that be okay with you?"

"Why . . . what about . . . what if he . . . ," she stuttered in confusion. She looked at me. "What do you think?"

I nodded eagerly as my head exploded.

"And we do stage shows up in your neck of the woods, too. He'd earn a nice paycheck for doing those from time to time."

"Mr. Foley," Mom said, "We can't thank you enough. Can we, Daniel?"

"No . . . I mean, yes . . . I mean, thank you!"

"You're both very welcome," he chuckled. "Just let me make a quick change in this contract and we'll be all set."

As he crossed out and scribbled something on the contract, my mind returned to the practicalities of the immediate future. Mom had promised to leave Larry, but I knew that wouldn't go down without a fight. This time, though, I would be ready. I had what I needed to settle his hash. It was wrapped in a t-shirt in my guitar case and I had the nerve to use it. I figured we would be safely out of his house and moved into Aunt Mae's the same day we got back to St. Joe.

Red Foley smiled at me as he handed the contract to Mom. "I seem to recall an energetic friend of yours with red hair just like mine. He said he is your manager, I think."

"That's my pal, Rusty," I laughed. "He kind of appointed himself. It's a long story." I remembered Rusty joshing with his dad in the theater lobby and his dad laughing every time Rusty opened his mouth. It felt good to know we would still be together in St. Joe.

Mom gave the contract back to Foley. He stood up and reached across the desk to shake my hand. "Daniel," he said, "Welcome to the *Ozark Jubilee*."

And that, my friends, is the way this story ends. I guess you could say I'm leaving you like a waiter who serves a glass of ice without any tea, but trust me, it might be best if you don't know exactly everything that happened after Mom and Willy and I left Springfield and went back to St. Joe.

I can tell you a few things that didn't happen. I never married Brenda Lee, for example, although if you know anything about her you figured that out already. I mean, she was cute as a kitten in a basket, but let's face it, she was only eleven years old that summer. We appeared on the *Ozark Jubilee* lots of times, and we stayed in touch over the years, but that was it.

Rusty and I stayed friends forever. He tried to be my manager, but we both kind of outgrew that little charade. He got married, a couple of times, in fact, but he never lost his sense of humor. Every time I see him, he still tries to get me to pull his finger to play a tune in the key of fart.

You should also know that Dad wrote me a letter not long after I got home and said he used the dope he stole from Little Eddie to pay his debt to Mike. He told me in the letter that he was in rehab and was getting clean. I was happy for him when I read the letter, but he never came home. I'm still pretty pissed about that. Some folks say, "once a junkie, always a junkie." That's a pretty small-minded way to look at it, but in this case I have my suspicions that it's true.

And Mom, well, you probably guessed that she made good on her promise to get rid of Larry. I won't go into any details about my role in the matter because I don't know nothin' about the statue of limitations or the statute of liberty or whatever you call it. Suffice it to say that Larry ceased to be a problem as soon as we got back to St. Joe. You can draw your own conclusions.

Like I said before, I've still got my guitar, bullet hole and all. I could have gotten it fixed, but the bullet missed all the cross bracing and everything, so it didn't hurt the way it plays none. Besides, the holes give it a little, I don't know, "character," so to speak.

Willy growed up fine, by the way. When I cross paths with him every once in a while, I get out my guitar and we sound real good when he plays along on his gitfiddle.

AUTHOR'S NOTE

My Gitfiddle Summer is a work of fiction. The *Ozark Jubilee*, though, was a very real, very successful country music variety show that aired live from the Jewell Theater in Springfield, Missouri, and was carried nationally on the ABC Television Network in the 1950s. Red Foley, one of the leading country music stars of the day, hosted the program, and other big names like Patsy Cline, Eddy Arnold, and Johnny Cash appeared as well. Brenda Lee was the Taylor Swift of her day. She sold more than 100 million records worldwide throughout her career and made her breakthrough national television performance on the *Ozark Jubilee* in 1956 at the age of eleven. I've taken many liberties with details about her and many of the historic characters for the sake of the story.

St. Joseph, Missouri, is a very real city, too. I was born there, as a matter of fact, and played my Martin D-18 guitar and sang in coffee houses and other venues in town. KFEQ Radio still broadcasts from studios there, too. I worked as an announcer at the station in the 1970s and my grandfather, Bunkhouse Bill Russell, performed live music on KFEQ in the 1930s and 40s. My mother and two brothers and I also lived for a couple of years in the dirt-floored cellar of the KO-Z-INN, a neighborhood tavern owned by my grandmother. I rode my bike all over town in the company of my best friend, Dick Crumpton, from the time we met in the sixth grade. Krug Park was one of our favorite destinations.

My Gitfiddle Summer is far from autobiographical, although parts of it were drawn from people and incidents in my early youth. Many of them can be found in my book, *Fathers: A Memoir.*

I owe a debt of gratitude to many people who helped this book along its journey from concept to completion. I will always be grateful to Nora Raleigh Baskin, my friend and mentor, who encouraged me to draw on my memoir to create a work of fiction. Thanks, too, to many early readers including Ary Hammerman, Joey Portocarrero, Rebecca Fitzgerald, Matt Sullivan, and Steve and Jeremy Donelson. And extra special gratitude to my wife, Nora Guzewicz, who patiently read through numerous drafts, offered so many good suggestions I can't count them all, and lovingly supported me in this as she does in all my endeavors.

About the Author

Dave Donelson is an award-winning writer and artist with some three million words in print. His career has taken him from the jungles of Australia's Cape York Peninsula to the minarets of Riyadh. He's climbed the spire of the Empire State Building and photographed the tree-climbing lions and mountain gorillas of Uganda. His work appears regularly in over three dozen national periodicals and he is the author of numerous books of fiction, non-fiction, poetry, and memoir. For more information, visit www.davedonelson.com.

ALSO BY DAVE DONELSON

Fiction
Heart of Diamonds
Hunting Elf
Blind Curve
Weird Golf

Non-fiction
Fathers: a Memoir
Provence Reflections
The Journal of My Seventieth Year
The Dynamic Manager's Guides

Poetry
Cityverse & Cityverse 2
Points in Time
Visions of a Certain Age

The Quick Read Ebook Collection
1 Short Stories of Suspense
2 Short Stories of Horror
3 Short Stories of Escape
4 Short Stories of Goofy Golf
5 Short Stories of Bizarre Golf
6 Short Stories of Monster Golf
7 Short Stories of Ghost Golf
8 Short Essays on Creativity
9 Short Tales of Memory